EMMETT SWAN

Cadaver Swords

Contents

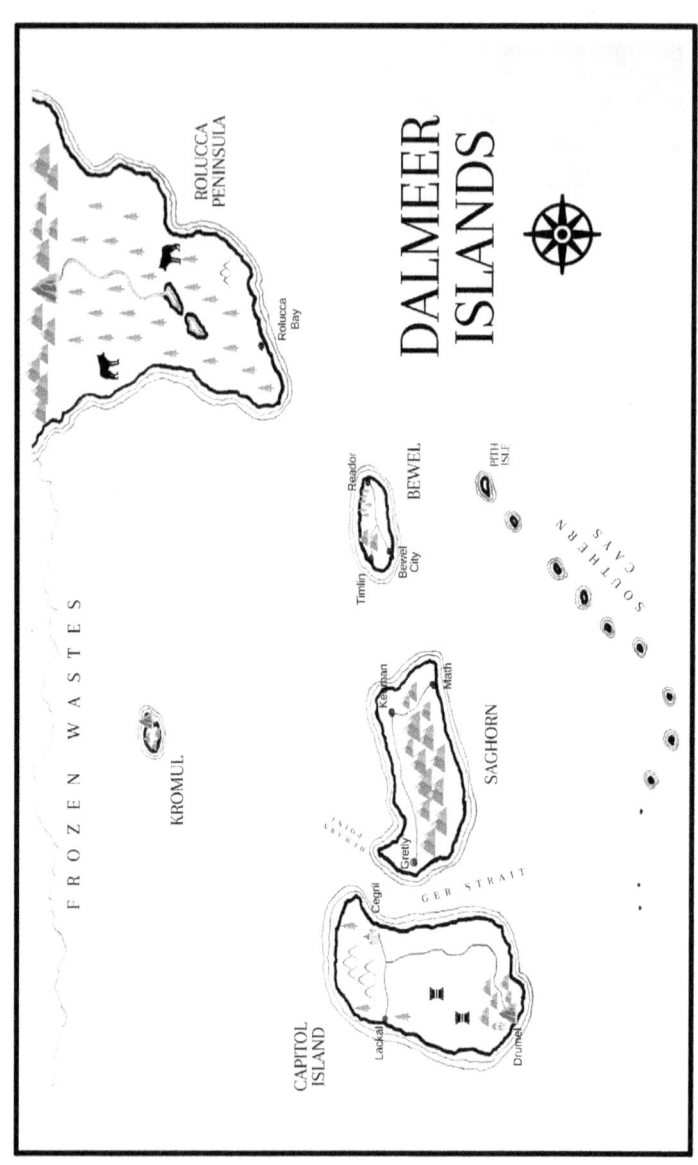

DALMEER ISLANDS

ROLUCCA PENINSULA

Rolucca Bay

FROZEN WASTES

KROMUL

BEWEL

Reador

Timlin

Bewel City

PITH ISLE

SOUTHERN CAVS

SAGHORN

Keyman

Math

Gretly

HINTON POINT

GER STRAIT

CAPITOL ISLAND

Cegril

Ladkal

Drumel

Sacred Covenant

Ferrin, the Medium of the White Mountain, leaned into the biting wind and marched doggedly forward. Behind him followed his retinue of twelve white-robed assistants, walking two by two, their hoods tilted into the stinging breeze to protect their faces. The featureless Plain of Nubinor extended in every direction, an expanse of short brown grass dusted with light snow. A brilliant sky vaulted the heavens.

Though his eyes watered profusely, Ferrin focused his gaze on the three stone pillars dead ahead, clear in the bright light and standing in stark contrast to the empty plain. His destination was near.

For four days, Mount Krin, the White Mountain, had lain dormant. For four days, its healing power had been rendered inert, failing the suffering people who had journeyed to its shadow for relief from their injuries. This unhappy state of affairs was a sign. Another Medium was dead. It meant that he would need to undertake the voyage to Bewel Island and then march to the center of its blustery interior plain. For there, in a natural depression marked by three pillars, stood the Covenant Stone.

There was no more important landmark in the entire land. It was at the Covenant Stone that the Mediums of the White

1

Mountain, the Blue Mountain, and the Gray Mountain were bound to one another and to their sacred duties.

As Ferrin reached the closest pillar, perched on the edge of the depression, he peered down into the recess and beheld the stone. A great crystal shard twice the height of a man, it stood in the center, surrounded by three stone benches. Small drifts of dry snow lay here and there, softly shuffled by the breezes that made their way into the depths of the recess. As he expected, he was the first to arrive.

He shielded his eyes from the bright sun and surveyed the surrounding terrain. He could make out two other groups approaching from different directions. To his relief, both were near. The one coming from the north was close enough for him to make out the details of their blue robes, and they would reach the Covenant Stone presently. The group coming from the northwest would arrive some minutes later.

"Thank Gludema," said Ferrin. The ceremonial protocols would be implemented without delay. With luck on their side, they would be homeward bound in a couple of hours. Ferrin thought longingly of his cozy hearth back home in Drumel.

He turned to his entourage and bade them to sit on the frozen grass just beyond the rim of the depression. Protocol allowed only the Mediums and their designated successors into the protected recess during formal ceremonies, so those sitting on the rim would be exposed to the wind. But, eight of the twelve were the hardened soldiers of the White Guard, his personal band of bodyguards, clad in white robes to reflect the solemn nature of the occasion. The other four were his assistants, used to the stoic ways of the temple that lay in the shadow of the White Mountain. They would all bear their discomfort without complaint.

He motioned for Tingle, his designated successor, to follow, and the two of them carefully crept down the icy staircase that led to the bottom of the depression. During their descent, the sound of the wind died down, a striking change from the chaotic cacophony above the rim.

At least now, I'll be able to hear myself think, thought Ferrin.

He reached the rocky floor and made his way to one of the stone benches before the Covenant Stone. Tingle sat on the ground behind him and remained silent.

As Ferrin waited, he bundled up tightly and looked up at the crystal shard before him, so clear it barely hindered the light that passed through it. As he peered into its depths, he tried to imagine what it was like, two centuries past, when Narr, the Dark Overlord, ruled the land. The entire Dalmeer Island chain had been held in his iron grip, the result of his brilliant manipulation of the powers of the Gludemic Mountains.

For forty-eight years, he had spread his unspeakable depravity across the land, destroying all who opposed him. But, as he became feeble with age and almost blind, the tormented populace had risen up, and they overthrew the wicked overlord. Determined to prevent a repeat of his odious reign, they instituted a Covenant wherein the powers of the White, Gray, and Blue mountains were to be placed in the hands of three separate individuals—the Mediums. This Covenant guaranteed their cooperation, for no one Medium could seize the power of the Gludemic Mountains against the will of the other two. It would be of no advantage to murder another Medium, because once one Medium passed, all three Gludemic Mountains would become dormant, to be revived only when a successor was duly sworn in—the successor officially designated by the deceased Medium.

3

Ferrin's thoughts turned to his many patients awaiting Mount Krin's reawakening, specifically Deralia, the beautiful and gentle wife of his eldest grandson. She had been injured in a riding accident, and now her life teetered on the edge. The sooner he returned to Drumel and focused the healing powers of the White Mountain upon her damaged body, the greater her chance of survival. Despite his anxiety over Deralia's welfare, he did not for a second question the wisdom of the Covenant.

Movement above the rim caught his attention, and he watched two figures clad in blue robes gracefully descend the stone stairway beside another of the pillars. The figures were small, and they made no effort to draw the flowing material of their garments more closely around their bodies. One of the blue-robed figures sat upon another of the benches facing the Covenant Stone while the other sat on the frozen ground behind it.

The figure on the bench grasped the folds of her blue hood and tossed them back, and Ferrin was pleased to behold the lined but elegant face of Er Lomith. She was an elderly woman, yet her great beauty was still evident. Ferrin smiled and studied her face, for it had been years since he had last seen her. Er Lomith returned the smile and pulled her long hair out from within her robe and let it flow in the light breeze. It was white as pristine snow. Her otherwise pale skin had a pronounced bluish tint around her neck and near her ears.

"Ah, Er Lomith, what a pleasure to see you again," said Ferrin. "I'm relieved to see it was not your demise that brought us here today. The years have treated you well."

"And it is good to see you, too, are still with us, Ferrin," responded Er Lomith. "Your hair has become nearly white as mine."

4

"I'm afraid age has taken its toll. A few years back, a journey like this would have been of no concern. Now, it is insufferable. Thankfully, they are few and far between."

He watched Er Lomith fan the folds of her hood to cool herself. "I would have thought these frigid winds would be to your liking."

"The heat could be worse, I suppose. But we are far from the Ice Shard Mountains."

Er Lomith was the Medium of Mount Lomith, the Blue Mountain. In its shadow, far from the villages of humans, lived the Lomitheri, a secretive tribe of beings. The Lomitheri loved the cold, and Er Lomith harnessed the chilling power of the Blue Mountain to serve the needs of her people.

Ferrin was familiar with their ways and knew that Er Lomith would respect human decorum and continue to suffer unless given a direct invitation to tend to her comfort.

"Please, Er Lomith, stand on no formalities around me, for I have known you too many years. Make yourself comfortable."

Er Lomith smiled and pushed back the edges of her robe, letting the garment fall around her waist and revealing her unadorned upper body. Now free from the constricting garment, Er Lomith's translucent wings, each twice as long as her body, unfolded and stretched in the air, maximizing their cooling power. Ferrin smiled as he watched her half-naked form, reminding him of the stirrings of his younger years. He had always found Er Lomith beautiful, but as desirable as she was, he knew that the heat of erotic passion was toxic to the Lomitheri.

After a moment, Er Lomith withdrew her wings. "Such a relief! So it is Grael who has fallen. Do you know the details?"

"About his demise? No." Ferrin, glanced up at the rim of

the depression, where he expected the last party to appear any minute. "But I'm sure that Clerith will fill us in."

Er Lomith also glanced up at the rim. "Grael's passing is a sad affair, but I hope today's procedures are completed quickly. Losing the Blue Mountain's power is already affecting my people."

"I agree. My people, too, suffer while Mount Krin lies dormant."

They heard a muffled command from above and watched two figures, this time clad in dark gray robes, descending the stone stairway near the third pillar. The first was of average height, but the second was smaller, even smaller than the two blue-clad Lomitheri. The first figure sat down on the last unoccupied bench while the smaller one sat on the ground behind it, as had the other two designated successors before them. After a moment's hesitation, the seated figure dramatically tossed back the gray hood obscuring his face and revealed not the fine features of Clerith, Grael's son and successor, but the bald, hook-nosed visage of his brother, Dran.

He gazed at the surprised looks on the faces of Ferrin and Er Lomith, his pointy chin becoming more prominent as he smiled. "Er Lomith, you're as lovely as ever. And Ferrin, how nobly you've aged."

"Dran!" managed Ferrin. "Where is Clerith? What has happened?"

"Dran, it was your brother who was designated," said Er Lomith. "Why are you here? If Clerith is ill, we should have—"

"Clerith isn't ill," interrupted Dran. "He's dead. He died in the same terrible accident that took my father's life."

The news shocked Ferrin. He and Er Lomith sat quietly,

frowns on their faces.

Dran stood up and looked solemnly to the northwest, the direction of the Gray Mountain. "It is a double tragedy that has taken much of the life from our small community. But the Gray Mountain lies dormant, and we must move forward."

He pulled out a gray crystal collar from the inner folds of his robe and laid it upon his stone bench.

"I'm all that's left, and I feel it is my duty to come here today to assume the responsibilities of the Krakul Gat."

"Dran, did you really think we would disregard the protocols and designate you Krakul Gat?" asked Er Lomith.

"This is most unfortunate," added Ferrin with a discernible note of irritation in his voice. He had made this arduous trip for nothing. "I regret your double loss, but we cannot accept you into the Covenant like this. Our ancestors established these protocols with good reason. One must be designated."

Ferrin paused and shook his head in exasperation and then looked at Er Lomith. "I'll return to Drumel and send word to Queen Cirmar to convene the Council of Sages." Turning now to Dran, he continued. "We must study on this and bring in the most qualified individual from your tribe."

"My tribe!" exclaimed Dran. "Do you realize the population of our island is down to forty-seven men, women, and children? And most of these are fishermen. The people of this land have entrusted the title of Krakul Gat to my bloodline for nearly a hundred years, and only I remain. I'm the only one qualified."

"Perhaps you are," calmly replied Er Lomith. "And in that case, you will be the one selected as a result of our researches."

"I don't wish to sound offensive," added Ferrin, "but we also must rule out foul play. We must investigate the deaths of your brother and father."

"Regardless of your wish, the suggestion is offensive," said Dran.

Er Lomith let out a sigh and stood up, hanging her head. "We must abort the ceremony and regroup after the investigation. My people will take the delay hard."

"As will mine," said Ferrin, also looking downcast as he rose. He did not cherish the thought of making this trip again in a few weeks, but of more concern was this unexpected delay in the return of Mount Krin's healing powers. "I wish, Dran, you had sent word. We could have planned this better."

Dran walked to the Covenant Stone and placed his hand upon it, looking up at its full height.

"My dear Ferrin," he began, still looking at the stone, "what will Drumel do without the powers of the White Mountain for several more weeks? I heard the tragic news that the wife of your oldest grandson lies near death because of an accident. And that her injuries could be healed in a matter of hours, should Mount Krin's powers be restored?" Dran turned to Ferrin, his face filled with pity. "Is this true?"

Ferrin slowly nodded. "It is. She will probably perish without the help of the White Mountain."

Dran turned toward Er Lomith. "And isn't it true, my dear Er Lomith, that the past season has been the warmest in memory for the Ice Shard Mountains? And that the Lomitheri, especially the fine group of young Lomitheri, are suffering greatly from the heat? How many will lose their lives before the power of the Blue Mountain is restored?"

"Some," said Er Lomith, shaking her head. "Too many—but that can't be helped. We have a great responsibility to proceed with caution. We've taken our most sacred oath to prevent a

8

repeat of history." As if the thought were a heavy burden, Er Lomith regained her seat upon her bench.

"It is only by protecting the integrity of the Covenant that we can protect our people," added Ferrin. "The scars of the Dark Overlord yet remain upon this land."

"Yes, Ferrin, I studied my school lessons along with all the other children. But is that the issue here?"

Er Lomith's voice was firm. "The protocols have been established to protect—"

"Yes, protect," interjected Dran. "We must be responsible to the people of the Dalmeer Islands and ensure they are watched over with good will. That is why our ancestors established the protocols of the Covenant Stone. I understand all that. But these protocols are mere procedures. They aren't the important thing, not in themselves. What matters is wise guardianship. As we pursue this investigation, the children of the Lomitheri perish from the heat, and people who have journeyed to the White Mountain suffer and even die from injuries that are curable once the Covenant is re-established."

Dran leaned on the Covenant Stone and gazed at the faces of his audience. "As you both know, I am the son of the last Krakul Gat. Grael, my father, designated my brother instead of me as his successor, but I suggest that the choice was a difficult one. We both have our merits, and my father knew that."

He pulled out a sheet of writing parchment from the folds of his robe. "A mining tunnel collapsed on Grael and Clerith as they were completing their inspections. Clerith died immediately. We dug my father out from under the debris still alive, but he survived only two days. As he lay dying, he called me to his side and asked this letter to be written. It's in a servant's hand, but he signed it himself."

Dran handed the letter to Ferrin, who read it attentively. After a few minutes, he passed it to Er Lomith and then studied Dran. "He speaks highly of you. He says you were even brighter than Clerith in your studies, and that you possess natural leadership."

"My father loved me, and as with all loving parents, was no doubt biased." Dran held open his hands in a humble gesture.

"Yes," said Er Lomith pensively. "One almost wonders why he selected Clerith at all."

"Well, as I suggested, the choice was not an easy one."

Ferrin also re-seated himself upon his bench. "It may be as you say. But the consequences of a misplaced step can be even more tragic than our current ordeals. Sometimes, sacrifices must be made to ensure—"

"But the Covenant that protects us is more than a protocol for selecting our successors," interjected Dran once again. "No one Medium can take control. If I were to break with the long tradition of my family's caretaking of the Gray Mountain and attempt to gain power over the dominions of the Dalmeer Islands, what could I do? The powers of Mount Lomith and Mount Krin will always be greater than that of the Gray Mountain alone. And one man can wear but one of the crystal bands. So, should I kill the two of you, then the Covenant would be violated and all three Gludemic Mountains powerless. There would be no point."

"That is true, but..." began Ferrin, but he allowed his sentence to trail away, his thoughts inwardly directed. Both he and Er Lomith were silent.

Dran rubbed his face with his hands and spoke soft, articulated words. "Our people suffer, and it need not be. By the time we complete our treks home, embark on a trip to Kromul Island, and complete the research, weeks will have passed. And then we must all retake the journey here to the Covenant Stone to install Grael's successor. Many will have died. Even on Kromul Island, our mines will lay untended while the Gray Mountain sleeps. Our population of fishermen is of no use in the mining tunnels, so our small economy is failing without our exports of tin and silver. Let us now set these procedures aside to preserve those we love. Let us re-establish the Covenant and return to our posts, where our people need us."

Er Lomith stroked her pure white hair as she looked into the distance. Ferrin was also far away in thought. Dran remained silent, apparently willing to let his case rest.

At last, Er Lomith spoke, her voice heavy and grave. "There are fourteen small children in our village, and many lay in agony as I left. And with the warmer temperatures, the mating rituals are dangerous. I tell you frankly, nothing less than the loss of a whole generation of our tribe is at stake." She studied Dran for a moment longer and then turned to Ferrin. "Ferrin, I will agree to this breach in protocol. I do this for my people. I believe there is, in fact, little risk. The Covenant is structured so we remain protected."

"Er Lomith!" exclaimed Ferrin. "You, of all people, sanction this?"

"I do."

Ferrin looked down and said nothing further. He thought about Deralia's face, and how it shone with delight as she examined a spring flower, and his grandson's expression of deep contentment as he held her close. Tears welled in the old man's eyes. He looked at Er Lomith and then Dran, and nodded.

11

"I, too, have loved ones in peril." His voice was hoarse. "And I also sanction this breach in protocol."

He stood up and walked to Dran's bench, where he picked up the gray crystal collar, and after a moment's hesitation handed it to Dran. "Dran, you may participate in the Covenant. Let us pray that we aren't putting the ones we love in greater peril."

Broken Covenant

Dran received the collar of gray crystal from Ferrin and nodded. They both returned to their benches.

"Once you enter the Covenant, you can never remove the band," explained Ferrin, his eyes riveted on the gray collar in Dran's hand. "And should you die, the powers of the Gludemic Mountains will become dormant in a matter of weeks and will remain so until we re-establish the Covenant. Whom do you designate as your successor?"

Dran stood up and beckoned the small figure seated behind him to come forward. "I designate Ilsher, my daughter."

"Have her pull back her hood so we may see her face," said Ferrin.

The small figure cast aside her hood, revealing a lithe young girl of twelve years. She had pulled her long brown hair into a ponytail. Her face seemed older than her frame, with large eyes and pronounced eyebrows.

"I am Ilsher." She said it simply, without flourish. Yet she exhibited a confidence that impressed both the Blue and White Mediums.

"Very well." Ferrin's official voice rang loudly. "Ilsher shall be your designated successor." He motioned for her to return to her seat on the ground, and turned to face the stone. "It is this stone that binds the Mediums to the Gludemic Mountains, and through Gludema's power, which the mountains channel from the land between, they are bound to one another. Only a Medium, by the grace of Gludema, can control the power of a Gludemic Mountain, and only one who takes part in the Covenant can become a Medium.

"I, the Medium of Mount Krin, the White Mountain, accept into our Covenant Dran as the new Krakul Gat, the Medium of the Gray Mountain." Ferrin inserted his left arm into an opening in the side of the Covenant Stone that faced him.

"And I," began Er Lomith, "the Medium of Mount Lomith, the Blue Mountain, also accept Dran as the new Krakul Gat." She also inserted her arm into the opening facing her then grasped Ferrin's hand at the center of the stone.

"Now," said Ferrin, "place the gray band around your neck and insert your left arm into the opening in front of you."

Dran placed the collar around his neck and clasped it shut, then inserted his arm as instructed. He grasped Ferrin's and Er Lomith's hands at the center of the stone, and as he did, the great stone glowed with a cold, soft light. The crystal collars around Ferrin's and Er Lomith's necks also began to glow.

"My collar is getting warm," Dran said, wonder in his voice.

Then Dran's collar, too, gave off a light glow, but of a grayish color. There was a pronounced click, and Dran felt the collar with his free hand.

"It is done." Ferrin removed his arm from the stone. "The Covenant is sealed. And you, Dran, are the new Krakul Gat. I welcome you to our fold, and may you wield your power wisely."

Dran was visibly moved as he continued to finger the band around his neck.

"The seam has vanished," he observed.

Er Lomith nodded. "It has been permanently sealed and can never be removed from your neck during your lifetime. At which time, the powers of the Gludemic Mountains will once again be interrupted until we meet here to re-establish the Covenant with your designated successor."

"Is that it? I'm the new Krakul Gat?" asked Dran as if he had difficulty believing it.

"It is done," said Er Lomith.

"I understood there was more ceremony."

"Well, there is the Litany of Limits," replied Er Lomith, "to be read now that the band is in place."

"But no one can change it?" he asked.

"No one," said Ferrin gravely. "Until you die."

Dran stood up and smiled at his daughter, who gave him a hug.

"You did it, my father."

Dran shook his fist in an excited gesture. "Yes!" He then looked sheepishly at the solemn faces of the other two Mediums. "Please excuse my excitement. This is a meaningful moment in my life."

"Quite so," said Er Lomith, "but let me assure you, your new title has more than its fair share of burdens associated with it. Once you know these more clearly, your enthusiasm may well be dampened."

"Time is of the essence, so let us proceed with the reading of the Litany of Limits," urged Ferrin. "It is important that you understand them thoroughly."

"Ah, the Litany of Limits." Dran looked up at the sun still visible above the rim of the depression. "And how long does this lecture last?"

"Why, an hour or so," answered Ferrin. "But they have to be discussed after they are read, which will take an hour or two longer. We must be certain you understand them. The reading of the Litany of Limits is a crucial part of your preparation to become a wise and competent Krakul Gat. This is especially so in your case since you weren't here for your father's ceremony, as you were not designated as successor."

"It's part of our Covenant," added Er Lomith. "We limit our powers according to the best interests of our people. You must understand what those limits are."

Once again, Dran looked up at the sun and then back to Ferrin and Er Lomith.

"I'm afraid I must delay this portion of the proceedings. My powers are urgently needed at home."

"What?" cried Er Lomith, her voice incredulous.

"Yes, that's true of us all," said Ferrin, "but there's much you must learn, much you must understand."

Dran stood up and adjusted his robe and hood. "Just consider this a necessary postponement. We'll get together soon and pick this up again." He smiled at the other two and walked toward the stone staircase leading back up to the rim of the depression. Ilsher followed. As he climbed toward the rim, he called down to Ferrin and Er Lomith. "I will send word, but in the meantime, a good journey to both of you."

Dran's followers stood up and fell into line behind him as he scurried down the path from which they came. Er Lomith and Ferrin watched with amazement, remaining seated on their benches.

After a moment or two of stunned silence, Er Lomith spoke up, shaking her head in disbelief. "It has occurred to me that a better arrangement would be to read the Litany of Limits *before* the collar is sealed."

"What have we done?" asked Ferrin.

"I don't know." Er Lomith pulled the folds of her robe over her bare shoulders. "But when it comes right down to it, the Litany is common sense."

"Hmm. Dran has plenty of sense," said Ferrin. "I hope his heart is in the right place."

"But he's right, you know. Even should he make some power play, what can one Medium do alone?"

"You don't know of anything, Er Lomith, and neither do I. Let us pray that Dran doesn't, either."

* * *

The Plain of Nubinor covered nearly all the interior of Bewel Island, the most northern of the Dalmeer Islands. Along its thin and fertile coast, several towns thrived on commerce and fishing, towns such as Bewel City and Trimlin on the west coast, and Reador on the east. These communities were protected from the incessant winds that bowled down from the frozen wastes farther north, either by the Balor Mountains in the west or the towering trees of the great Ronin Woods that spread in a northwesterly direction from the outskirts of Reador.

But the interior plain, a barren expanse of sparse grass and dry snow, was subjected to the full brunt of the northern winds. No crops could grow there, and because of its sacred status, horses and other animals were forbidden to tread upon it; though, no animal could derive much sustenance from its meager ground cover. Consequently, the citizens of the coastal cities rarely entered far into the interior. Should the need to visit other coastal communities arise, they relied on the more comfortable and celeritous ships that carried supplies and passengers along the coast of Bewel Island.

After the aborted ceremony, Ferrin and his retinue had traveled for two days in a southeasterly direction across the plain. But now the snowy heights of the Balor Mountains loomed on the northwestern horizon. Bewel City was not far. There, they would embark on their xebec to begin their two-day voyage home.

They still had several hours of brisk walking ahead of them, however, so they took a rest to break bread. Ferrin sat on the snowy grass and was soon miles away as he absentmindedly gnawed on his hardened trail bread. He was thinking of his ailing granddaughter-in-law when a large shadow blocked out the sun. He looked up to see Huskar, the Captain of the White Guard.

"Riders," he said. "To the north. They are moving quickly and heading in this direction." As always, Huskar spoke directly and with little emotion.

"Horsemen? Out here?" Ferrin stood up and peered off into the distance, barely able to see the swirling cloud of dust and powdered snow.

"How much farther to the walls of the city?" he asked.

"If we were to march with no rest, perhaps three hours."

"Then let us hurry. I'm uneasy about these approaching riders."

"Aye," replied Huskar, "I'm uneasy, too. But, My Lord, they will reach us in an hour."

Ferrin scanned the surrounding terrain. To the southwest, a group of low-lying hills in the direction of Bewel City were visible, but they were too far away to be used for defense.

As were the Balor Mountains, several hours' march to the northwest. Otherwise, the plain was unbroken flatness. "It may be nothing," he said. "But let us prepare the best we can. Deploy your men, Captain, and draw your weapons."

"Aye, My Lord. We will be ready."

* * *

At about the same time, at the opposite end of the Plain of Nubinor, Er Lomith and her fellow Lomitheri were ascending a rising slope as their trail neared the village of Reador, a fishing community at the southern lip of the Ronin Woods. Being unused to the warmer temperatures, they suffered from the exertion of climbing the hill. All were breathing hard by the time they reached the top. Before them, the edge of the Ronin Woods was a few hundred yards away, and the buildings of the village several miles farther.

"Not far now, my comrades," said Er Lomith, looking back at her panting followers. "We reach Reador in an hour."

"I cannot wait to shun these garments," whined Schmie. "I have sweat to the point of exhaustion."

Er Lomith looked at Schmie with affection and sympathy. Schmie was the most capable of the younger generation of Lomitheri, a mere sixty-five years old, and Er Lomith had designated her as her successor. But, as young persons were want to do, she desired to have things her own way.

"But not yet, my dear," warned Er Lomith. "We all know the stir we create among our human brethren when we disrobe. We don't want trouble to delay our return."

"Just until the ship," replied Schmie. "A few sailors could do no harm."

"That is true. However, since I have seen you wield a sword, it is the welfare of the sailors that would concern me, not yours. So please, disrobe only in your berth."

"As you wish." Schmie bowed her head in submission.

The group made their way down the opposite slope of the hill, meandering past an occasional towering evergreen as they neared the edge of the forest proper, a welcome change to the unbroken plain they had just traversed. Old Halinan, walking near the front of the party, abruptly halted. As she did, a few of the band bumped into her. But, the Lomitheri were a good-natured race, so they merely giggled and walked around her. Er Lomith, however, did not giggle. She paused and watched her with concerned curiosity.

At one time, Halinan had been Er Lomith's main rival for the leadership over the Lomitheri. She had been famed for her wondrous talents, one of which was her perceptiveness, so sharp that many thought her clairvoyant. Now, she was but a shell of her former self, having come unraveled from losing the power struggle. She remained reserved and awkwardly quiet, never speaking to anyone unless they spoke to her first. But although her peculiar ways sometimes made her the object of ridicule from the younger generation, Er Lomith never lost respect for her.

As Halinan stood staring into the direction of the woods, where a spur of the forest crossed the trail, Er Lomith gently took her hand. "What is it? Are you okay?"

"There is something amiss," Halinan whispered.

"What do you mean?" asked Schmie, who was standing next to Er Lomith. "Do you think we have lost our way?" She had a slight smirk on her young face.

"No. This is our way," replied Halinan. "But up ahead, in

the trees, something is amiss. I can sense it."

A few of the Lomitheri softly giggled in mellifluous tones. Er Lomith, however, stood silent, studying the edge of the forest.

"Disrobe," she commanded the members of the band, her voice stern. "Be prepared to take flight at a moment's notice."

She peered back at the woods and drew her sword.

Chimber Gets an Assistant

Chimber rested on the handle of his sweat-covered shovel. He was halfway finished digging his third grave of the morning and was quite spent. There was no one to blame but himself. He had scheduled all three burial ceremonies for this afternoon, so the graves had to be ready.

At least it'll be a profitable day.

He pulled his tall frame out of the partially completed grave and reached for his pigskin flask, letting his youthful but well-formed muscles relax as he sipped the warm water. His black shoulder-length hair, dripping with sweat, stuck to his bare and darkly tanned shoulders. Years of digging graves had made them broad and strong.

As he rested, he surveyed the burial grounds. He had dug nearly all the newer graves scattered about, and he was proud of that fact. Anyone could dig a hole in the ground, but Chimber knew his customers valued his professional approach and his solemn rendering of the Gludemic rites during the burial ceremony. Word got around, and his customers kept coming back for more. With the White Medium missing, more people were dying in the town of Math than ever before. Although Mount Krin emanated *some* healing energy, even without the White Medium at the helm, it was not strong enough for people with serious injuries to make the journey to Drumel. Most chose to avoid the rigors of travel and stay home, hoping their injuries would heal on their own. And often they didn't. Chimber didn't want people to die, but when they did, he might as well be the beneficiary.

He heard the tower bell and sighed. He would have to finish the grave after lunch, and the sun was coming on strong.

He stashed his water flask under the shadow of the mound of soil piled up beside the grave and left Math's cemetery, which was on the outskirts of the village. Math had a good harbor and good soil, but because it was located off the main commerce lines of the island chain, stuck in an unfrequented corner of Saghorn Island, it had never grown large.

Like all provincial villages throughout the Dalmeer Islands, the midday market took place in the central plaza. As Chimber passed by the cluster of stalls, the sound of rickety carts banging over cobblestone streets was everywhere. The towns-folk were busy running last-minute errands before breaking for lunch. As he walked along, he greeted several of his acquaintances but would not allow himself to be drawn into conversations. Otherwise, he would have hell to pay when he returned to his labors with the sun looming even higher in the sky. He would just grab a quick bite and return to the cemetery in good time.

His simple cottage was a few steps from the harbor under the shadow of a giant rock outcropping, which kept its rustic confines cool on hot summer days. Its walls were made of stacked stone, and the interior, two large rooms with a few pieces of humble furniture, retained the smoky odor of the previous night's repast.

As it always was, the cottage was empty. He lived there alone and often felt the dull pinch of loneliness. While collecting a few items for his simple noon meal, he thought wistfully about meal times when he was young.

His father had been a quiet man and would rest after cleaning up from his hard day's work. Chimber remembered him as a steady, stable, and hard-working provider. His brothers often became boisterous while waiting for dinner, especially after a tipple or two of ale. All the same, the house was full.

Both brothers and his father were lost at sea when he was still a young lad, leaving him and his mother to bear the grief and support one another until she, too, passed gently.

He sought to follow his father's example by building a solid reputation for himself, saving up his resources for the future. This modest starter cottage was just a stepping stone. Soon, he hoped to own a larger house, suitable for a family, and possibly a little land for farming. As he glanced around his meager abode, he couldn't resist envisioning a wife and children living there with him. One day, if he worked hard and steady, that life would be a reality. The love and laughter of a family would keep him company.

But first, he had to have something to offer his future bride—whoever she may be. *It's coming*, he thought. Patience, prudence, and hard work would soon pay off. He'd hardly had a day off these past two years, but his coffers were filling quickly.

He sat down and assembled a meal of coarse bread and cold beef. He had just taken a small swig of beer when there was a sudden and loud knocking on the partially-closed wooden shutter behind him. The abrupt knock startled him, and he jumped up from his table and angrily flung open the shutter, ready to tell whoever was so rude about proper manners.

But when he saw Jern standing there grinning back at him, Chimber's anger subsided.

Jern was Chimber's best friend and had been for years, yet they were in striking contrast. Chimber's frame was robust and solid while Jern was short and thin, though his wiry limbs possessed their own sort of athleticism. He had large green eyes, almost elf-like, and his face displayed a mischievous smirk at all times.

"How goes it, Chimber?" Jern said.

"Blast it, Jern, you scared the life out of me!" exclaimed Chimber. "Can't you knock on the door?"

Jern chuckled. "You were sitting next to the window. I didn't want you to have to get up."

"Very considerate of you," said Chimber. "What if I had a mouthful of food? I would've choked to death."

"Ah, well, I'll try to time it better next time."

"*Ha, ha,*" said Chimber sarcastically.

"Hey, Chimber, Lerla and Sajia have asked us to give them a hand stacking apple crates over at their orchard. The southern orchard. You know, the one beyond the bend of the river, hidden from Old Man Rackley's prying eyes. What do you say we give them a hand? Consider it your good deed for the day."

"Sajia, huh?" said Chimber, contemplating her spirited personality and voracious appetite. Then he recalled his half-completed grave. "I can't. I've got three burials this afternoon, and I'm still digging the last grave."

Jern stepped back from the window in mock amazement. "You're kidding me! You would rather drop dead bodies in the ground than frolic on the riverbank with Sajia?"

"Er, no. I wouldn't. But this is what being a professional

is all about, Jern. People count on you, and if you provide a reliable service, they'll keep coming back for more." He looked at Jern thoughtfully. "Which reminds me, why aren't you over at the town corral? Aren't you supposed to be exercising Klapid's horses?"

"Well, no, not really. That's, um, off for now," managed Jern.

Chimber slapped the windowsill with his palm. "I knew it! When I saw you going into the tavern with Lerla yesterday, smack in the middle of the afternoon, I wondered if you had screwed up again. I said to myself, 'Chimber, I bet that slacker Jern has skipped out of his work.' Were you a no-show?"

"You know, Chimber, Sajia asks about you all the time," replied Jern in an obvious attempt at evasion. "You should spend more time with her."

Chimber returned to his chair and sat down, solemnly shaking his head.

"I would love to," he said, attempting a fatherly tone, "but I have a job to do, for which I am well paid. That's how it works, Jern. You have to sacrifice to keep a job. You have skills with horses. No one in Math is better, and everyone knows it. But if you don't show up when they hire you, it won't matter. They'll go elsewhere."

Jern shrugged. "I know all that. And I can get work if I need it. I always can. But sometimes, you know, you've just got to break free. Step outside the narrow path. You should try it yourself sometimes. You're letting life pass you by."

Chimber noticed Jern glancing at the food on the table as they spoke, so he waved him around. "Come on in and have a nibble." Jern ambled in and sat down at Chimber's table, one at which he had sat many a time.

Chimber leaned back in his chair and folded his arms. "I'm not letting life pass me by, Jern. I perform an important service in the lives of the people of this town. Plus, I'm saving for the future. When the right girl comes along, I've got to be ready with something more than this place to offer her. I wouldn't want my future wife to run off with another man who's better equipped."

"Oh, no need for me to prepare for that," quipped Jern. "I'm already perfectly equipped for the ladies." He punctuated his remark with a wink.

Jern surveyed the table's offerings and assembled a sandwich. "You know, it's odd to say that you perform a service in the lives of people by presiding over their deaths."

"I put away their decaying bodies, that's true," replied Chimber, "but it is to the living I'm important. They need to know that the spirit of the deceased is protected from unsavory forces on its downward journey to the land in between. And it is more than that. It's about the deceased's loved ones bidding a proper farewell; it's about completeness."

"Maybe, but it sounds like you're full of yourself," mumbled Jern with a mouthful of food. "And what are you going to do if they ever find Ferrin, and Mount Krin begins healing people again? You'll be scraping for work, just like me."

"I'd be happy for the return of the White Medium, just like everyone else. But it has been two years now, so he may never return. No one knows. In the meantime, I'll be available whenever my services are needed. Besides, lots of people die from things besides injury. We all get old. My business isn't going anywhere."

"Chimber, you have a strange way of—"

A firm knock on the door interrupted Jern's comment.

Chimber scowled. "I'll get a headache with all this knocking." When he opened the door, he found Elder Lumm, one of the old bureaucrats who ran the town of Math. His rich brown beard was immaculately trimmed, and his leather lederhosen, as usual, were spotless. No small feat given the fact that his belly protruded far enough to intercept most dropped food.

"Elder Lumm!" said Chimber, pleased to have a member of the Council of Elders in his home. "Come in, come in. Have a seat. What can I do for you? Would you care for some lunch?"

Elder Lumm glanced at the rustic spread of food and then at Chimber. "No, thank you. This will only take a minute. I received a request from Warden Kruuger at Pith Isle Prison. It seems several prisoners have passed away, and while they usually just bury them themselves, several of the deceased's relatives have insisted on a proper burial. Pith Isle is under our administrative jurisdiction, so it falls upon the Council's shoulders to provide a proper gravedigger. Naturally, Chimber, you came to mind. It's your call, but you would have to set sail on the morning tide. The pay would be generous."

Chimber rubbed his chin for a moment, thinking about the three afternoon ceremonies in front of him. He'd be exhausted by the time he'd finished, but it was a good opportunity.

"Pith Isle, eh? How many?"

Elder Lumm scratched his chin. "A handful. Maybe five or six."

"Hmm. Am I allowed to take an assistant?"

"That seems a reasonable request," said Elder Lumm, weighing a bag of coins in his hand. "And I have a small retainer to get you started. Interested?"

"Yeah, I'll do it," said Chimber.

Elder Lumm tossed him the bag of coins. "Well, here's your

retainer. Is your xebec available, or would you need to use the city's sloop?"

"Ah, no thanks," said Chimber. "I'll use my xebec."

He showed Elder Lumm out and walked over to the table, lost in thought. He absentmindedly tossed the bag on the table, where the coins spilled out in front of Jern.

His friend's eyes widened with interest. "So. Who are you taking?"

"Hmm? As my assistant? Not sure. I gotta round someone up in a hurry."

"Hey, Chimber, why don't you take me?" cried Jern, jumping up from his chair. "I could use a few coin in my pocket."

Chimber eyed his friend.

"Well, I guess so, since you bailed on your last job. And this proves my point. I've worked hard to earn my reputation. Did you notice what Elder Lumm said? He 'naturally' thought of me. I have a reputation at stake, so I can't take an assistant that would be unreliable."

"Chimber! What a painful stab!" said Jern with mustered, but not wholly convincing, indignation.

"Well, if it walks like a duck and quacks like a duck..."

"No quacking, I promise." Jern jerked up his right hand and held it rigidly as if swearing in for duty. "I give you my word. If you hire me as your assistant, I will do your bidding."

Chimber frowned and rubbed his chin. Jern had real potential and he wanted him to succeed. But he could be so damned inconsistent and flippant. Sometimes Chimber wondered if he should advise his friend more than he did, but Jern didn't receive advice well. So instead, he tried being a quiet example, like his father had been for him.

"Okay, Jern, as long as you can dig a hole when requested. I wouldn't need you for the ceremonial services anyway."

Jern sat on his chair with an air of satisfaction, once again eying the coins spread upon the table. "Dead bodies, digging holes, weird ceremonies. It sounds like fun."

Chimber put the coins back in their pouch. "We leave early tomorrow. Before dawn. We gotta have our supplies packed by early light. We should be prepared for a journey of four days, counting return time."

"Okay, but might I have a few of those coins sent my way in the meantime? You know, for my own supplies?"

Again, Chimber regarded Jern. He wanted to trust him, but too many times Jern had left him in the lurch. Six graves would be a lot to handle on his own in one day, and this gig was good pay; he couldn't afford to let anything ruin it.

"You get paid after the job is done," he asserted. "In fact, meet me here at sundown. We'll gather up our supplies tonight, and you can sleep on my floor. That way, I know you'll be here on time."

"Ah, Chimber, don't you trust me?" asked Jern. When he got no response from a stone-faced Chimber, he continued. "Okay, fine, I'll do it." He stood up and brushed off his clothes. "So how do I look?"

"Um, like Jern, I suppose."

"Great! Thanks for the compliment. Well, I'm off to the apple orchard to do a little work handling crates with two lovely ladies. I will do my best to fill in for you."

At the word *fill*, Jern smirked and cupped his chest with his hands to simulate breasts.

"You do that," Chimber said, forcing his thoughts not to linger on Sajia's voluptuous form.

"Enjoy digging your holes," said Jern as he bounded out the

door. "See you at sundown."

Chimber shook his head and looked out the window. The sun was riding high in the sky with no clouds in sight. It would be a long afternoon.

The Strange Sight of Morning

The next day, dawn broke over a placid, warm sea. Chimber's xebec left the cozy confines of Math's small bay, and as he rounded its windward arm, the full rush of the open sea breeze blew across the deck of his craft. Invigorated by its moist coolness, he grasped the tiller more firmly and felt the craft surge forward. He felt exhilarated and alive—his craft one with the elements as he steered it before the breeze.

He loved his little hometown, but he equally enjoyed the adventure of leaving it from time to time, especially on sailing jaunts in his xebec. She was his one treasure. To be on the open sea just as the sun was coming up, riding the expansive waves with her sails responsive to his touch—there was nothing like it. Standing firmly on the wooden floor with feet planted, he softened his knees to absorb the movement and speed while expertly maneuvering her through the water. It felt similar to riding a horse. He could feel its power through his hands—steering her, riding her. It was a fantastic feeling.

He smiled as he looked down at Jern, wrapped up in a blanket and peering over the gunnels. He seemed in a trance-like state as he gazed at the rising sun.

"I figured you would be sound asleep by now," said Chimber.

"Yeah," said Jern rather flatly. "So that's what the sunrise looks like. I didn't know what I've been missing."

"Yep, it's there every morning, believe it or not."

Jern looked around at the expanse of the open sea. "I'm sure it is. But out here, it all seems intensified."

"That it does. Nothing is as exhilarating as sailing on a clear day with a favorable breeze. In fact, if this breeze keeps up, we should reach Pith Isle in a matter of hours."

Jern draped his blanket over his shoulders and wandered over to a large leather duffel bag sitting on the deck, rummaging around until he found a piece of cheese. He returned to his post at the back of the boat and nibbled on his breakfast. "A matter of hours, huh? So, we'll get there early this afternoon?"

"Yeah. If the wind holds."

"And we begin our burial duties tomorrow morning?"

"That's right," said Chimber.

"Don't get me wrong, Chimber, I'm enjoying this whole sunrise thing and the wind and the sea. But we'll reach Pith Isle with hours to spare. Yet we were up before dawn, had to fiddle with your very organized—some would even say overly organized—packing of supplies in the dark. We could have taken our time, reduced our stress level, and still have made Pith Isle landfall before sundown."

"Perhaps," returned Chimber. "Or perhaps our weather would have turned bad, or we would have had contrary winds—"

"But if the weather was bad enough, we would have had to delay our trip no matter what time we got up. And if it made us late, then we're late. But that would be a rare occasion, and we would have a good reason. With no one else to do the burials, they would just have to wait. And they're dead. They aren't going anywhere. So why fret so much?"

"You and I have differing viewpoints about these things, Jern. I prefer knowing I have minimized the chances of unexpected mishaps. Preparing for the worst but still being dependable. That's why I have my reputation. You would rather not worry about things to begin with and then worry if something happens."

Jern leaned back on the deck with his hands under his head and peered up at the mainsail. "I don't know, Chimber. You worry too much. You can't control everything."

"Hey, look at those porpoises!" exclaimed Chimber, pointing toward the eastern ocean.

"Yeah," said Jern, sounding sleepy and not even turning to look. His eyes remained fixed on the flapping mainsail. "Do they have a women's ward at this prison, I wonder?"

Chimber grinned and shook his head in disbelief. "I don't know, but we can find out. See? You and I will have something to do with our extra time after all."

The Saber Slash

As the sun heated the atmosphere, the invigorating morning breezes lost their potency, so it was close to sundown by the time the tiny craft tied up at Pith Isle's mooring dock.

Chimber tossed their two duffel bags to his sailing companion, who received them standing on the wharf. There were several other sea craft docked along the pier, one of which had an active crew on board, moving their day's catch to sea-filled tanks mounted in the center of the pier. Chimber and Jern glanced over the tiny village, a typical fishing community with wooden buildings, smoldering fires burning under fish racks, and nets mounted on the facades of several buildings.

"Now, aren't you glad we didn't dilly-dally this morning?" asked Chimber. "It would've been pitch black by the time we got here."

Jern shouldered one of the bags. "I suppose. But I need a thirst-quencher. What do you say we visit yon tavern?"

"Aye, I could use a tipple myself."

They walked across a small plaza of slimy cobblestones to a well-maintained two-story building close to the wharf. The only other buildings visible, aside from the large prison compound situated upriver, were small dwellings. The one exception was a large home just below the prison walls. It was three stories high, and ornate. The amber tones of the fading light cast a warm glow upon the facade of the home, accenting its contrast to the crude houses in the town.

"Nice house," commented Chimber as they crossed the threshold of the tavern and entered its candlelit interior. The air smelled of yeast and soot. Dark wood lined the walls. It took a few minutes for their eyes to adjust to the dim light, but the surroundings had that familiar coziness, which wayfarers would recognize in taverns throughout the Dalmeer Islands.

The open room had a scattering of tables and chairs, with two side stairways going up to a landing lined with doors to what Chimber assumed were rooms for rent. There was a long table positioned before a wall with a doorway behind it leading to the inn's kitchen. On the long table sat numerous empty and reasonably clean pewter mugs. Behind the table and on either side of the doorway were mounted two large casks, both marked "Saber Slash" in white chalk. Chimber and Jern sat at a table near the casks. A few patrons occupied other tables. A busty but hard-edged woman came over, and they ordered a round of the Saber Slash's house ale.

Jern savored the frothy mug. "So, what exactly will you be using me for?"

"Ah, you can help me test the cadavers," replied Chimber.

"Okay. What does that mean?" Jern peered about the tavern as he held the mug to his mouth.

"Well, you can't go burying bodies that aren't dead, now can you? So, you got to test them, to make sure."

"Yeah, being buried alive is bad. I can see that. So, what do you do?"

"Mouth to mouth," said a somber-faced Chimber.

"What?"

36

"You have to attempt to resuscitate them by breathing air into their lungs. If they are alive, hopefully they will revive."

"And you want me to...you aren't serious, are you?"

Chimber looked him dead in the eye. "Do you want to earn your wages or not? This is the profession. You are my assistant. Breathe air into these dead men's lungs if you want to be paid."

After a moment of consternation, Jern relaxed and took a long gulp of his beer. "You had better be kidding me."

Chimber smirked. "Well, tomorrow will tell."

"Can I breathe air into *her* lungs?" asked Jern, pointing to a lovely petite lady who had just come through the kitchen door and was examining the spigot on a cask of Saber Slash.

"Well, well," said Chimber, admiring the woman's form. "She is quite fetching." She had pulled her brownish-blonde hair into a ponytail, revealing her bare shoulders and graceful neck. Her eyes sparkled with intensity as she focused on the spigot.

"Hello, bar wench!" called Jern. "Over here, please." Jern's loud, scratchy voice caught the woman's attention. She left the spigot and came over to their table.

She looked them over. "Off-islanders, I see. What can I do for you?"

"Well," said Jern, "we would appreciate another round of your delectable ale and a jot of your company, if possible."

"About the ale, you will need to have Merriblan retrieve that for you. I'm not a 'bar wench,' as you so adorably put it. This tavern belongs to me and my husband. And as far as my company, I fear my talents at repairing casks will make me unavailable to you."

"So you're the taverness? My pardons," said Jern.

Chimber stood up. "I'm Chimber, and this is Jern," he said

in a polite voice. "We just arrived on an assignment at the prison. Sorry if my companion was rude."

"Oh, not at all. My name is Saffral, and in fact, I am the wife of the prison warden."

"I got it, ma'am," announced a voice from behind the long table. They all turned to Merriblan, who had set the cask spigot to rights. The ale was free-flowing again.

"A round of three, please, Merriblan," said Saffral, smiling at the two travelers. "Maybe I will give you that jot of company while I wait for my husband."

"Absolutely," said Jern with unveiled enthusiasm. "Please, have a seat."

"Do you live here in the tavern?" asked Chimber.

"No, no. We have a house near the prison walls."

"The grand house we saw up on the hill?" asked Jern.

"I've seen nothing like it, even on Capital Island," added Chimber.

"Well, it's big and lavishly embellished. But if you want to know the truth, it's not to my taste." Saffral received the ales from Merriblan and handed a fresh mug to Chimber and Jern.

"Doesn't the thought of sleeping so near all those criminals frighten you?" asked Chimber.

"It doesn't," she replied. "Perhaps it should. But my husband is a rather strict disciplinarian. I don't believe anyone would dare harm me."

"But if they hate him and someone escaped..." said Jern rather boisterously. He was already halfway through his second ale and was obviously feeling its effects. The Saber Slash Tavern was proud of the potency of its house ale.

"Well, maybe," she said, thinking it over. "But that's unlikely. The men are pitiful wretches. Prison life is hard.

The food is coarse, and punishment is severe. Most of them can hardly walk, much less scale the walls."

"I see," said Chimber, noticing that Saffral had replaced her friendly smile with a look of concern. "And how do you feel about it?" he asked, but added, "My apologies if the question is too personal."

"No, it's okay," she replied. "Well, my husband is wealthy and powerful, and I have everything I want. What more do you need to know?"

"Yeah!" offered Jern warmly.

"Hmm," responded Chimber, studying her. "True love, is it?"

"Love, bah! A fantasy." She looked over the two men once again. "And just what brings you two to our little slice of paradise?"

"We're professional gravediggers," blurted Jern. "You stab 'em, we plant 'em."

"*I'm* a professional gravedigger," corrected Chimber. "Jern here is my assistant on this trip."

She looked Chimber over. "I see it in your physique. Broad shoulders, dark tan. Nice."

"What about me?" asked Jern. "I get down in those holes, too."

She beamed a smile at Jern. "Yeah, you're kinda cute, too."

"Thanks for the kind words," said Chimber. "And sure, we—I should say I—dig a lot of holes in my profession, but the term 'gravedigger' is a bit misleading. It comes from the old days when a 'gravedigger' did little more than that—dig graves. Nowadays, a gravedigger must be an accomplished professional. Not only does the body have to be buried, but the gravedigger must be a performer, a psychologist, and a holy man. You help the living deal with their loss."

"Chimber is an officer in the Gravedigger's Guild," said Jern, slightly slurring the word "officer."

"Is he, now?" asked Saffral, smiling at Jern. She turned back to Chimber. "You seem very proud of your work."

"I am proud, but many people have a poor idea of what we do."

At that point, a man entered the doorway, catching Saffral's attention. He was a fastidious-looking individual who scraped his shoes and hung his coat on a rack near the door. He glanced over at Saffral with a scowl and made himself comfortable at a table.

"I'm sorry, gentlemen," said Saffral in a somewhat embarrassed tone. "My husband is not the friendliest of people. I must join him at his selected table. Perhaps I'll see you two again before you leave."

"I hope so," said Jern.

"Thanks for your company," said Chimber.

They watched her join her husband, who hardly looked up from a set of papers he was reading. She handed him an ale and mutely sat down.

"Did you hear that; she thought we were cute!" said Jern in a loud whisper.

"She's married, Jern. It doesn't matter what she thought about us."

"Maybe...maybe not. How long will we be here?"

"Just two days. Unless there are unexpected problems."

"Not a lot of time." Jern turned his pewter mug upside down and watched as a single drop of ale formed on its rim. He licked it off just as it was about to fall. "Well, are you ready for another round?"

"No, we need to go. We have to find someone at the prison to set us up for the night."

"Couldn't we stay here?" asked Jern.

"It would cost us," replied Chimber. "And I'm certain they'll have free quarters for us on the prison grounds."

"Why don't we ask Saffral's husband? He's the warden," suggested Jern.

Chimber studied the pinched-face man. "I don't think so. We'd better just check in at the prison compound."

As they walked out the doorway of the tavern, Chimber heard the sharp sound of a pewter mug being slammed onto a tabletop and glimpsed the prison warden's angry face before crossing the threshold.

"How could anyone be angry at a woman like that?" pondered Chimber.

Prison Ain't for Fun

Chimber and Jern made their way through the small cluster of crude houses and headed up the hill to the prison compound, along a road paralleling the small river that ran through town. The prison was perched on a bluff that rose high over the river. Just before reaching the compound, they passed in front of Saffral's ornate home, positioned on the scenic riverbank.

"Yeah, the warden is doing pretty well for himself," commented Jern as he looked over the home.

Chimber grunted in agreement. "I wonder how a prison warden acquired so much wealth, not to mention a beautiful wife?"

"It makes one wonder if there is a job open on the prison staff. I could work my way up."

"He must have inherited it," said Chimber. "I don't think a warden's salary would do it. And I don't think his wife automatically comes with the job."

Jern sighed. "You're probably right."

A stone wall enclosed the prison, appearing as a low-lying stockade. They approached a pair of battered and dusty wooden doors and clanged on a metal knocker. A panel opened in the center of the door, and a man in a helmet looked at them through the bars in the window.

"Yeah? What's your business?" he asked with a touch of boredom in his voice.

"I'm Chimber, and this is my assistant, Jern," replied Chimber. "We've been sent from Math to bury several deceased prisoners."

"The gravediggers, eh? Well, hold on."

He closed the panel, but in a moment another man, also in a helmet and a full uniform, creaked open the heavy wooden doors and stood before them. He was heavyset, with curls of unkempt, fiery red hair protruding beyond the edges of his helmet. His doublet depicted the double-diamonds of a military captain.

"I'm Charkol, Captain of the Guard," he announced, clearly not impressed as he looked them over. "Come with me, and I'll get you settled."

Saying nothing more, he led them across a dirt-packed and nearly empty interior courtyard. The inside of the prison differed from what Chimber and Jern had expected. There were no holding cells visible. Just a large L-shaped administration building toward the back of the open area, a stable with the garrison barracks attached, and an assortment of small utility buildings.

"Where are all your prisoners?" asked Jern.

"In their cells," responded Charkol with a matter-of-fact tone. "They don't come out here."

"But where are their cells?" persisted Chimber. "This one building doesn't seem large enough..."

"All cells are underground," said Charkol, pointing to one of the small buildings. "The entrance is inside there. The prison has four underground levels."

"No windows, no circulation—wouldn't be much fun,"

observed Chimber.

Charkol spat on the ground. "Well, now, prison ain't for fun, is it?" He brought them to the door of a small storage building. "You two will have to put up here. Nothing else is available unless you want to stay in a cell. We have several that have been recently vacated," he added with a smile.

"Um, this will be fine," said Chimber. "We would like to get started early tomorrow, before the sun gets too hot."

Charkol gestured toward the back of the building with his jutting jaw. "Be my guest. The bodies are stacked behind your building, next to the woodpile. The families will arrive on tomorrow's ferry, which gets here in the late afternoon."

"Thanks for all your hospitality," quipped Jern. "When will dinner arrive?"

Charkol spat again. "When you dig it out of your bag, I suppose." He made to leave, but looked back over his shoulder. "At this hour, there is no leaving the compound now that you've checked in."

Chimber and Jern looked at each other, shrugged in unison, and went inside the building. After lighting a beeswax taper near the doorway, they found two musty cots positioned between sacks of grain and large clay pots.

Jern slapped at one cot a few times, creating a dust cloud and sending several mice scurrying off. "At least we don't have to sleep on grain sacks. Done that already—not fun."

Chimber dusted off his cot. "Yeah, gravediggers are treated like royalty. Usually we are fed, at least. Good thing we came prepared, eh, Jern?" He dug out several packages from his duffel bag and unwrapped some smoked beef and more cheese.

"Well, I guess a good night's sleep is our only option. How many holes do we need to dig tomorrow?"

"Don't know," said Chimber. "Why don't you go around back and count the bodies?"

"No, thanks. I would rather just forget they were there for now." He lay on his cot, munching on dinner.

Chimber stood up and took the candle out of its base. "Some assistant you are. I guess I had better go. I've got to plan out our day."

"You do realize they won't go anywhere before morning?" asked Jern.

"Yeah. But I would rather know what we have in store for us."

Chimber left the shed, cupping his hand around the flame of the candle. Making his way around to the back in the dim light, he discovered a small mound covered with pieces of canvas. *Awfully small pile for six bodies*, he thought. *Maybe Elder Lumm was wrong about the number.* He pulled away the blankets and counted the heads.

There were, in fact, six cadavers—emaciated, pitiful speci-mens. They had been thrown one on top of the other, willy-nilly, face down. Chimber was accustomed to people taking better care with the deceased, if not out of love, then at least out of respect for the dead.

Certainly these poor souls weren't loved. At least not by anybody around here.

He moved the candle closer to the pile and frowned. The body on top had pale skin stretched over his bones. The spine arched toward him, with every vertebra easily visible, even in dim light, and the rib cage swelling under the skin on either side. Two sharp shoulder blades jutted out conspicuously. The back was covered in long thin scars, some still red. Chimber figured they were from the bite of a whip.

He gently rolled the top body over to examine the others. They were all equally scarred and scrawny, and all stacked face down. Various bruises and cuts, some red from infection, covered thin skin. Their faces were gaunt. Some wrists still had tatters of rope bound around them, cutting into the flesh, with dried blood caking the knots.

They hadn't even bothered to untie the poor fellows, Chimber thought, looking around himself protectively. He felt a chill along his spine in spite of the warm weather, and fought back a wave of nausea.

He gingerly laid all six bodies flat onto one of the pieces of canvas, face up and side by side, and covered them with the remaining section. He was aghast at how light each was. Given the appearance of the bodies, these poor souls may have been relieved to die. But criminal or not, every man deserved a proper and decent burial. He would give them that.

Jern's eyes were closed when he returned to the cots.

"How many?" Jern asked, his question punctuated with a yawn.

"Six."

"It took that long to count six bodies?"

Chimber sat on his cot and said nothing at first. Jern sensed something was wrong with his friend and sat up.

Chimber looked at him and bit his lower lip. "I've seen plenty of dead bodies in my profession. Sick ones and injured ones. But these men..." His voice trailed off.

"What is it?" asked Jern.

"Thin. Pale. Covered in lacerations. Pathetic. This is not a good place."

"Well, jail ain't for fun, now is it?" said Jern, mimicking Captain Charkol.

"No, I guess not," replied Chimber in a humorless tone. "Well, let's try to get some rest." He lay back on his cot and tried to relax. As the minutes passed, he heard Jern's breathing deepen with sleep. But he lay awake, restless, troubled by a dread he couldn't shake.

The Black Cloud

As Marshal Brechlin approached the harbor watchtower, she saw the harbor captain and his officers standing at attention near the entryway. As commander of Cegril's standing army, it was her duty to conduct periodic inspections of all aspects of Cegril's military resources—a dull, uninspiring task. But she had always liked Captain Labrok and the way he conducted harbor affairs. Not only were the harbor taxes collected in an efficient and fair way, his men were always disciplined and tended to their responsibilities with professional care. Brechlin hoped to bring him into her inner circle sometime in the near future.

She paused before the captain, and they exchanged military salutes with formal rigidity. Brechlin gave a quick nod to the other officers attending, grouped just behind Labrok. Although her build was slighter than those of the officers assembled, Marshal Brechlin was as tall as most, and none of them could mistake the authority with which she carried herself. She was a handsome woman with sparkling eyes full of intelligence and hair as black as coal; but, every soldier in the ranks, down to the lowest militiaman, knew that an inappropriate remark in her company would have dire consequences, as past instances of demotions and punishments had demonstrated.

She followed Labrok through the tower doorway, and the other officers respectfully filed in behind as he led them up the winding staircase to the watchtower's observation deck. As Brechlin stepped onto the platform, the full force of the cool sea breeze struck her face-on, much appreciated on a day as hot as this one. She stepped toward the ocean-facing merlons and looked out over the great expanse of the sea. From this vantage point, she had a panoramic view of the busy harbor. Numerous merchant brigs were docked next to Cegril's extensive moorings, and Cegril's small fleet of warships, three sleek sloops painted light blue and beige, were anchored apart from the activity of the harbor.

The sloops were, to all appearances, ready for action, but Brechlin knew that they were understaffed and the crews in need of training. Except for the occasional pirate and even rarer rebellion, there wasn't much demand for the services of this small navy. Whether or not the fleet should be dismantled was a constant bone of contention between her and Tarmot, Queen Cirmar's lover and recent adviser. He wanted the ships decommissioned and sold, netting the city a few dollars from their sale and saving the city the maintenance costs.

After giving Marshal Brechlin a few moments to take in the view, Captain Labrok directed her attention to a distant black band low on the horizon.

"Do you see that low-lying cloud bank?" asked Labrok. "It was heading in this direction an hour ago, but due to a shift in the wind, it's now moving due east."

"I see it," replied Brechlin. "It looks nasty; I've ever seen clouds so dark. Too bad it shifted, though. Our farmers could use the rain."

"True," said Labrok respectfully. "But this cloud—well, I'm not sure it's a storm cloud."

"What else could it be?"

"To be honest, General, I don't know. But there are experienced seamen under my command perplexed by its behavior. A merchant craft that passed near it reported there was no lightning, no wind, nor change in the sea. And our barometer readings have held steady. Odd for a storm. It seems, for lack of a better word, inert. I sent out a scout ship to sail into it and determine its nature. If it bodes evil, I thought it best to know in advance."

Brechlin studied the distant band but had difficulty appreciating Labrok's concern. "Hmm. Perhaps you should confer with the astrologers. I'm sure they would have something to say about it. It's not always wisdom, but they do have opinions. Anyway, as you pointed out, it now heads away from us, so it is of no serious concern."

"Not for us," replied Labrok. "But it heads toward Bewel and Saghorn islands. If it harbors some ill element, they will encounter it."

The Dalmeer Islands were a chain of islands that extended into the sea southward from the Rolucca Peninsula. Beyond the southern tip of the peninsula was Bewel Island, then Saghorn Island and then, separated by Ger Strait, was Capital Island itself, which was where Cegril, the nation's capital, was located. Farther south, a long necklace of tiny islands formed the Southern Cays.

"Perhaps," returned Brechlin, somewhat impatiently. "Surely we are overly concerned with a mere weather phenomenon. What of the collection of harbor tariffs? Do the merchants approve of our restructuring the assessment procedure?"

Labrok did not answer but was gazing out to sea. Something had caught his attention.

"Pardon me, General," he said after a moment. "I see our scout ship returning. The one I sent into the cloud. And it appears to be towing another craft behind it."

Brechlin's sharp eyes spotted the two ships, appearing like children's toys from this distance.

Brechlin shaded her eyes from the sun. "Curious. The ship being towed looks undamaged, yet it doesn't seem manned."

"It is curious," replied Labrok. "Something may have happened to the crew."

"This doesn't bode well. Perhaps the Southern Pirates?"

"But they would have taken the ship."

"Bilge fever?"

"It may be," said Labrok. "No need to take chances. I'll have an armed detachment meet the boats at the dock and quarantine all crew members. Shall I have you notified if it is bilge fever?"

"No need, Captain. You know your business. Let's continue with our inspection of the harbor, shall we?"

"Yes, General."

* * *

Brechlin and Labrok completed the dockyard inspection two hot and dusty hours later. As usual, the details were tedious, and as she had come to expect from Captain Labrok, everything was in perfect order. She began the climb up the hill through the lower town to barracks headquarters, where her administrative office and personal quarters were located.

As she approached the main entrance to the building, she spotted a court messenger lounging near the door. As soon as the messenger recognized Brechlin, he jumped up and bowed his head.

"Marshal Brechlin," said the messenger. "I have a note for you from the Counselor General."

Brechlin took the note with a puzzled expression. "The who?"

"From Tarmot, the Counselor General," returned the messenger, somewhat self-consciously.

"Oh, he's Counselor General now. Where did he come up with that title, I wonder?" replied Brechlin, obviously to herself, but the messenger shrugged anyway. As the messenger stood waiting, Brechlin read through the note. It requested her presence in the Counselor General's reception chamber as soon as possible.

"Tell the, um, Counselor General, I will see him as soon as I have refreshed myself in my quarters. It's been a hot morning."

"Very well," replied the messenger. He bowed and withdrew.

Brechlin entered her personal quarters and sat at a table made of a thick slab of weathered and nicked wood. She poured herself a cool ale, and while she sipped, she began tossing her knife into the wooden surface of the table, withdrawing it, and tossing it again.

She thought about how difficult it had been getting to where she was now—at the top of the ranks. It had been a mighty struggle within a male-dominated profession, but she hadn't minded working harder and smarter than her rivals. Her father taught her well, but she still had to prove her loyalty, courage, and determination time and time again. And she sacrificed any semblance of a "normal" life to become who she was, not only a military leader but the well-trusted and intimate confidante of Queen Cirmar.

I'll be damned if I'm going to let that weasel Tarmot screw this up for me, she thought and firmly embedded the knife into the wood.

After downing the last few swallows of her ale, she gathered herself up and began the ascent to the crest of the hill, where sat the Royal Palace, the political heart of all the Dalmeer Islands.

The Queen's Pleasure

Marshal Brechlin slogged up the hill to the Royal Palace, past a row of tidy administration buildings lining the roadway leading to its main gate. As she crested the top of the hill, she paused to look out at Cegril's harbor and catch her breath. Sweat drenched her skin.

At least the new palace will be a little more accessible.

She looked below at the construction site where the new palace lay nearly complete, an easy stroll from the harbor. She could see the piles of rubbish lying around the palace grounds and the row of worker shacks yet to be dismantled. Its new stone walls were a brilliant white, and its young gardens were already lush and colorful.

A few more days of preparation and cleanup, and the new structure would be ready to receive the queen and her court.

She climbed the steps to the front gate of the old palace and approached the guards who stood on either side. They allowed her to pass only after she formally stated her purpose for entering. A ludicrous routine, as the palace guards were technically under her command. But since Tarmot's ascendancy, he had instructed them to answer only to him and Queen Cirmar. Over the last few months, Brechlin had become used to such breaches in protocol and went through the motions without comment.

She entered the gate and crossed the inner courtyard. As she peered around the old, familiar building, she saw signs of neglect. The general maintenance of the inner buildings left much to be desired, but with all the realm's construction resources directed toward erecting the new palace, maintaining the old one had become a low priority, or forgotten about entirely.

Still. You would think they would replace the missing shingles on the palace roof. It looks shabby.

The old palace was not large, at least not compared to the new structure down the hill destined to replace it, but Brechlin had always appreciated its character. It had a notorious history. The Dark Overlord himself had occupied it and committed many of his odious acts within its walls, but it had housed generations of the ruling family over many centuries. Only in Drumel, in the convalescing wards surrounding Mount Krin, were there buildings of greater age on all of Capital Island. It was a shame to tear it down, but that was the queen's plan—at Tarmot's urging.

Just another symptom of misguided leadership.

She entered a large, long entry hall with a dark coffered ceiling and lined with matching hand-carved oak chairs. She turned down a side hall to Tarmot's reception chamber.

The chamber was ornate, filled with colorful and busy tapestries. Tarmot, wearing a yellow camicia covered with a purple-dyed leather jerkin, sat behind an elaborately carved desk and studied a ledger sheet while making no acknowledgment of her entrance. She recognized this as a juvenile attempt to emphasize her subordinate station, but it had happened so often that the gesture bordered on the ridiculous. In fact,

Brechlin doubted that Tarmot could read.

She studied the handsome man behind the desk with contempt. He was certainly clever but entirely interested in his own gain. Yet his charm had won over Queen Cirmar, a confident queen in most ways. Tarmot convinced her he thought she was beautiful, despite a prominent scar from a childhood accident, and she allowed him into her bed. The queen of the land needed human intimacy as much as any other member of the Imperial Realm, and there was nothing wrong with her taking a lover. But the problem was that Tarmot also had the queen's ear.

"Ah, Marshal Brechlin, thank you for responding to my summons so promptly," said Tarmot finally and with obvious sarcasm.

"Tarmot, you really—"

"That would be Counselor General, if you please," interjected Tarmot. "I must insist on formal titles."

"*Counselor General* Tarmot," returned Brechlin with obvious overemphasis, "I spent the entire morning in that steaming sun inspecting the waterfront. I trust you kept yourself cool and comfortable in the shade of the palace."

Tarmot gave Brechlin a complacent smile and shrugged. "It's here that the cogs of the imperial machinery are manipulated. This is where my queen wants me, where I can do the most good."

"One can only hope the queen is pleased with your manipulations," responded Brechlin, smiling internally at her little joke.

"She must be," continued Tarmot, missing Brechlin's innuendo. "She entrusts me to reassess the imperial budget. Which brings me to why I have summoned you." At this, Tarmot stood and deftly swung a new robe over his shoulders in a showy display, apparently deeming it a part of the Counselor General's proper ensemble. He walked to a window that allowed him a distant view of the palace construction site.

"As you know, our new palace is a tremendous enterprise, requiring extensive outlay of resources," he said after a moment's pause. "It will elevate the status of the queen throughout the Dalmeer Islands and will provide her with a residence more fitting to her station than this"—Tarmot waved his hand dismissively at his surroundings—"old pile of stones."

"Yes, I am aware of these motivations. You may recall, Counselor General, having enumerated them for me on several occasions."

"Yes, but I was not always certain of your acceptance of them," said Tarmot, looking down at the sheet before him. "But the importance of the new palace for the Imperial Realm is without question. And the debts the queen has incurred while having it built are justified. But now, the craftsmen and suppliers must be paid, since the palace is nearly complete, so we must dig deep for additional monies. Which brings us to the question of Cegril's military arm. It costs plenty to maintain the various branches of your command, certainly at the high level of readiness upon which you have insisted. Yet, and I don't know how to say this more clearly, we have no enemy at present. There is no reason for such elaborate city defenses. So, I would like you to review your..."

"You want to cut back on our defense budget again?" Brechlin asked in an incredulous tone. "You have already sliced it to the bone! Does the queen know of this?"

"The queen has empowered me to determine the best way

to generate the needed funds to pay the debts associated with the construction of the palace, not to mention the cost of landscaping the grounds," said Tarmot with a defensive tone in his voice. "And that's what I'm doing."

"And what if the citizens of Drumel stage another uprising?" asked Brechlin. "The White Mountain has been without its Medium for nearly two years now, and their city is suffering its worst economic crisis in recent memory. The rumblings of its city leaders are a reality. Or what of the Southern Pirates? It's true they haven't attempted a land raid in several years, but they are more than capable. And since Desmondi is still at large, that moment may be at hand."

"These are minor worries," returned Tarmot, again waving his hand in a dismissive gesture. "It's a matter of assessing priorities. Sure, disgruntled nobles could stage a coup to over-throw the queen, but should we divert our imperial resources for such a scenario? Of course not—that would be silly."

"You have no good reason for believing the Southern Pirates will remain quiet. They often attack in grouped assaults after lying low for several years and, frankly, the timing is right—"

"Marshal Brechlin, please," interrupted Tarmot. "Please allow the queen and her advisers to make these policy de-cisions and you focus on doing your job." He fiddled with one of the many tassels that embellished the sleeve of his robe. "I will give you three days to submit an outline of your recommendations for trimming the maintenance costs of Cegril's army by forty percent."

"Forty percent!" exclaimed Brechlin. "Are you out of your...we will see what Queen Cirmar has to say about this."

Brechlin spun around and stomped out of the chamber in a fury, heading for the queen's private suite. Tarmot dashed out from behind his desk and caught up with her, walking in stride.

"Brechlin, I wouldn't disturb the queen right now if I were you. She has had a trying morning," insisted Tarmot. "It would be best if you waited."

Brechlin shook her head but did not look at Tarmot. "I know there is no way Queen Cirmar has authorized you to cut back our military resources by forty percent. In fact, I believe she will be rather aghast when she hears about it."

Brechlin picked up the pace as she walked down the long hallway to the queen's antechamber, and Tarmot followed suit.

"You are mistaken," he replied, but he had lost his smug confidence. "We were discussing it this very morning."

Brechlin abruptly stopped and looked Tarmot squarely in the eye. "And she said to cut back the military by forty percent?"

"Well," stumbled Tarmot, "not exactly. But she knew I was looking at the military budget, and I believe she would agree."

"Tarmot, you have no conception of what that would involve. None. At least Queen Cirmar has a better handle on it." She returned to her brisk stride toward the queen's antechamber.

"Besides," continued Tarmot, "she's out this morning. She rode to the Merchant's Guild to hear grievances."

"Well, she has more grievances to hear, and I will wait on her until she returns," she said as she plopped down on a silk-upholstered settle placed opposite the entryway to Queen Cirmar's private suite.

At that moment, the door swung open at the far end of the hall. They turned to see Queen Cirmar enter along with her handmaiden. She wore her riding ensemble of leather breeches and a silk split-sleeve shirt with an embroidered doublet. She looked flushed but radiant from her morning's exertions.

"I could hear you two argue from the bottom of the stairs," she announced as she walked toward them. "Pray tell, what is it this time? Why can't I have peace between the two of you?" Queen Cirmar's voice thinly veiled her exasperation.

"But my dear queen," began Tarmot, "it's just that Marshal Brechlin is less than cooperative in pursuing the cutbacks necessary to pay for our new palace."

"It's just that General Counselor Tarmot has asked me to cut back the military budget by forty percent!" replied Brechlin, standing up as Queen Cirmar approached.

"Forty percent?" repeated Queen Cirmar. She looked at Tarmot apologetically. "I'm sorry, dear, but we can't do that. That would make us too vulnerable to riots and pirates and such."

"But, *dear*," oozed Tarmot, "I was only thinking of our new home. I'm convinced that with a little creative restructuring, we can still find a way to fund the garden vestibule and promenade. Wouldn't that be a delightful spot for our breakfast?"

Queen Cirmar looked at him affectionately. "I know you are only thinking of our little nest together, my love. And yes, it would be delightful. But we'll have to come up with some other means of funding it."

"But, my darling..." began Tarmot.

Queen Cirmar walked over to him and kissed him on the cheek. "Don't fret, my dear. We'll get it worked out. But for now, I need a few minutes with Marshal Brechlin. Do you mind?"

Then, turning to Brechlin, she gave her a weak smile. "Just give me a moment to freshen up—it's been a hectic morning—and then you and I can meet in my antechamber. Does that suit?" Without waiting for an answer, she looked at the guard standing by the entrance to the chamber, who nodded in acknowledgment, and entered her suite, leaving Brechlin and Tarmot in the hallway.

Tarmot looked at Brechlin with unveiled hatred. "Don't think you'll get away with this affront to my authority," he hissed and turned to walk away.

"Tarmot, just please focus on your manipulations, and let the rest of us run the realm," called out Brechlin as he proceeded down the hallway. Tarmot hesitated, apparently picking up Brechlin's innuendo for the first time, but continued on in an angry gait.

Brechlin watched Tarmot stomp down the hall for a moment before shaking her head and letting out an exasperated sigh. She then stepped inside the queen's antechamber to wait on Queen Cirmar. The space was familiar to her, with nothing to capture her attention, so her thoughts wandered to Queen Cirmar's character.

In her opinion, the queen was a beautiful woman despite her scar. It had always perplexed her why she allowed Tarmot to get involved in the realm's policy decisions. She was not incompetent, so she must recognize his administrative shortcomings. Yet, she still listened.

Queen Cirmar's appearance interrupted her reverie. She gave Brechlin an apologetic smile and gestured for her to be seated on the settee by the wall as Queen Cirmar sat down next to her, taking Brechlin's hand.

"My dear Brechlin, please forgive Tarmot's awkward attempts at pleasing me. He is intent on making our new home an inspiring place."

As Brechlin watched the queen's face, she observed a gleeful light in her eyes. Edging closer to Brechlin, Queen Cirmar briefly looked around the empty antechamber before continuing. "I've informed no one yet, but Tarmot and I have agreed to be married."

"Married?" gasped Brechlin.

"Yes, I know it is surprising," said Queen Cirmar, misinterpreting Brechlin's concern. "As you know, Tarmot and I have been romantically involved for only a few months, but we have been swept away by it all! It's so exciting!"

"My Queen," began Brechlin, "a few months isn't that long. Are you sure of his intentions?"

"Oh, as to that, I'm sure," responded Queen Cirmar. "He really loves me. I can sense it."

Brechlin considered how little experience with love the queen had. She felt sad for her, for she was equally confident Tarmot's intentions had nothing to do with love. But, Brechlin was more concerned with the welfare of the realm than the queen's broken heart.

"I hope you're right, my Queen," she said. And then, feeling it was expected, she searched for something encouraging to add. "I can see how happy he makes you."

"Oh, he does," said the queen, beaming with delight. "And you don't know the half of it. There is more to him than meets the eye."

"I'm sure of it," said Brechlin, holding back a smirk.

Queen Cirmar squeezed Brechlin's hand and looked earnestly into her eyes. "I hope the two of you become better friends and colleagues. I don't understand the grudge he bears against you. He doesn't understand your value to our kingdom."

"Thank you, my Queen," said Brechlin. "It gratifies me that you do understand my value. And I hope you appreciate the value of the kingdom's standing army."

"Oh, that," replied the queen. "I don't know, Brechlin. Can't you dismantle some of it without harm?"

"We have already cut things to the quick the last time Tarmot got involved!" exclaimed Brechlin. "There's no fat left to cut. By reducing our military any further, we are putting our realm in real danger. Why, if any of the—"

Brechlin was interrupted by a vigorous knock on the door. Relieved to have the discussion postponed, Queen Cirmar quickly opened the door herself.

"Sorry to interrupt your conference, my Queen, but it is Captain Labrok," said the timid attendant. "He asks for Marshal Brechlin and says it is urgent."

"It's all right, Sigmund, let the captain in," said Queen Cirmar.

Labrok walked into the antechamber, hat in his hand, looking awkward.

"My Queen," he said, bowing. "Excuse my impertinence, please, but I thought Marshal Brechlin should know about the ship that was towed in."

"The ship?" questioned Queen Cirmar.

"Yes, my Queen," returned Labrok. "Marshal Brechlin and I spotted it being towed in from the black cloud this morning. Well, it has arrived, and I have examined it." He looked at Brechlin, his face somber. "Everyone on board was dead, and I don't think it was any kind of fever, bilge or otherwise. They were, um...perhaps you should just come and see for yourself."

"They were..." persisted Brechlin, irritated at having her conversation with Queen Cirmar interrupted just as she had begun to present her arguments for the military budget.

"It was the black cloud," replied Labrok, conscious of Brechlin's impatience and speaking quickly. "It coated the bodies, the ship, everything with...something. I think that's what killed them."

"The cloud?" questioned Queen Cirmar.

"Yes, my Queen. The same cloud that is heading toward the eastern islands," said Labrok.

Brechlin stood. "Well, Captain, I suppose I should have a look."

Naked Concern

After their uncomfortable and smelly night in the storage shed, Chimber and Jern were up early to labor under a cloudless sky. The noonday sun found them drenched in sweat as they worked on digging their fourth grave of the day. The crowded cemetery was in an open area outside the prison compound opposite the river. There was no shade, and the red soil was dry and brick-like. As he pulled himself up to the edge of the partially completed grave, Jern sat down and shook his head.

"Chimber, the only saving grace I can think of for being here today is that without me you would've been digging these holes all by yourself. Those gold coins have lost their shine."

"Yeah, it's a tough job," agreed Chimber, "but six graves at once is unusual. Besides, you'll get to sit back and relax later while I conduct the burial ceremonies."

"I hope they have the sense enough to wait until the sun goes down before everyone gathers."

Chimber nodded. "Kruuger said the proceedings should start in the late afternoon."

After letting out a sigh, Jern grabbed his shovel and began once again shoveling dirt onto the growing pile next to the grave site. But, after a moment, he stopped and studied his left hand, working the fingers back and forth.

"I'm getting blisters," he observed.

"We can find you some gloves at lunch," said Chimber, whose callused hands were beyond needing gloves.

"Lunch...yeah, that sounds good. Chimber, we have plenty of time to finish these last two graves. What do you say we finish up this hole and take a dip in yon river before lunch? I'm covered with salt and stink."

"Tell me about it," sniffed Chimber.

"Well, you're no fragrant bouquet yourself."

"Yeah. Okay. After we finish this one. The cool water would be nice."

After digging out the last layers of soil, which, being farther down, were less hard and dry, they then climbed out of the grave, tossed their shovels aside, and strode shirtless around the prison compound to the river on the other side. A thin but long copse of trees and undergrowth ran along the bank of the river. Chimber and Jern discarded their breeches, tossing them on the branches of a bush, and plunged into the flowing water.

"Oh, yeah! This is more like it!" cried Jern.

"Very nice," agreed Chimber as he backstroked a few feet and then allowed his lower body to sink to the shallow river bottom.

"Maybe we can come back this afternoon and..." began Chimber, but he stopped and listened. "Voices," he said. "Someone is coming along the path."

"That's the path to Saffral's home," said Jern excitedly.

"Yeah, Saffral *and* Warden Kruuger's home," said Chimber. "We had better duck behind those bushes. We don't want the warden to think we're goofing off."

Chimber and Jern dashed over to a spot behind a cluster

of lush riverbank growth. The animated voices grew louder, and by peeking through the branches of the river brush, they could see Warden Kruuger and Saffral walking together along the pathway from their home. They were in a heated discussion and stopped on the path, just a few yards from Chimber and Jern, who were crouched low in the water. They watched as Kruuger put his hands on his waist and sighed in an exaggerated manner. "Saffral," he began, "you have everything you could want. It's a good life, you must admit. So can we dispense with these tedious arguments and make things easier for both of us?"

"Yes, let's do," said Saffral. "Just honor the vows of our matrimony."

Kruuger shook his head and spat on the ground. "I'm not talking about that. It's time for a change."

"What does that mean?"

"I'm talking about my so-called infidelity you keep haranguing me about. You and I both know how little you care for me on a personal level. So, let's be honest and just accept it as a part of our lives. It will not change, and quite frankly, I am tired of having to fake it."

"Are you seriously suggesting—"

"I'll keep you around," interrupted Kruuger. "You are respectable and a social asset and, well, you look good on my arm. But let's be realistic here."

"I...I can't believe you're saying this," managed Saffral. "You're not even going to pretend to be faithful? What about your vows? Is our marriage a joke?"

Chimber and Jern, both embarrassed and outraged to be privy to such a personal conversation, stooped even lower into the shallow river.

"Saffral, darling, I still find you attractive, and we will sleep together every night, as always. But the time has come for change. No longer will you ask me to sacrifice personal opportunities that come along. I worked hard for what I have, and I plan on using it. I will no longer attempt to hide my conquests from you."

"Your *conquests*?" screamed Saffral. "What kind of creature are you? You bastard!" In a rage of fury, she struck Kruuger's thin body with her fists. "What kind of fool was I to marry you?"

For a moment, Kruuger fended off her blows, but one struck home on his jaw. His odious smirk turned into an angry sneer as he pulled back his arm and slapped her in the face with all his force. Saffral crumpled to the ground in a spasm of sobs and tears as Kruuger stood over her.

Jern began to step toward the bank, but Chimber forcefully grabbed his arm. He knew Jern wanted to defend Saffral. He felt the same impulse. But reason kept him still.

"We can't," he whispered into Jern's ear. "Kruuger can cancel our assignment."

"Let me go, Chimber." Jern didn't take his eyes off Saffral and Kruuger. "I couldn't care less about those coins."

"No, Jern! It's not just the coins. We could be thrown in jail. You don't want to wind up like those poor blokes we're burying, do ya? We'll report Kruuger to the Council of Elders when we get back. We can't do anything to help her now."

Jern tugged his arm away from Chimber's grasp, but just as he did, Kruuger walked away from Saffral, leaving her prostrate and sobbing on the riverbank.

"Pull yourself together," he called back at her as he trod up to the rear entrance to the prison compound. "I expect dinner at the usual time."

As soon as he was out of sight, Jern ran over to the distraught Saffral.

"Are you okay?" he inquired, kneeling next to her. She looked up at him with surprise. "It's Jern," he said. "Remember me from the tavern yesterday?" She nodded and looked back down, calming her convulsions.

"I'm okay," she managed after a moment.

"I saw him hit you," he said. "What a vile being."

"It's happened before," she said, looking up again at Jern, and for the first time, noticing his lack of apparel.

"You're...naked," she said, becoming frightened. But, at that moment, Chimber walked up—dressed—and handed Jern his breeches.

"Sorry, ma'am," Chimber said. "We were taking a swim when you and the warden came along."

"I see," she said while Jern slipped into his pants. "Thank you for your concern."

There was a trace of blood on the side of Saffral's mouth as she stood up and massaged her jaw.

"I'd better be getting back to the house," she said, her eyes moist with tears.

"What are you going to do?" asked Jern, his voice kind. "You won't stay with him, will you? No one should be treated like that!"

"Jern, that's not our business," cautioned Chimber.

"No, it's okay," replied Saffral. "You're sweet, Jern," she continued, looking at him warmly. "But I must endure it."

"But why?" asked Jern. "Is it the wealth? The house? Do those mean so much you would sacrifice your self-respect?"

Saffral glanced toward the turrets of her home, just visible above the trees growing along the riverbank, and then at Jern and Chimber.

"If the two of you would escort me to my home, I'll explain the situation to you. If you are interested, that is. It's only a little ways down this path."

"We're interested!" asserted Jern.

"Okay, follow me." She led them down the riverbank path, saying nothing at first. After a few minutes, she let out a breath and spoke.

"My father was a good man, but he was always a risk taker. He bought the rights to a tin mine in the hills just outside of Gretly at a good price. Too good of a price, as it turns out. After buying equipment on credit and hiring a crew to work the machinery, the mine produced only low-grade ore. My father wasn't even breaking even when, for reasons unknown, a group of vandals entered the mining camp one night—there was no reason to guard a tin mine—and destroyed all the equipment. Without the means to generate an income, the authorities placed both he and my mother in the Gretly Debtor's Prison. It was so unjust. Mother had nothing to do with Father's speculating, but they found her name on one of the papers and imprisoned her, too.

"Kruuger had been a business partner of my father's in earlier ventures, and I knew he had his eye on me from the beginning. It always made me uneasy, but I suppose it's not unusual for men of his age and character. Well, after they imprisoned my parents, he approached me and offered to pay off my father's debts if I would marry him. That was two years ago. He didn't seem so bad at that time. And yes, the lifestyle had its appeal, I confess. I accepted his offer. So, you see, because he freed my parents, I'm bound to stay with him."

"But he's not honorable!" said Jern. "You don't have to respect your agreement with someone like that."

Saffral bit her lip. "But he did honor his word and had my parents freed."

"If it's not offensive to ask, how did he make his fortune?" inquired Chimber. "Surely prison wardens aren't paid that well."

Saffral looked at Chimber blankly and with some embarrassment. "I know this may sound odd, but I can't say. He is very secretive about it. I suspect it resulted from some shady business venture he got away with. But I know the funds continue to come in. Somebody somewhere is paying him a lot of money."

They followed the path away from the river and up the steep bank to the back door of her large home. She stopped at the threshold of the door and turned to them. "Well, that's personal information, but I guess you wanted to know. Anyway, that's my life. Thanks for the company."

Then she turned to Jern. "And thank you, Jern, for your naked concern," she said with a sly smile.

"Maybe we'll see you around before we leave," suggested Jern.

"Yeah, come down to the tavern to say hello—that's where you'll usually find me."

After they departed, Chimber and Jern were quiet as they walked back up the river path. When they reached the spot where they had taken their swim, Jern turned to Chimber. "Do you want to continue our swim?" he asked.

"Nah, best not," said Chimber. "I promised Kruuger we'd have the graves finished by five bells."

"Kruuger!" spat out Jern. "Chimber, you should've let me

confront him. I would've loved to crush his ugly face."

"Yeah, maybe I should have. Although, I wonder if it would have mattered, except to get you in prison."

"It would have been right, Chimber. That's what would have mattered."

"Well, let's redirect some of that angry energy toward finishing up those two grave sites. We owe it to the pathetic sods who died under Kruuger's command to see that they have a decent burial."

Prison Manners

Later that day, a crowd gathered around the six freshly dug grave sites as the sun ventured low in the sky. A cooling northern breeze made everyone comfortable as they listened to Chimber's solemn recital of the burial rites, sending the souls of each deceased prisoner deep into the land between to spend eternity at Gludema's side. After he completed the ceremony for each, Kruuger's guards lowered the body into the grave. At Kruuger's insistence, each was thoroughly wrapped in burial shrouds, hiding the bodies from the view of those outsiders attending.

For the first couple of speeches, Jern listened to Chimber's somber reading of the burial rites, but as they were all the same and Chimber had no need of him, he became bored. He wandered around the burial ground, examining some of the older grave sites. As he was trying to read the name on one of the few marked gravestones, he spotted someone approaching the prison gate carrying a small bundle. Although the figure was a hundred yards away, he recognized Saffral's petite form.

Saffral must be bringing Kruuger his dinner, he thought, realizing that the warden was not taking part in the burial ceremonies.

Jern shook his head in disgust and tried to turn his attention to Chimber's droning. But, he decided that he was hungry and resolved to sneak back to their storage shed for a bite or two. Just maybe, along the way, he would have a chance to say hello to Saffral.

By now, the guard monitoring the gate was used to seeing Jern come and go and allowed him through. He took a quick glance around the prison grounds but saw no sign of Saffral. He walked in the general direction of the storage shed, but swung wide of the small building the covered the entrance to the underground cells. Its reek was overpowering. But this took him near the main doorway to the administration building, which was left partially open. As he passed by, he heard an angry voice coming from inside. It was Kruuger, and Jern was immediately concerned that once again he was venting his spite on Saffral.

Unable to stop himself, he approached the dusty doorway and peered inside but saw nothing. He then stepped into the dark inner hallway, quietly following the sound of Kruuger's voice, which led him down the hall and to a doorway. The door was slightly ajar, and Kruuger's angry words were pouring out.

Jern stopped a few steps away from the door and listened. Kruuger was making points similar to those he had made on the riverbank. About how he had earned his position by hard work, which entitled him to certain rights, and that someone to whom he had shown so much generosity should respect those hard-earned rights. Kruuger's voice had a smug, tinny quality that Jern found unpleasant. The more he heard it, the more disgust he felt for the man. Then he heard Saffral's agitated yet subdued voice.

"You have made the way you feel about me perfectly

clear—about us…"

"It's not about us!" Kruuger interjected. "It's about my rights. I run this place. This is my domain. I expect my wife to be tolerant of my indulgences. No! I expect my wife to accept my indulgences, and that means treating me with proper respect when she brings me my dinner. I cannot go on and on about this every time we meet!"

"I just said…"

"It's not just what you said. It's how you said it! It's how you conducted yourself when you came into my office. You may not show your displeasure with me by the tone in your voice or your attitude. You will not try to arouse my guilt. You will oblige me as you have given your word you will do. Don't think I wouldn't return your parents to that prison."

"What is that supposed to mean?" said Saffral, her voice now rising.

"Well, you keep yourself in line, and you won't have to worry about it."

"What kind of man do you call yourself?" asked Saffral. "You're no man at all!"

"I call myself your husband. A man who freed your parents from prison. Now this argument has me agitated and stressed. Close that door and come. I'm in need of your services."

"You bastard!" cried Saffral. Jern heard the crash of a tray as it fell to the ground, plates clattering. "Now," said Saffral. "Your dinner is on the floor. Eat it like the dog you are!"

Saffral's steps approached the doorway, and Jern started to retreat into a shadowy recess, but he had only taken a step when a body slammed into the opposite side of the wall.

"You will obey me, wench!" shouted Kruuger. "I said serve me!"

Saffral released a tearful sob, and Jern could stand no more. He burst into the room to find Kruuger standing over Saffral, who was trying to prop herself up on the floor. Jern walked up to the tall but thin warden and shoved him, sending him to the floor.

"If you touch her again, I will kill you with my bare hands!" cried Jern. He turned to Saffral. "Are you okay?"

It took Kruuger but a moment to recover his composure.

"Guards!" he called. "Captain Charkol!" Moments later, Charkol and two more men in prison uniforms walked into the room.

"That man attacked me!" Kruuger shouted. "Restrain him!" The prison guards, used to dealing with unruly prisoners in the course of their duty, grabbed Jern by either arm while the third held him securely in place by locking his arm around Jern's neck.

"Now who, may I ask, are you?" inquired Kruuger, now standing and dusting himself off. "A secret lover to the disgusting heap on the floor, perhaps?"

"He's one of the gravediggers," said Charkol. "They call him Jern."

"Well, Jern, I see you need to be taught your manners." Kruuger walked over to Jern and backhanded him across the jaw.

"Leave him alone!" blurted Saffral. "He was just trying to help me."

"Shut up!" shouted Kruuger, and kicked Saffral, still on the floor, squarely in the side.

In a sudden and violent outburst of anger, Jern wrenched his wiry frame free of the guards' grasp and jumped on Kruuger's back, hurling fists into his face and sides. The guards recovered from their surprise, pulled Jern off Kruuger's back, and pinned him down on the hardwood floor. They began pummeling him with kicks and blows.

"Beat him!" screamed Kruuger. "Teach him who he is dealing with!"

After a few minutes of swirling pain, Jern lost consciousness.

* * *

Chimber smiled and nodded as he received his customary compliments from the assembled families of the deceased. With several burials, one after another, and with the obvious character shortcomings of the deceased, his abilities as an orator had been tested. But, he had placed a somber yet positive note over the whole affair. The family members were genuinely moved.

Chimber had just shaken hands with the father of one of the deceased prisoners when he spotted Captain Charkol walking toward him from the prison compound. He was covered in sweat.

"You'd better take care of that bundle over there and clear out," said Charkol, pointing over his shoulder to an object lying on the ground near the front gate of the compound, wrapped in bloody burial cloth. "And consider yourself lucky that you and your buddy aren't staying put for a while."

"What?" asked Chimber, peering at the bundle. "Did I miss someone? No one informed me—"

"He's not ready for burying yet. But, if you take your time, who knows?" said Charkol with a smirk. "Now, I said clear out!" he spat and tossed a coin bag in the dirt by Chimber's feet. Puzzled, Chimber glanced at the coin bag and then he stared at the bundle by the gate. His concern rose.

"Have you seen my assistant?" Chimber called out to the retreating Captain, who chuckled and pointed at the object by the gate as he continued to walk away.

Now alarmed, Chimber dashed to the bundle. He bent over the body and pulled back the folds of the cloth to see Jern's unconscious and bloodied face. Anguished, he stood and looked around him, uncertain what to do. He picked up Jern's limp body and gently propped him over his shoulder. It was obvious Jern needed immediate attention, so he struggled with his burden down the hill to the little cluster of buildings huddled around the harbor. Not having any better options, he burst through the doors of the Saber Slash Tavern.

Ship of Death

Marshal Brechlin and Captain Labrok hurried down the hill to the city harbor in silence. The vigorous walk did Brechlin good. She was still fuming over Tarmot's attempt to reduce the military budget and felt frustrated because Queen Cirmar didn't fully share her concerns.

As they approached the ship in question, Brechlin saw that a curious crowd had gathered nearby. At least they had enough sense to keep their distance while peering at the vessel. Bilge fever, if that was the problem, could easily spread.

Several of Labrok's men cleared a path as they approached, and they cautiously walked to the side of the silent ship, now tied securely to the dock. The gunnels were just low enough for Brechlin to peer over them when standing on her toes, and she had a clear view of the boat's deck. There were several bodies lying around, and even from where she was standing, she saw no signs typical of bilge fever. Victims of that malady had bloated white faces with purplish-red rings around their eyes. Moreover, although bilge fever struck suddenly and often took the life of its victim in a day or two, the afflicted victims would have to the opportunity to retreat to their beds before the end came. But these men had died quickly, expiring near where they stood. Whatever had killed the members of this ship was

79

not bilge fever.

As she studied the deck, she noticed that everything was covered with a thin grayish powder, including the bodies of the deceased crew members. She ran her finger along the top of the gunnels and looked at her fingertip. A layer of grayish residue stuck to her skin.

"Grand Marshal!" cried Labrok. "With all due respect, it was probably that gray powder that killed these men. Do you think it wise to touch it?"

"I wonder," said Brechlin, peering at the gray glob on her fingertip while keeping her arm fully extended away from her. She turned to Labrok. "It looks like volcanic ash but has the wrong texture—more like powdered stone. We need to find out what it is, so have your men collect some and take it to Alipharem's lab. He can analyze it and give us an idea of what we are dealing with.

"And Captain," she added while swishing her finger vigorously through the harbor water, "don't let them touch it directly."

"Oh, I don't think there will be any problem," replied Labrok. "This ship has given everyone here the frights. Should we assume the powder came from the cloud?"

"Maybe," said Brechlin. "Or maybe something hidden by the cloud. I don't know."

"At least we can be thankful the wind shifted," said Labrok. "The cloud was headed straight for Capital Island."

"But other islands are in its path," said Brechlin, looking out at the dark mass still visible on the horizon. Then, looking up at the observation tower at the edge of the harbor's mooring district, she nodded toward its deck. "Captain, let's see what we can determine about the current progress of the cloud."

"Yes, Marshal," replied Labrok. He turned to a military officer standing nearby. "Two men only," he stressed. "One on the deck to collect the samples and another by the boat's side to receive them. The rest of you stay back. And keep these civilians out of the way!"

Brechlin and Labrok made their way up the path to the observation tower, and then up the long staircase to the platform. Both of them were out of breath by the time they arrived. Brechlin paused for a moment while she breathed, gazing to the east.

"It's difficult to make out the cloud's course," she said. "I wonder if it has reached Saghorn Island."

"I've spent many hours on this platform," said Labrok, "and I'm familiar with what can be seen in the distance. Saghorn reaches its most easterly extent at Hewarn Point, and even now I can just make out the outlines of its high headland. I would suppose that the dark cloud would obscure our view had it reached Saghorn."

"Yes, I can just see it," said Brechlin. "Since the cloud has had ample time to reach it, I think we can surmise it is passing to the north of the island. But what about Bewel?"

"Hmm," pondered Labrok. "I would say that if the cloud stays on its current course, it will strike Bewel Island dead on. But the wind may change its course before then—not an unusual occurrence."

"Well, let's hope so," replied Brechlin, looking into the distance. "Besides, the cloud may be harmless. Something else may have killed those crewmen."

"General Counselor!" cried Labrok, turning around and saluting. "I am honored."

Brechlin turned to see Tarmot standing on the platform. He

acknowledged Labrok with a slight nod and walked to the edge of the observation deck next to Brechlin.

"Well, Marshal Brechlin," he began, "just what is all the commotion about? You seem to have the whole harbor running scared."

"Yes, Tarmot, I personally assaulted the crippled craft and killed all the crew members aboard. They should be scared." She had little tolerance for Tarmot's meddling.

"You should have assured the harbor personnel that nothing serious is wrong. You realize that these kinds of distractions disrupt the normal economic functioning of the harbor?"

"Tarmot, do you believe I have any say in the rumor mongering that always runs rampant along the docks?"

Tarmot shrugged his shoulders. "You can help defuse it. Besides, why all this commotion over what must be another case of bilge fever? As long as it is quarantined, there should be no...no reason to...hey! Is that the ship over there, the one with the crowd standing around it?" said Tarmot, now looking down from the tower toward the crippled craft.

"It is, General Counselor," said Labrok sharply.

"Good Gludema, Captain, one of your men is on the boat! It should be quarantined. And all those people standing around—surely they're too close."

"We are investigating, sir," returned Labrok.

"Captain, if you spread bilge fever among our dock workers with your incompetence, losing your commission will be the least of your worries!"

"He's not being incompetent," said Brechlin. "I don't think this is a case of bilge fever."

"Since when, Marshal Brechlin, did you become qualified to make medical assessments?"

"There is clearly something else going on here. I asked Labrok to have samples taken from the ship for Alipharem to analyze."

"Alipharem? Samples of what, may I ask?"

"Of the grayish powder that covered the deck of the ship," replied Labrok. "It's on everything, even the dead crewmen's bodies."

"Yes, an odd thing," added Brechlin. "We believe it may have come from the dark cloud you can see in the distance."

"What is it? A volcanic ash cloud, perhaps?" asked Tarmot, peering at the low dark horizon.

"A sensible guess," allowed Brechlin, "but the gray powder is not like ash. It has a different consistency."

"I see," replied Tarmot. "And you believe this cloud, not bilge fever, took the lives of these men. And that is why you sent men aboard in complete disregard to quarantine protocols?"

Brechlin's customary irritation toward Tarmot rose once again. A part of her suspected that his concerns were justified, and she secretly hoped she hadn't made a careless mistake. She could ill afford to give Tarmot ammunition for questioning her actions.

"Like I said, the cadavers exhibit none of the symptoms of bilge fever. I saw them myself. I'm not concerned the disease will spread."

"You were on board the ship?" asked Tarmot, taking a step back.

"No. I didn't go on the ship, but I saw the cadavers. And I examined the gray powder. We hope that Alipharem will tell us what it is. And it may interest you, Counselor General, that the same cloud that may have resulted in the deaths of these crew members is, as we speak, heading for Bewel Island. So, unless there is a sudden shift in the wind, the inhabitants of that island will be subjected to what those sailors experienced."

"I see," said Tarmot, looking vaguely toward Bewel Island.

"So, we thought it important to find out what the substance is. Or would you prefer that we not investigate the cause of these deaths and just leave the inhabitants of Bewel Island to their fate?"

Tarmot studied the distant black band for a few moments. "Bah," he said. "Mere coincidence. These men died of fever and entered a volcanic cloud of dust."

"Then Alipharem will determine just that, and we can all relax," Brechlin assured him.

"Ridiculous!" returned Tarmot. He abruptly turned and walked toward the doorway leading back to the stairs. "You and that old coot Alipharem can fiddle with your theories if you like," he called over his shoulder. "Just make sure those men don't spread the fever among our dockworkers. They're needed to keep our city running smoothly."

"We will do our utmost to make sure progress on the new palace is not hampered," quipped Brechlin as Tarmot exited.

The Gray Mountain

Ilsher leaned on the window rail and peered down at the violent sea as its waves crashed into the crags many feet below. She found the release of energy at each resounding slap of water invigorating.

She was waiting on Dran in the Ascension Chamber while he descended from heights of the Gray Mountain. A long, narrow bridge crossed the gap over the turbulent waters to a narrow set of stairs that wound steeply up the Gray Mountain to a large cleft near its peak. Her eyes followed the thin ribbon of stairs winding its way up until, near the top, she spotted a descending dark figure near its upper reaches. It would take Dran a while longer to reach her, so she wrapped her woolen shawl tightly around her shoulders. It would be less wet and cold away from the window, but she enjoyed the stimulation.

The hexagonal Ascension Chamber crowned the very top of the Krakul Gat residence. The building itself was many stories high and was built into one side of the Gray Mountain. Ilsher idly watched the crashing ocean as the spray spread with its usual intensity, coating the bridge and the lower sections of the stairway with a slimy residue, testing the attentiveness of the Krakul Gat as he made his daily trips up and down the Gray Mountain.

"It's a wonder that father doesn't slip off those steps to his doom," she said to herself as she watched the latest great wave hammer on the huge rocks.

The Gray Mountain, a giant tooth of smoky gray crystal protruding among a cluster of craggy, granite mountains, was the largest feature on Kromul Island. A tiny village on the opposite side of the island spread out near a small sheltered bay where a few fishing trawlers anchored near the mossy pier. Closer at hand were the openings to three mine shafts, which tunneled down to rich deposits of tin and silver, the mainstays of Kromul Island's economy.

The mine shafts were dank and full of noxious gases and crumbling supports. Rarely did anyone go far into the tunnels, for they were hazardous, at least to the living. The tin and silver mining operations underneath Kromul Island were productive not because of working laborers, but because of a crew of mining cadavers.

It was the power of the Gray Mountain that made this possible. In the shadow of the mountain, its power prevented the decay of all organic matter. No refrigeration was needed to keep food products wholesome anywhere on the island. But, with a talented Krakul Gat at its helm, the power of the Gray Mountain could be harnessed to animate deceased bodies, which then could be directed according to the will of the Krakul Gat.

For centuries, cadavers from all over the Dalmeer Islands were shipped to Kromul Island. The Krakul Gat animated them from the bowels of the mountain and directed them to enter the mining shafts to dig for ore. Eventually, despite the lack of decay, the corpses would deteriorate from accidents and general wear and tear and would need replacing. Usually, there was a greater demand for fresh corpses than were available. For most families, the thought of the bodies of their deceased loved ones working in the mining tunnels was repulsive. But the compensation was not insignificant. And lately, with the absence of the White Medium to control the healing powers of Mount Krin, cadaver availability was on the rise.

As Dran finally completed his descent down the stairs and entered the Ascension Chamber, Ilsher approached her father and brushed away the damp gray dust from his bald pate with a motherly gesture.

"You work so hard, my father," she said.

"I try," he replied, shaking the water off his cloak and hanging it on a nearby hook. He walked over to the fire pit in the center of the room and held his hands near the flames.

"I watched the cadavers assembling this morning," said Ilsher. "It was encouraging. Soon, you'll have as much control over them as did Grandfather."

Dran did not respond right away but just shook his head while peering into the fire. "Ilsher, why do you keep saying that?" he said after a moment, irritation in his voice. "I already have complete control over the mining crews. Production levels are as high as they were under my father's control."

"I was just trying to be supportive, dear father," she added slyly. "I can only guess how it grieves you that so many cadavers were damaged this week."

"No, I don't think about it," Dran replied.

"Well, I know it must bother you that Grael maintained production levels using the same shipment of cadavers for months. But you will be there soon, I'm sure."

"No, it doesn't bother me, but thank you for your confidence," said Dran rather curtly. "Now, where is Ginthar? I need his report."

"I spoke with him a few minutes ago in his lab," said Ilsher. "And I am afraid…" She paused while she put her small hand on her father's face and gazed into his eyes. "You missed. Not by much, but you missed."

Dran steadily returned Ilsher's gaze, but she saw the disappointment on his face. She knew he hated for her to see him fail. He took a long slow breath, then walked over to the open window and peered out at the mountain's mists.

"Missed completely?" he asked a bit too casually.

"Yes, completely," replied Ilsher with mocking glee. "And Saghorn, too."

She waited a moment for it to sink in.

"Damn!" he exclaimed. "Our efforts wasted. So much of the mountain destroyed, and for nothing…"

"Not to mention the cost of the poison. What did we use? Fourteen thousand gallons?"

Dran didn't bother to respond. "You didn't mention Bewel Island. Did we miss Bewel, too?"

"Um, Ginthar thinks the cloud might strike Bewel Island if the wind doesn't shift."

"Well…that could still work. It would be more difficult, sure, but it could still work."

"If you say so," Ilsher replied.

They both looked up as Ginthar walked into the chamber. A short, thin man with a food-stained robe and an arched back, he spoke in a loud whisper, his words incompletely formed. His eyes were brilliant, ever scanning his surroundings.

He walked up to Dran and handed him a document.

"My Lord," he began, "our observers…our observers…"

"Please, Ginthar," said Dran. "Speak louder, man. I can't

hear you over the sound of the waves."

"Yes, My Lord. Our observers have been tracking the course of the cloud. Due to a last-minute shift in the wind, we missed Capital and Saghorn islands. Though Bewel Island is still...is still in the cloud's path."

"So I heard," replied Dran. "And what of the poison? Will it remain potent?"

"Yes, I think so," whispered Ginthar. "The only concern I have is the effect of heat. The process of combusting the gray crystal may have overheated the poison, partially...diluting its potency. We shall see soon. On its present course, the cloud should reach Bewel's coast within an hour. Assuming...the winds don't shift."

"We didn't plan on Bewel. Do you think this could still work?" asked Dran.

"Perhaps," offered Ginthar, "but difficult."

"Ah, the whimsy of the winds," sang out Ilsher. "All our hopes rest on the whimsy of the wind and the wild scheming of you two. What would Grael say if he were still here?"

"Well, he isn't still here, now is he?" replied Dran tartly. "Unless you want to find his corpse laboring away in mining shaft number two, alongside my fine brother."

"Yes, he is dead, and you are now the Krakul Gat. And let us pray that the winds don't change," she responded sweetly.

Dran gave Ilsher a sour look and left the chamber for his midday meal already awaiting him in the dining chamber. "Keep me informed," he said to Ginthar as he departed.

Once Dran had left, Ginthar looked down at Ilsher's tiny frame. "Why do you torture him so?" he asked. "All of this...he does for you."

"Well, he is my father. So, isn't it my duty to push him to

succeed? And," she continued, looking up at Ginthar with expressionless eyes, "isn't it your duty, Ginthar, to serve our family rather than asking inappropriate questions?"

"My apologies," muttered Ginthar, bowing to the young girl. "I had best return to my observations."

"Yes. That would be best."

The Tear of Life

Chimber, still holding Jern's inert body, looked around the interior of the Saber Slash and spotted Merriblan serving ale to a small group of fishermen on the far side of the tavern.

"I need a room, quickly!" he announced. Merriblan looked up with blank surprise and peered curiously at his bundle.

"I need a room!" Chimber urgently repeated.

"Upstairs. I'll show you," she said, still staring at the bundle.

Chimber followed her up the stairs where she opened the door to an empty room. He handed her a few coins and she left immediately to return to her duties. Chimber laid Jern's limp body on the bed and carefully unwrapped the burial cloth. As he looked him over, he saw raw and bloody marks all over his body and a steady trickle of blood coming from the side of his mouth. He was still breathing, but as he looked over Jern's injuries, Chimber's concern grew more urgent. Powerful men had viciously worked over Jern's body. Purplish swellings around an arm and one of his legs suggested broken bones.

He began to feel overwhelmed. What could he do? Jern was dying, and he possessed no knowledge of medicinal herbs or treatments. And with Kruuger's animosity aroused, he suspected they would receive little help from the occupants of the village. Kruuger was the only authority on Pith Isle, and it was his henchmen who had done this deed.

Chimber's anger surged, but as much as he wanted to go after whoever had done this to Jern, he was realistic enough to know he was but one man against Kruuger's small personal army. It would be better to get back to Math, care for Jern, and take appropriate action later. But would Jern survive the trip? Or even live through the night?

As these thoughts raced through his brain, he retrieved a basin of water and wiped the blood and dust from Jern's skin. As he was finishing up, there was a soft rap at the door, and it began to open. As he was expecting no one, Chimber started up and braced himself for action but relaxed as Saffral's petite form entered the room. She had two reddish swollen areas on her face and was holding her side as she walked across the floor to the bed.

She looked down at Jern's face. "How is he?"

"He's bad! What's going on?" demanded Chimber in a sharp tone.

"It was Kruuger and his guards. He tried to protect me," said Saffral, tears welling up in her eyes. "He struck Kruuger, and the guards beat him."

Chimber softened toward her as he saw her wounds more clearly. "Are you okay? Did they beat you, too?"

"Just Kruuger," she said, studying the marks on Jern's body. "I'll be okay. I'm not so sure about Jern. This blood coming out of his mouth—it's not from anything external. I think he's been severely injured."

"No, no, he'll be fine," said Chimber, worry distorting his face. "I need to get him home. If we can get him—"

"No," asserted Saffral. "He wouldn't survive the trip."

"What can we do, then? Do you know medicine? Is there an herbalist on the island?"

Saffral looked at Jern quietly for a moment, then pulled off her necklace, which had a tear-shaped white pendant attached. She sighed as she looked at it and placed it over Jern's neck. She looked at Chimber. "Kruuger took it from a prisoner, a special prisoner they keep in an isolated cell on the lowest level. It's called the 'Tear of Life.'"

"What is it? Will it help?" asked Chimber, looking dubiously at the little pendant.

"It may save his life," she responded. "It has special powers. Kruuger gave it to me after he confiscated it from the prisoner, thinking it was just a pretty ornament. But it soon became clear it was no ordinary piece of jewelry. It is imbued with healing powers."

"God, I hope you are right. Jern needs any help he can get right now."

Saffral put her hand on Jern's forehead. "I have to leave. When Kruuger gets home, he will expect me to be there. And, without the protection of the pendant, I dare not provoke his wrath further."

"You're leaving? What should I do?" questioned Chimber.

"If he is beyond the power of the pendant, nothing we did would help anyway. If he's not, then by tomorrow morning, he'll be better. Let him rest, and I'll come at first light."

Saffral limped across the room to the door and looked back at Chimber standing by Jern's bed.

"I'm sorry I brought this on you two," she said and closed the door.

Chimber did his best to make Jern comfortable, but there was little he could do. He paced the room for several hours, listening to Jern's erratic breathing and thinking about their past together.

They had been friends for so long, he couldn't remember a time when he wasn't there. And even though they were different from one another, Chimber had come to need his witty sidekick. Jern was his comic relief in a world of serious adult responsibility, his reminder to be spontaneous and carefree.

As he paced back and forth, furtively studying Jern's sleeping form, his mind went to Jern's family. How could he explain what happened? How could he tell Jern's mother her only son died helping him? He felt responsible for this terrible situation and wished now he had refused Elder Lumm's offer.

Already exhausted from the day's strenuous labors, Chimber drifted to sleep as he sat beside Jern's bed.

* * *

The first rays of light were seeping into the room the next morning when, to Chimber's surprise, he heard Jern's voice.

"I know we are on friendly terms, Chimber, but do you have to use my leg for a pillow?"

"Jern!" shouted Chimber, sitting up. "You're awake!"

"I'm awake," he replied. "But I'm not sure what happened."

"Never mind that, how do you feel? Can you move?"

"Um, yeah. I'm pretty sore, but nothing broken, at least," said Jern, moving his arms and legs. "I remember those thugs working me over."

He slowly sat up, spitting out bits of dried blood from around his lips.

"Whose blood is this?" he asked, now seeing the dried

splotches of red all over his bedclothes.

"Yours, Jern," said Chimber, his voice somber.

"But...I'm not wounded." Jern looked himself over. "Just sore and bruised."

Chimber gaped at his buddy. "Jern, last night you were...well, you were close to leaving us. That's all I can say."

"I was dying?"

"You have Saffral to thank for your amazing recovery. She gave you this," said Chimber as he fingered the pendant around Jern's neck. "It worked. I'm amazed."

"This stone? Saffral? How?"

"After the guards did their work on you, I brought you here. Yes, you were dying. I'm sure of it. But Saffral came and put this pendant around your neck. She called it the Tear of Life. She said it had healing power."

"Saffral!" exclaimed Jern. "Where is she? Is she okay?"

"I'll be okay," said Saffral, entering the room. She limped to Jern's bedside.

"Saffral!" cried Jern, looking at her bruised face. "That bastard! God, he'll pay!"

Saffral looked at Chimber. "See what I mean? He's already himself again. In another few days, he'll be recovered completely."

"It's wondrous," said Chimber. "We owe you much."

Saffral shook her head. "You owe me nothing. It was for my sake that Jern is like this."

"This pendant...I thank you," said Jern, for once at a loss for words. "You saved my life. But now, you must take it back. You have your own wounds to heal."

Saffral smiled at Jern and clasped his hand.

"You are still much worse than I, Jern. I want you to keep

it—a gift from me. To remember me by."

"But—your wounds."

"I'll be fine," insisted Saffral. "You still have to survive your journey home." Turning to Chimber, she added, "You two had best depart. I wouldn't put it past Kruuger to cast his malice toward you again should he hear of you two still in town."

Chimber bit his lower lip and nodded. "Time to get the hell out of this place."

"Come with us!" cried Jern. "Leave that tyrant and come to Math. We'll get you set up."

Saffral smiled at Jern once again. "With protectors such as you, a woman is sorely tempted. But I cannot. Until I can find a better way to ensure my parents' safety, Kruuger will have his way with me, and I will not resist."

Jern shook his head in wonder. "I will return," he said in a confident voice. "This island is not far. I will return to you with this pendant. And then," he continued, gazing into her eyes, "I will take you away from here."

She took his hand again. "Well, I must go. Perhaps we will see each other again. Have a safe journey."

She left the room, and Jern looked at Chimber. "I'll be back for her, Chimber. I swear it."

"I know you will, good buddy. But for now, let's get you home."

Homeward Bound

Chimber helped Jern make his painful way to the xebec, loaded up their gear, and unmoored as quickly as possible. They got underway before many were stirring in the little hamlet. Jern, exhausted from the effort, lay on the deck wrapped in a blanket and went immediately to sleep.

Chimber kept a close eye on his best friend, occasionally adjusting his blanket, checking his breathing, and making sure the Tear of Life was still in place. He felt like a protective father, but it felt good to him. As he looked pensively out over the ocean, he thought about how close he'd come to losing Jern. He loved that little guy more than he'd realized. They owed a great debt to Saffral, and something told him this wasn't the last time they would see her.

The winds were less favorable on the return trip to Math, keeping Chimber at the helm throughout the day. But, as the sun neared the horizon, they were approaching home.

"There she lies," said Chimber, noticing that Jern, who had slept the whole way, was stirring.

The xebec had just passed the jutting headland of Math's harbor, and the cluster of tan and brownish dwellings came into view, though still at a distance.

Jern, already gaining his strength, sat up on his bench and

peered quietly ahead. He was absentmindedly fingering the Tear of Life, still dangling from his neck. "Can you believe she gave this to me? What a generous person."

"Are you sure you should sit up?" asked Chimber. "Don't exert yourself."

"Yeah, I'm sore, but not too bad. This arm," he continued, holding the arm in question in the air, "was woefully painful this morning. I thought it might be sprained. But now...it's just sore."

"She's right about that pendant's healing powers," observed Chimber.

"Yeah," said Jern, his voice trailing off. Then, abruptly, "I'm going back for her, Chimber. She doesn't belong with him."

"I agree," said Chimber, "but it's not like you would be rescuing her. She didn't want to leave."

"She wants to leave. She's just worried about what Kruuger would do to her parents. That's the kind of person she is. She would rather sacrifice her own happiness to keep them safe. Get rid of Kruuger, and you get rid of the threat. Then she can leave."

"What are you going to do, Jern?" asked Chimber. "Just murder the man in cold blood?"

Jern shrugged. "Whatever it takes. I will set her free. I will make her mine."

"Well, you have a lot to do. So, we had better get you well first. As soon as we dock, I'll send for Lerla. I know she'll take good care of you."

"Chimber, please take me seriously about this," insisted Jern. "Lerla is a nice girl, but Saffral...she's set apart."

"Okay," replied Chimber. "In that case, I'll send for your aunt Murgor. She would love to pamper you over at her shop."

Jern hesitated for a moment. "All right, send for Lerla if you must. But, it won't change anything."

"I know, Jern. I know. But you might as well enjoy pretty company while you get better. Right?"

Jern kissed the pendant and placed it inside his shirt. He then looked at Chimber, who was still sitting at the tiller. "When are you going to find love, Chimber?"

Chimber looked amazed. He smiled a sheepish smile and shrugged his broad shoulders. "I'm not ready yet. As soon as old lady Sheeker passes, I'll move into her cottage by the river, and then, when I have set aside some money, I'll be in a better position to think about such things."

Jern managed a weak chuckle. "Aren't you being a little structured? Take advantage of opportunities that cross your path."

Chimber kicked at a rope end lying on the deck. "I just want to be ready. I'm not really looking in the meantime."

Jern shook his head. "I couldn't live like you, Chimber. Life can't be parceled into neat packages, with certain things happening at certain times. Break free."

"Maybe I find freedom in my structured packages," replied Chimber. "And look," he added, pointing toward shore, "there's Lerla, already standing by the dock. See her waving?"

"Just change the subject. Fine," Jern said and managed a weak wave at Lerla. "We will return to this conversation."

"You get well, and we can pick it back up again. Deal?"

"Sure, deal," said Jern.

As they glided up to the mooring pier and the xebec nudged the dock, Chimber observed the immediate concern in Lerla's face as she saw Jern lying on the deck. He knew she would take good care of him. His main task would be to keep Jern from making good on his promise of going back. He didn't want the same thing or worse to happen again. Kruuger wielded absolute power in his little kingdom. And, such an outcome would be an easy thing for Kruuger's thugs. Hopefully, Lumm and the other members of the council would closely look into Kruuger's actions. There were limits on what someone like that could get away with.

He tied off his trusty craft and looked over the familiar little town. Familiar felt good to Chimber. There was safety in familiar. Something in him gave a slight sigh of relief as he stepped onto the dock.

It didn't matter where he'd traveled, Math was his home. It had been his whole life. Towns had a collective personality, and good or bad, Math was no different. Chimber was born into it, but today he took Math in with a special gratitude. He and Jern were safely home again.

The Gray Powder

By the next morning, Brechlin had received no word from Alipharem about his analysis of the gray powder. Concerned over the path of the black cloud, she climbed the ladder up to the top of a narrow tower that extended beyond the ramparts of the garrison headquarters. Since the building was halfway up the city's central hill, she had an unobstructed view of the sea and beyond. No dark band was visible. The cloud had moved on or dissipated. That was good news, but she would have to find out what had happened farther east. Had the cloud struck Bewel Island? If so, did it have any harmful effects?

Every afternoon, a ship from Bewel City left carrying mail and cargo to Cegril and usually reached the city's dock by midmorning the next day. She hoped the crew of the ship would provide her with information.

She descended the tower and headed down the hill, but as she reached the harbor area, she veered off the main lane and up a long and narrow side alley paved with large and mossy cobblestones. As the alley neared its end, she found the door she was looking for, marked with nothing but a large question mark etched into the wood. It was the entrance to Alipharem's working laboratory. She knocked loudly and entered, not waiting for an invitation.

A feeling of comfort and ease came over her as she passed through the familiar doorway. A long-time friend of her father, Alipharem was a true ally, yet he was more than that. He was a sage adviser and mentor in life. Over the years, he had been the only one she confided in about her aspirations and dreams, and she trusted him implicitly. Alipharem was progressive and open-minded, encouraging her to dream.

She remembered how he looked deep into her soul as she told him, years ago, of her goal to become marshal. One eyebrow arched and a knowing partial grin flashed across his face. "The first female Marshal of Cegril's army." He spoke the title as if he were announcing her. "Yes, my dear, it's coming. And you would raise the bar of that position, you know."

She remembered how his confidence had ignited her. And every time she encountered discouragement, she would visit Alipharem.

As usual, the inner chamber was dark and smelled of chemicals and unwashed skin. She spotted Alipharem hunched over a thick-planked desk positioned under a small window, the only significant light source in the room. Brechlin spotted samples of the gray dust sitting on the desk, along with magnifying lenses and tumblers filled with various fluids. It took a moment for Alipharem to acknowledge that someone else was in the room, but when he did, he stood up and put his hands on his hips, his flushed face smiling with pleasure. Brechlin attempted a formal salute, but as usual, Alipharem advanced and gave Brechlin a generous hug.

"Brechlin, my dear," he exclaimed. "Always a delight to see you."

Brechlin returned his embrace, which was no small feat considering Alipharem's ample girth, but her expression quickly turned serious. She gestured toward the samples. "Have you figured it out? What is that stuff?"

"It's just pulverized quartz," he replied. "Completely common and completely inert. Very similar to the crystal material that makes up the Gludemic Mountains."

"But it's gray," Brechlin noted. "Did the Gray Mountain erupt or something?"

"The Gludemic Mountains are not volcanic," Alipharem replied while shaking his head. "No. In fact, I don't believe a cloud on the scale you described could be formed through any natural process."

"Then how?"

"You say it came from the north, from the direction of Kromul Island?"

"Yes. Should I be worried about the community on that island?"

"I don't know," pondered Alipharem. "But, I have known old Ginthar for many years."

"Dran's mining engineer?" asked Brechlin.

"The same. Although, he is much more than a mining engineer. His is a very ingenious mind. The thought has occurred to me that he may have created this cloud by some process involving the Gray Mountain."

Brechlin frowned. "But why? What would be the point?"

"Why, indeed? You have not asked me how the crew members perished. It wasn't the dust."

"What, then?" asked Brechlin.

Alipharem picked up a container holding the gray dust and gazed at it in the window's light. "The crystal granules that make up the dust have a viscous substance adhered to them. This substance is made from a solution of metallic salts and other elements I cannot identify. It's a very potent poison. I hope you didn't come in direct contact with it."

"I touched it but cleansed my hand immediately," replied Brechlin, absently wiping her fingertip on her jerkin. "Should I be concerned?"

"Hmm," said Alipharem, looking at her hand. "You'll probably live. Although I wouldn't recommend touching the powder, the real danger is when the tiny granules are breathed into the lungs. It is inside the lungs that the poison would be most dangerous."

"If the cloud wasn't formed by some natural process, then should we conclude that it was designed to kill? Would Ginthar do something like that?"

Alipharem shrugged. "Who has experience with metallic salts? Who knows about pulverizing rock? These questions suggest the mines of Kromul Island. Do I think Ginthar would do something like this? Yes, I do. I suspect that the Krakul Gat and old Ginthar are up to something."

"But I don't get it," said Brechlin. "How would creating such a lethal instrument benefit Dran? Even with many of our population dead, the community on Kromul Island is too small to launch an attack. An alliance with the Southern Pirates, perhaps?"

"It's possible," said Alipharem as he rubbed the ragged stubble on his chin. "I don't think it's likely, however. The Southern Pirates may receive some immediate benefit if coastal communities were made vulnerable to attack, but it would not be in their interest in the long run. They thrive on raiding our shipping. So, I have no idea why Dran would want to kill the citizens of our islands. Unless..." Alipharem's voice trailed off.

"Unless what?" asked Brechlin.

"Ah, never mind. We can fret all day about possibilities. Baseless pondering will do us no good. We should see for ourselves what damage this threat has caused."

Brechlin glanced up at the sun through the laboratory window. "Bewel City's post ship should be at the harbor by now. I'll head there to see if there is any news. I'll keep you posted."

"Brechlin," said Alipharem, grasping Brechlin's shoulder as she was about to walk out the door. "I don't believe Dran harbors any kind of grudge against the Imperial Realm. So, if he is behind this, the cloud was no act of mere vengeance. It was some kind of power play. A stratagem for his own gain. So beware."

"If I find that this cloud has caused harm on Bewel Island and that Dran is responsible, he will soon pay penitence in our cells!" said Brechlin with surprising enthusiasm.

"Perhaps we are getting ahead of ourselves," consoled Alipharem. "Let us calmly investigate the situation on Bewel Island, and we can rationally draw our conclusions."

"I will. Let us pray by the Guardians of Gludema that this is all a false alarm."

Alipharem nodded, walked to a large piece of red crystal mounted on a table in the center of the room, and massaged its surface idly. Brechlin observed that it gave off a soft light. "Let us hope," he said. "For if it is not a false alarm, the black cloud is only the beginning."

* * *

By the time Brechlin reached the harbor and made her way

up to the observation deck with Captain Labrok, the sun was approaching its zenith. Bewel City's post ship had not arrived, and as they looked out over the vast sea under a crystal blue sky, they spotted no sailing vessels heading toward the harbor.

After keeping watch for over an hour with no sign of the craft, Brechlin found her impatience and concern growing.

"What do you think?" she asked of Labrok, breaking a long silence.

Labrok shrugged. "The winds are favorable. The seas are calm. Captain Harley is a reliable and competent old seaman. The post ship should have been here by now. Something must have delayed it."

"We've waited long enough. Captain, have one of the war sloops manned and prepared for a trip to Bewel City. Have it stocked for four days of travel. Let's see what happened for ourselves, shall we?"

Cataclysm

As the sun rose the next morning, Marshal Brechlin was comfortably resting on a pile of folded sail canvas near the bow of Cegril's sloop. She was no sea officer but had full confidence in the abilities of Captain Labrok and his subordinates in getting the ship to where it needed to be.

Fine weather had aided their progress, so from her perch the Bewel Island coastline was already in view. She studied its details as the craft rounded the headland and smoothly glided into Bewel City's quiet harbor. Brechlin's impression was of peaceful serenity.

"Such a calm setting would belie any evil afoot," she said to herself as she gazed at the rows of moored sailing craft and the precipitous rim of limestone bluffs along the northern shore, formed where the sea had cut into outliers from the nearby Balor Mountains. The white bluffs were reflected in the quiet waters of the bay.

Yet, as they came nearer, the tranquility of the scene made her suspicious. There were no craft sailing in the bay, and her sharp eyes spotted three smaller vessels aground along the beaches that covered the southern shore. She watched them gently sway back and forth, pivoting as they dug into the loose sand. Her stomach muscles tightened. That which had seemed to speak of peacefulness a few minutes ago had become an ominous harbinger of doom.

Her fears were reinforced as the sloop approached the mooring pier. There was no activity to be seen. Normally, at his hour, labor crews would be loading and unloading the freight ships moored alongside the pier. Idle sailors and workers would mill around near each craft. But, despite the ships and the visible piles of cargo ready to be loaded, no movement was visible.

Then she saw them. What had at first appeared to be small bundles of cargo distributed along the pier took on the shape of human bodies. None of them were moving.

Following Brechlin's order, Captain Labrok dropped the sloop's anchor a hundred feet from the pier and lowered a rowboat. Brechlin, Labrok, and six crew members climbed down into the boat and cautiously rowed to the edge of the pier. As they tied the boat off, she ordered the crew members to stay put and stepped up.

The gray powder dusted the wooden planks, so she pulled a pair of gloves out of her vest pocket and kneeled to examine the nearest body. It was a dead laborer. He had dropped the burden he had been carrying; its contents, a parcel of combs with mother-of-pearl inlay, were scattered across the pier. He had died quickly.

She walked back to the crew members still sitting in the rowboat.

"Captain, have your men fan out and search the area for survivors," she commanded. "And be careful of the powder—it's poisonous. Wear gloves, and do not let it come in contact with your skin. If that happens, try to cleanse it off as fast as possible. And do not stir up the dust by disturbing anything.

Breathing it could be deadly. See what you can find, and report back here at high noon."

Cautiously, and with obvious concern on their faces, the crew members climbed onto the pier and looked apprehensively at the bodies lying around them.

* * *

"We searched Bewel City thoroughly, and we spent two days touching at other major ports along the island's coast," said Brechlin, now standing before Queen Cirmar and Tarmot in the queen's antechamber. "The story was the same at all of them. Everyone was dead. No survivors. The gray dust coated everything."

"But how can that be?" asked Queen Cirmar. Her brow wrinkled with concern and puzzlement.

"Alipharem suspects Dran and his assistant Ginthar had something to do with it. That they created the cloud and made it poisonous," replied Brechlin.

Tarmot snorted. "That's dubious. How is it possible for someone to create a poisonous cloud of gray ash? And why would Dran want to kill the citizens of Bewel Island?"

Brechlin sighed. "My dear, astute General Counselor, you may recall that the cloud was directed toward Capital Island before the wind shifted."

"Bah!" returned Tarmot. "Speculation. It sounds like you are trying to draw attention away from your glaring incompetence dealing with what is a natural phenomenon. When you saw the cloud, why didn't you warn the citizens? Why didn't you do something?"

"What are you suggesting, Counselor General? That when

I spotted the cloud, mere minutes before I showed it to you, I should have sped to Bewel Island and evacuated its entire population in a few hours' time? Even though some individuals, whose name I need not mention, doubted it was dangerous."

"My dear Tarmot," said Queen Cirmar rather abruptly.

"Yes, my Queen?"

"Would you please leave Brechlin and me alone for a few minutes?"

Tarmot's face showed surprise and then open hostility toward Brechlin. But, he bowed slightly and walked out of the room without uttering a word. Queen Cirmar sat down and looked gravely up at Brechlin. "When you say 'no survivors,' do you mean that literally? Is everyone on Bewel Island dead?"

"Everyone," replied Brechlin solemnly.

"And what about the peninsula? Did the cloud reach Rolucca Peninsula?"

Brechlin shrugged. "We didn't have sufficient provisions to allow us to investigate the peninsula firsthand, but we intercepted a fishing boat while we were on the east side of Bewel Island. The captain said he had left Rolucca Bay that morning, two full days after the cloud had made landfall on Bewel, and reported nothing out of the ordinary."

Queen Cirmar nodded. "If this is the work of Dran and that greasy old Ginthar, we'll get to the bottom of it. We should be thankful, I suppose, that Capital Island escaped Bewel Island's fate. If it weren't for something as whimsical as a shift in the wind, well..." She silently looked at a nearby window, lost in thought.

"My Queen?"

"I'm sorry, Marshal Brechlin. I wandered off," returned

Queen Cirmar weakly.

"My Queen, there is the issue of all the dead. Thousands of them. Something must be done."

Queen Cirmar covered her mouth with her hand. "My God! You're right. They must be buried somehow. Call up the Gravedigger's Guild. All of them. And gather volunteers. Send them to Bewel Island right away."

"I will," replied Brechlin.

"And what of the harvests?" continued Queen Cirmar, her concerns now running away with her. "And the mining operations in Reador? The ship works at Trimlin? All of it will have to be manned. How can we—"

"I'll take care of everything, my Queen, don't you worry," interjected Brechlin in a soft voice. "We'll salvage what we can. And, in the meantime, we'll find out who was behind this. Justice will be served."

"I know," replied Queen Cirmar, looking up at Brechlin. She smiled. "Thank you. I put my faith in your capable hands. And I'll make sure Tarmot stays out of your way."

The queen looked up at the door. "I guess I had better go to him," she said. "Come back with a full report once you have the situation in hand. Try to get a count of the dead. My Gludema, how does one repopulate an entire island? Are you sure the poison has lost its power? We don't want to lose anyone else."

"Yes, my Queen," replied Brechlin. "Alipharem tested the samples we brought back, and the poison is inert. That may explain why Rolucca Peninsula suffered no harm. The poison must have lost its potency by the time it reached its shore."

"Let's hope," said Queen Cirmar. "And if Dran is responsible, we'll send an expedition to Kromul Island. I don't care if he is the Krakul Gat. We'll teach that man what it means to harm the people of my realm."

"Yes, my Queen," said Brechlin. "Kromul Island's famous cliffs will offer no protection."

Burial Detail

Chimber tried Jern's front door, but it was off the hinges and jammed between the sides of the door frame. There was no way to remove it without tools. Sighing, he backed up and looked for alternative means of entry.

"How in the hell does he get in and out of his own house?" Chimber wondered.

"Jern!" he yelled. "Jern!"

"Around back," came Jern's voice from the other side of the building.

Chimber stepped over a fallen slab of wood—a gate in its former life—and made his way to the backyard of the ramshackle cottage. There he found Jern sitting next to a small stream with his feet propped up on a log and a pipe in his hand.

"Chimber!" said Jern. "Welcome! You haven't visited in ages. Have a seat." He pointed to a log.

"I can see why you prefer your backyard. Entrance to the interior of your house is somewhat problematic."

"Oh, that," answered Jern. "I use yon window. It's big enough for me. But I like it better out here. Listening to the water relaxes me."

"Well, it's time you got un-relaxed. We have a public duty to perform."

"What public duty?"

"There has been a disaster on Bewel Island. Some kind of freak weather phenomenon. I'm not clear what. But they have called out guild members from all over to bury the bodies."

Jern sat up. "A disaster? On Bewel Island? How many are dead?"

"Very many, I'm afraid. I have been told there may be hundreds of bodies lying around. The queen has mustered guild members from Capital Island, Saghorn, and even the Rolucca Peninsula, and all are converging on Bewel Island. And we'll need all the help we can get."

"Hundreds of dead?" asked Jern. "My Gludema! What kind of disaster would do that?"

Chimber shrugged. "All I know is there are dead bodies that have to be buried. Are you in?"

"I have family on Bewel Island. Yeah, sure. I'll help."

"Okay, good. Pack up for a couple of weeks. Even if we use mass graves, it'll take us a while. And, after a few days, things won't be very pleasant, so be prepared."

Jern wrinkled up his nose. "No, I suppose not. Will there be pay for this public service? Just asking."

"I don't know yet. But let's not worry about that for now. Let's just get the job done. We leave in the morning."

"I'll meet you at the docks."

"We leave at sunrise. Please be on time, Jern," urged Chimber. "There will be others on board with us."

"I'll be there," assured Jern.

* * *

The bright morning sun found Jern at the docks, sleepy and

disheveled but on time. He climbed aboard Chimber's xebec, gave a brief hello to the other guild members—he knew them all—and settled down on the deck. Chimber eased the craft out of Math's harbor with the morning tide, its lateen sails glistening with morning dew. The journey to Bewel City, the area to which the queen had assigned Saghorn Island's guild members, was a short one. They had fair seas and steady winds and docked at Bewel City's mooring pier the same day they set sail.

As they secured the craft and the gravediggers clambered onto the pier, they were mildly surprised that the bodies they had expected to see lying about had been moved.

"Did another crew get here before us?" wondered Chimber.

They wandered toward the quiet town, hailing as they went, but no calls were returned. Yet neither were any bodies visible in the streets around the taverns and shops that were clustered near the pier.

"Where are all the people we're supposed to bury?" asked Jern.

"I'm not sure," replied Chimber. "It looks like somebody got here before us."

"Well then, where are *they*?"

Chimber shrugged. It was perplexing since a cadaver was no lightweight object. The effort of moving so many bodies in such a short time would have been considerable.

"I'll check in here," said Jern, pointing to a large tavern. "Perhaps the other gravediggers went in for a spot. You gravediggers indulge in an occasional drink, don't you?"

Chimber and the others spread out into the various buildings surrounding the dock area. Chimber entered a warehouse, where partially unloaded carts were scattered. Marcox—another guild member—and his nephew he had recruited to help followed behind.

Chimber scanned the interior. "There would've been workers unloading in here. And if they perished, where are the bodies?"

Marcox shrugged. "Beats me."

Jern came into the building. "No sign of anybody, dead or alive."

"Were the bodies moved to the communal burial ground?" asked Marcox's nephew.

Chimber nodded pensively. "I guess so, but that would have taken quite a bit of time. And we got here pretty quickly."

"Maybe local survivors are working on it," suggested Marcox.

"Maybe," replied Chimber, "but I was told there were no survivors."

"No survivors!" exclaimed Jern. "On the entire island? You never mentioned that."

"Well, the task was daunting enough," was Chimber's weak reply.

"The largest cemetery is outside of town on the Trimlin road," offered Marcox. "Perhaps we should head in that direction."

"I heard something!" cried Jern.

"Yeah, behind those bundles," said Chimber, pointing to two unloaded stacks of wood posts near a back wall.

They dashed toward the sound and discovered, lying on the ground, a cadaver dressed in a simple smock and breeches.

Jern bit his lip. "He looks like a dockworker."

"Look!" exclaimed Marcox. "He's moving!"

They all stared as the body began to move its limbs in an

erratic, jerking motion. Then it bent at the waist like it was trying to sit up.

"He must be snapping out of it," said Marcox's nephew. "He survived!"

Chimber closely eyed the awakening worker. "Maybe. But something isn't right."

Jern took a step back. "I strongly agree. Something creepy is going on here."

"Well, let's help the guy up," said Marcox. "I think he's trying to stand."

The worker had sat up to an upright position and was leaning on a large crate. His eyes were open, but they didn't seem to focus on anything in particular. There was no indication he had any awareness of the four men standing around him. Chimber and Marcox stepped closer, holding out their hands.

The worker's limbs moved in a violent jerking motion once again, causing the two men to step back in surprise. They watched in amazement as the body stretched out his legs, folding them in and out, and then awkwardly attempted to stand.

"Please, mate, take it easy," said Jern, putting his hand on the body's dusty shoulder. "Let us help you."

The dockworker took no regard of Jern's caution. His jerking motion flung Jern's hand aside, and he attempted to climb up on his legs. Using the crate to prop himself up, he shifted all his weight to his feet, tottered for a second, attempted a couple of steps, and fell on his face.

The four men all reached to help the man back up but again backed off as the body once again began a series of violent convulsions. Apparently unfazed by his fall, the worker climbed to his feet and teetered for a moment but this time remained erect.

"Are you okay, friend?" asked Jern. Still, there was no acknowledgment from the revived dockworker. He spun to face the doorway and began walking. Further entreaties by the four men seemed to have no effect. The man seemed oblivious.

"He seems to be well enough," suggested Marcox's nephew. "A sick man couldn't walk around like that, right?"

"I don't know," replied Chimber. "He doesn't seem right. It's like he's in a trance."

"Perhaps it's the aftereffects of whatever hit this place, and it will take a while before they fully recover, like a hangover," offered Jern.

"It may explain the absence of the other bodies," said Marcox. "They simply awakened from whatever the affliction was."

"Okay, but if they all have re-awakened, then where *are* they?" asked Chimber.

"I don't know, but maybe he does," said Jern, pointing to the revived dockworker now shuffling through the doorway in an awkward stride. "Let's follow him."

They all four filed out of the warehouse and followed the dockworker. He led them through the streets of Bewel City, not once stopping or acknowledging those around him in any way. Most of the other gravediggers joined them and walked alongside the dockworker to the outskirts of town toward the Plain of Nubinor, where they encountered a woman coming from another part of town but heading in the same direction as the dockworker and shuffling in the same awkward manner.

The members of the guild asked her questions, but she was no more responsive to their inquiries than was the dockworker. Just like him, she steadily faced forward as she walked. Exasperated and perplexed, the gravediggers trailed along behind the two figures.

As they passed the last few buildings on the edge of town, the group crested a rise in the road and looked down onto the barren Plain of Nubinor. And there, huddled in a dark mass, they beheld a thousand people. They all stopped and stared as the dockworker and the woman kept on walking.

Jern's forehead furrowed. "Well, we know where the towns-folk went."

"Why are all these people just standing out there?" asked a guild member.

"I don't know," said Chimber, "but there's something strange happening."

The gravediggers approached the throng of people, and as they got closer, they saw that they were certainly the towns-people of Bewel City. They were of all ages and professions. As Chimber and the others asked questions of those people along the edges of the huddled mass, once again they were entirely ignored. No one acknowledged their presence to the slightest degree.

Chimber recognized a small child as the daughter of a merchant he knew but saw no sign of her parents. He knelt in front of her and smiled, but the little girl's eyes made no movement toward Chimber's face. Rather, she kept staring off into the distance.

"My name is Chimber," he said. "You're Layem's little girl, aren't you? Where are your parents?"

There was no response, no acknowledgment. Chimber reached out and brushed the gray dust from the child's face and was immediately struck by how cold the child's flesh felt.

"Guild members," said Chimber loudly as he stood up,

"touch the flesh of these people. They feel cold...lifeless. These people are not well."

The gravediggers reached out and touched nearby towns-people, none of whom responded to their attentions.

"Cold, and kind of hard," observed Marcox.

"Yeah," said another gravedigger. "It feels like they're dead."

"What do we do?" Jern asked Chimber.

"Well, we're gravediggers," replied Chimber. "And there are no graves that need digging here. I think it is best to report this to the authorities and have these people treated for whatever this strange illness may be."

"We leave them like this?" asked Jern.

Chimber shrugged his shoulders. "What can we do? The authorities will send people over who will know what to do."

Perplexed and unsure, the group wandered back toward town, gathered up their gear, and boarded the xebec. All were silent as they sailed out of Bewel City harbor.

"I was prepared for death and gore, but this..." said Jern, gesturing over his shoulder with his thumb. "This, I was not prepared for."

Chimber set his jaw. "Nor were any of us. But someone will find out what is wrong with these people, and all will be back to normal."

"I guess sick is better than dead. Right?"

"Yeah," said Chimber. "Right."

Kromul Island Vista

Perched atop the Gray Mountain, Ilsher took in a sweeping view of Kromul Island many feet below her. It was a rare day, for the ever-present fog had lifted, and brilliant sunshine rained down. She looked out to sea and shifted her gaze to the far edge of the small island where she saw clusters of buildings near the harbor. Almost straight down below her, she saw her palatial home, toy-like from this height.

"It's quite thrilling up here," she said to Ginthar, who was standing next to her.

"Quite," whispered the somber Ginthar.

Ilsher closed her eyes as the breeze brushed past her face, laden with the scent of the sea. It had a cold bite, but she found it pleasing. She opened her eyes and saw Dran emerge from the entrance to the narrow tunnel that led to the interior of the Gray Mountain. He was haggard and covered in sweat. He gave them a quick nod and collapsed on a bench near a hut he used for rest.

Ilsher tried to imagine how much concentration it took to control the movements of hundreds of cadavers. The effort took its toll on Dran, whose eyes were already closed.

After watching him doze for a few moments, Ilsher turned once again to Ginthar.

"Just how are things proceeding, my dear Ginthar?"

Ginthar looked down at the beautiful, precocious little girl. Experience had taught him to treat her as an equal, despite her youth.

"Things are proceeding reasonably well, considering," he told her. "The cadavers are gathering on the plains near the towns, and soon Dran will direct them to begin the campaign."

Ilsher looked at Dran with curiosity. "It must be difficult to control so many at once."

"Yes, it is. But with the experience he has gained from operating the mining crews, he has become quite adept. He's a natural talent."

"What about the rain?" wondered Ilsher. "What if there is a storm and it washes away the remnants of the gray ash from the cadavers? Will Dran lose control?"

"No," answered Ginthar. "They breathed in the vapors of the cloud, so there should be enough of the crystal residue in their lungs to control them. But we must act without delay, for the powder will lose its virtue over time."

Ilsher looked around her immediate vicinity—a platform carved into the mountain. Besides the flattened area where Dran's hut was located, there was another recessed area nearby. A large irregular gorge, with signs of recent hammering and cutting.

"Things look different up here," she observed. "That gash is so ugly."

"Yes," agreed Ginthar. "It took a significant chunk of the mountain to form the cloud."

"I wonder, with the bulk of the mountain reduced, is the power of the Krakul Gat affected in any way?"

"Yes, somewhat," replied Ginthar, looking at Ilsher with

surprise. "Did Dran tell you that?"

"No, but it seems logical enough. The mountain's power is channeled and amplified by the gray crystal from which it is formed. With less crystal to amplify, there is less power."

"That is a concern, but the power has not been diminished to an extent that would compromise our efforts. As long as we act while the crystal particles are still active, the Krakul Gat's powers will be sufficient for our needs."

"I hope the sacrifice was worth it. If the scheme doesn't succeed, the Krakul Gat will have a more difficult time controlling the corpses in the mines," pondered Ilsher.

"If the plan doesn't succeed, Dran's ability to manipulate the mining cadavers will be the least of our concerns. But success seems assured. And without the power of the White Mountain to heal their wounded warriors, the army of Capital Island will have no chance against an army of the dead. It will be a matter of time."

"You can't kill the dead," said Ilsher with a sing-song lilt. "And then, after we destroy Cegril, Dran will be ruler of all the realm? With you at his side?"

"That is the plan," said Ginthar in a somewhat guarded tone.

"Then, one day, I shall be queen," added Ilsher.

"I'm sure of it, my dear Ilsher," said Ginthar. "That is, if the plan succeeds."

"What would stop us?"

Ginthar walked over to the wall of the recess in which they stood and caressed the gray crystal. "The power of the Krakul Gat is unique among the other Gludemic Mountains. And as long as we hold Ferrin, the power of the White Mountain is a mere shadow of itself. But it is the Medium of the Blue Mountain who is the wild card. With Er Lomith still free, it is possible for the Lomitheri to come to the aid of Cegril."

"Is that likely?"

Ginthar shrugged his shoulders. "The Lomitheri live far to the north, almost as far as the frozen wastes. They may never hear of our struggle."

"Even should Er Lomith use the power of the Mount Lomith to support Cegril, I don't see how that would matter. Freeze a cadaver solid if you like; once it defrosts, it's as good as new."

Once again, Ilsher watched Ginthar raise his bushy eyebrows. "Yes. Dran and I agree. It seems, at best, the involvement of Er Lomith could only delay our ends. But there is a long tradition about the balance of power among the Gludemic Mountains. The Litany of Limits, which are read as part of a new Medium's induction ceremony, refers to it. Since all three Mediums are equally powerful, one Medium would always be defeated by the other two. And if the Lomitheri intervene, and the power of the Blue Mountain is equal to the power of the Gray Mountain, then there is the possibility of our failure."

"If only your henchmen had captured Er Lomith when they took Ferrin, this would all be a moot point," said Ilsher with a clear note of accusation in her voice.

"It's true," allowed Ginthar. "That's a failing that must be regretted. But now we roll the dice. In a conflict with an equally powerful adversary, either side can win. We have to be smarter."

Ilsher toyed with a lock of hair. "And we will be smarter. I'll see to it."

The Cadaver Host

Brechlin knocked on the door to Queen Cirmar's private dining chamber. The queen and Tarmot were enjoying their usual quiet breakfast together and had given strict orders not to be disturbed. So, when the door was slightly opened, she wasn't surprised to see Tarmot's angry and scowling face peering at her.

"Marshal Brechlin!" exclaimed Tarmot. "Have a little respect for the queen of your country. You interrupt us a mere hour after sunrise? Queen Cirmar and I will be in our official chambers at our normal time. Whatever it is you deem so important can wait until then!" He began to close the door, but Brechlin placed her heavily-booted foot in the door's way, blocking it from being closed.

"I must see the queen now," she said with an even tone. "It is of the utmost urgency."

"I said later!" cried Tarmot, who viciously slammed the door into Brechlin's foot. Her foot did not budge, however. She looked at him with contempt for a moment and then suddenly pushed open the door and rammed her armored shoulder into Tarmot's broad chest. The unexpected blow sent him tumbling backward onto the floor of the dining chamber. As Brechlin stepped in, Tarmot jumped up. "I will kill you, woman!" he howled and reached for his sword hilt, but he only found the satin belt of his morning robe.

"Tarmot!" cried Queen Cirmar, quickly standing up from their breakfast table and holding Tarmot back with her hand. "Please relax. Let's see what this is all about."

She turned to Brechlin. "Marshal Brechlin, really! This is rather rude. Couldn't it wait?"

"My apologies, my Queen," Brechlin replied. "I assure you I would not have disturbed you this morning were it not of the most pressing importance."

"Well, go on, then. What's so important?"

"Very early this morning, I received a messenger from the city leaders of Keeman. An army is gathering outside their city. Troops are being ferried over from Bewel Island. Alipharem thinks they are being controlled by Dran and that they will attack Keeman as soon as the army is deployed."

"Where in God's name would Dran get an army?" asked Tarmot with disdain. "It's ridiculous. Are you drunk?"

"It seems implausible, Brechlin," agreed Queen Cirmar. "Where would Dran get the men?"

"Not just men, but women and children, too," replied Brechlin rather somberly. "At least, they *were* men, women, and children. They are the former citizens of Bewel Island. Now, they are cadavers controlled by Dran."

"The story gets better all the time!" exclaimed Tarmot. "Now you have Dran projecting the power of the Gray Mountain over the sea to Bewel Island!"

"How is that possible?" asked Queen Cirmar, keeping her palm on Tarmot's chest.

"It was the black cloud. Alipharem believes that Ginthar and Dran had part of the Gray Mountain pulverized and made into a cloud. He then laced the particles of the cloud with poison. The cloud killed the citizens and coated them with the dust of the Gray Mountain, which retains its virtue. Now, Dran can use the mountain's power to control them."

Queen Cirmar was visibly flustered as she sat back at her table. Tarmot retained his doubting sneer.

"Is this possible?" managed Queen Cirmar. "How big of an army?"

"The cloud killed, and coated, every person living on Bewel Island. We should expect the army to contain every deceased citizen," replied Brechlin.

Queen Cirmar put her hands to her face. "My God! There were thousands of people living on Bewel Island. What do we do?"

"The first thing we must do is to call a general muster. Every available soldier needs to report to duty as fast as possible. And while the troops are gathering, we need to devise a strategy for Keeman. It has city walls, but they are not strong. Just a rough wooden palisade. And the citizens of Keeman alone cannot mount a defense of the city. Since there isn't time to send the full army to Keeman before the attack, I suggest that we send out an advance force. Once in place, they could delay the attacking army long enough for the citizens of Keeman to escape along Saghorn Island's shore road to Gretly."

The queen bit her lower lip. "That sounds sensible. Let's get the people in Keeman to safety. But if Keeman falls, then what?"

"I suspect Dran's cadavers would follow Keeman's citizens down the coast road. I recommend that as soon as we can field our full army, we send them to Gretly. There, they can deploy in the open area to the northwest of town and meet Dran's army. I believe that we would enjoy significant defensive advantages at that location."

"Marshal Brechlin," began Tarmot, "that is all very interesting. But if what you say is true, and Dran has an army of cadavers under his control, what happens if the army fails to stop them at your chosen spot outside of Gretly?"

"I suspect they would take Gretly and attempt to cross Ger Strait. If they succeeded, then they would march on Cegril."

"So why risk our force at Gretly?" asked Tarmot. "Our city has stout walls. We would do better to keep our mustered army here for our defense."

"And leave the citizens of Keeman and Gretly to their fate?" asked Brechlin rather heatedly.

"They could head up into Saghorn Mountains," said Tarmot. "They can hide there until it's over."

"You want the entire population of Keeman and Gretly to hide in the wilderness while their cities are being sacked?" asked Brechlin incredulously. "Are you serious?"

Tarmot shrugged. "Many would survive. Perhaps most."

Brechlin turned to Queen Cirmar.

"Surely, you wouldn't consider such an outlandish suggestion. Those mountains often drop below freezing at night. There is no food, and wolves are abundant. We can't just allow thousands of our citizens to perish. Don't you think the disaster on Bewel Island is sufficient loss of life for our realm?"

"This is a decision for the Council of Sages," Queen Cirmar replied.

Brechlin's expression hardened. "Perhaps, but time is of the essence, and that council, wise as it may be, deliberates slowly. We would need to transport the army to Gretly immediately."

"But why the area northwest of Gretly?" asked Queen Cirmar.

"It is an open area, so our cavalry would have the advantage. And with the sea on one side and Saghorn Mountains on the other, Dran's larger force could not outflank us."

"And if our army is destroyed, don't we all perish?" asked Tarmot.

"Perhaps," replied Brechlin.

"Then we should minimize the chance of that happening by fighting behind solid walls, not in an open field," pressed Tarmot.

"Isn't there merit to what Tarmot is saying?" asked Queen Cirmar.

"We are better defended behind stone walls, yes. But we have the lives of thousands of people at stake. And, consider this. I have seen the control the Krakul Gat extends over the mine workers on Kromul Island. It is sufficient for the tasks at hand but not refined. I don't think an army of animated corpses will be able to maneuver quickly. That is why an open plain gives us an advantage. And if things do not go our way, I believe we could disengage and retreat to Capital Island without significant losses."

Tarmot snorted. "That's pure speculation, Marshal Brechlin. If you should prove wrong, the consequences are unacceptable."

Queen Cirmar rubbed her forehead as she looked down at her feet. "All of this requires careful consideration. But I can assure you, I am not inclined to leave the people of Saghorn Island to their fate."

"My Queen," said Brechlin, "I took the liberty to interrupt your morning tranquility because things are coming to a head.

This force, this...cadaver host...is gathering as we speak and may attack soon. The wind is out of the south and a few points to the west. The advance force I spoke of should be able to reach Keeman tomorrow morning, Gludema willing. They, along with the Keeman militia, should be able to delay Dran's army until the citizens evacuate. We need to act now."

Queen Cirmar ran her fingers through her hair. "Okay, Brechlin. You have my blessing. Let it be so."

"I will have Captain Wilart prepare the sloops and other transport craft. And I will place Captain Labrok in charge of the advance force. He is an excellent leader."

Tarmot scowled. "The Harbor Captain! In charge of an assault force?"

"As I said, he is an excellent leader."

"No, no, my dear Marshal," said Tarmot with a smug tone of voice. "This is much too important to leave in the hands of the Harbor Captain. We need *you* to lead the advance force."

Brechlin turned to Queen Cirmar. "I would be honored to lead my men in the field, my Queen," she said, "but my place is here to oversee the general muster. We must get our army ready as quickly as possible."

"Nonsense!" said Tarmot. "I can call out the muster as well as you. No, no. We need your leadership in the field!" He was barely holding back a sinister grin.

"Yes, you go, Brechlin," said Queen Cirmar. "See to things firsthand. Tarmot and I will see to the muster."

Brechlin bowed. "Yes, my Queen," she said.

Tarmot smiled at Brechlin. "A brave gesture!" he exclaimed. "The citizens of Keeman will be forever grateful, I am sure."

Brechlin looked at Tarmot suspiciously.

"In the meantime, I will convene the Council of Sages,"

said Queen Cirmar. "We will decide on the best path to follow after the citizens of Keeman have evacuated the city and are on the road to Gretly. I will not let them perish. If we must make a stand in the fields outside Gretly, then so be it. But perhaps they and the citizens of Gretly could all be evacuated to Cegril. We could then mount a defense of the city with all of our citizens safely inside."

"Well," began Tarmot, "all those people here? Our food supplies are limited, my Queen. Are you sure it is wise to—"

"I don't have the time to stand here and debate our nation's strategy!" interjected Brechlin. "Much is unknown anyway. I leave to assemble the advance force and make sail for Keeman. After we make contact with this army, we will have a better idea of our strategic options."

"Agreed," said Queen Cirmar. "Brechlin, I give you leave. Tarmot, assemble the Council of Sages and the army generals. We meet in one hour."

Tarmot glanced at his barely touched breakfast and hastened out of the room alongside Brechlin.

"I wish you much success, Marshal Brechlin," he said as they paced side by side down the hallway. "And, pray, be careful of your own skin. It would be difficult to replace a leader of your caliber."

"I know your thoughts, Tarmot," replied Brechlin. "But rest assured, I will return."

First Assault

The next morning, the sun rose over an agitated but manageable sea. During the previous night, Brechlin had fought seasickness as the sloop, filled with an advance force of Cegril's regular garrison, beat into a headwind toward Saghorn Island.

Two ships. One hundred twenty men. Against an army of thousands of cadavers. Is it enough? The upcoming hours will tell.

She swallowed her nausea and stood at the gunnels, peering out at the throng of Keeman citizens gathered around the town's mooring area. They formed an indistinguishable mass in the poor early light, but it was clear they were pressing to board a freight ship docked at the pier. As the sloop got closer, she could make out a stream of people making their way along the coastal road, heading west toward Gretly.

Captain Wilart was standing nearby at the rudder wheel, watching with obvious concern the horde of citizens on the pier. "Keeman's citizens are panicked. We must be careful. They may try to swarm our ships."

Brechlin nodded and looked back across the sea toward the transport ship following the sloop. It was bulky and barely seaworthy, but it had a lot of room.

She was sworn to the crown, and the crown was ultimately

sworn to its people. *What good is a crown that cannot protect its inhabitants?* She and the queen always agreed here, and her duty now was clear—to get these people to safety. After all, the protection of the kingdom was her chief responsibility.

She turned to Captain Wilart. "It's okay, Captain Wilart. Let them board. Our troops will police the embarkation."

"But...how will your men evacuate?" he asked in surprise.

"Return as soon as you can. If we can't hold out, we'll retreat along the coast road, hopefully to meet up with the mustered army near Gretly."

"But Marshal Brechlin, the attacking forces might cut off your escape. You would be trapped."

"Our mission is to delay the enemy long enough to enable the citizens of Keeman to get a safe distance along the coast road," said Brechlin. "That is our primary concern."

"But my primary concern is the safe retrieval of you and your—" began the crusty old Wilart, but Labrok, who had overheard the exchange, stepped up.

"The Marshal has given you an order, Captain," he said firmly, cutting off Wilart in mid-sentence. "Get as many citizens as possible escorted to safety."

Captain Wilart looked at Labrok and then at Brechlin. "I understand," he replied.

Brechlin gave Labrok an appreciative glance. "Get your men disembarked, Captain Labrok. Then help oversee the boarding of these citizens. Don't let them rush the ships. Keep it orderly. Feeble and non-ambulatory citizens get first priority. In the meantime, I'll head to the city walls and reconnoiter the situation. Follow me as soon as the ships are under way."

Brechlin entered the mass of people and pushed her way up the short road connecting Keeman with her port. It was sweaty work. She had to squeeze around people, animals, and carts all heading in the opposite direction. But, as she got closer to the city, the traffic on the road began to thin out.

That's good, she thought. *Most of the citizens are already on their way west.*

As she approached the wooden palisade that surrounded the city, she encountered a logjam of vehicles and animals at the gate, with several drivers desperately trying to push through at the same time.

Where are the constables?

She climbed up on the nearest stalled wagon, ignored the maniacal jabbering of its owner, and scampered over three more carts, which allowed her to enter the city proper. As she walked down the main avenue, she noted trash strewn everywhere and piles of abandoned belongings, but there was comparatively little traffic. She pressed on to the eastern wall, where she spotted a young officer speaking to a group of men holding weapons and a few farm implements, none of whom looked happy to be there.

"Who's in charge here?" she demanded.

The young officer pivoted to see who had interrupted his instructions, but his expression of harried irritation changed to formal respect as he recognized the woman standing before him.

"Marshal Brechlin!" he cried. "Welcome. Glad to see you. I'm Mimmers, sir—er, ma'am. Chief Officer of the City Guard." He saluted briskly and glanced over her shoulder. "Do you have troops with you?"

"An advance guard of one hundred and twenty men," replied Brechlin. "They're supervising the embarkation of citizens at the port and should be along."

"One hundred and twenty men?" asked Mimmers in a respectful but disappointed tone. "I was hoping for more."

"It's okay, Chief Officer Mimmers. We've conceded the city. We merely have to delay the attacking forces long enough for the citizens to evacuate. Once we fall back to Gretly, the full army should be mustered, and we will make our stand."

"Once we defeat this horde, then we can retake Keeman," said Mimmers, nodding hesitantly. "But what will this enemy do to the town?"

"Probably not much," suggested Brechlin. "They're cadavers. They won't need to pillage. They don't even need shelter."

She looked over the group of men Mimmers had been instructing. They were obviously militia, with little armor and an assortment of weapons. She could discern a look a fear on many of their faces.

"What is the status of your men, Chief Officer Mimmers?"

"We have twenty-five police officers and over a hundred trained militia along the wall, with another fifty volunteers interspersed among them," he replied.

"I see." She surveyed the placement of the men along the wall and nodded. "Well, let's check out our enemy."

She climbed a crude ladder up the wooden wall to a narrow platform, where she had a view over its top. Mimmers joined her. The land beyond the city walls was flat, broken with short hedges, stone fences, and a number of minor streams. Several hundred yards away, she saw a dark mass of huddled beings, with a long stream of more cadavers connecting the horde with the distant seashore at the eastern end of the island.

"They've been gathering all day," said Mimmers. "As soon as they reach the shore, they march to that gathering point."

"From here, it looks as if they are barely armed!" exclaimed

Brechlin. "Some have swords, but many have staffs or pitch-forks. How do they plan to take the city walls?"

"I don't know," answered Mimmers. "But I fear it wouldn't take much." He hammered his armored elbow onto the top of the wall for emphasis.

Brechlin's military mind was racing. "Have you attempted any probing attacks?"

"None. We felt the sensible strategy was to remain behind these walls until help arrived or until they came at us."

"Hmm," pondered Brechlin, regarding the horde. "I take it your police officers have mounts available."

"Yes, ma'am."

"I have an idea. While these things are gathering and before they deploy for an attack, let's use your mounts to see what they're made of. Probe their flanks. If they're as sluggish to react as I suspect they are, then we may not have much to fear."

"You're going out there?" asked Mimmers in a surprised voice. "Why, there must be more than a thousand cadavers."

"And there will be thousands more before it is all said and done, so we had best be quick about it, correct, Chief Officer Mimmers?"

Mimmers stood up straight and saluted. "Correct, Marshal Brechlin. I will attend to it immediately."

He scampered down the ladder to collect the police officers and their mounts, while Brechlin continued to stare at the growing horde of walking cadavers—men, women, and children. The enemy's army of undead soldiers.

"How do you kill a dead soldier?" Brechlin asked no one in particular.

To Bie Pass

Chimber let out a slow, frustrated breath and looked around the meeting hall. Everyone seemed to listen attentively to the frightened ramblings of the man at the podium. Elder Lumm was there, and the other leaders of the community. They sat around two large banquet tables, riveted to what the speaker, Old Man Rackley, had to say.

That's what fear will do for you. Grasping at whatever straws are dangling within reach.

Only Jern seemed as disengaged as Chimber. He sat near a window, staring out at the range of mountains that ran the length of Saghorn Island and separated Math from the northern coast. Chimber wadded up his note sheet and tossed it at Jern. It scored a direct hit, bouncing off the top of his head and through the open window. Jern's surprised and accusing glare sent a wave of mirth through Chimber's body. He convulsed with submerged laughter. When he turned back to the podium, he saw that Old Man Rackley had stopped speaking. Others around the room were looking at him with scowling faces.

Elder Lumm stood up, clearly exasperated. "How is it possible, Chimber, that you can be so jocular at a time of such peril? Do you not take our situation seriously?"

"Sorry, Elder Lumm," meekly replied Chimber. "I...please, Mr. Rackley, continue your observations."

"This is wasting everyone's time!" blurted Jern. "What's the point of sitting here listening to worried prattle?"

"Jern!" exclaimed Chimber.

"Well, it's true! What's the point?"

Jern's remark set off an outburst of chatter from all quarters of the meeting hall.

"Order, please!" cried Elder Lumm. "We must have order!"

Elder Lumm's words had little effect. The members of the town council, assembled to discuss how to deal with the threat of the cadaver army gathering outside Keeman, were very much on edge. Keeman was less than a day's trek over the mountains and through Bie Pass.

Chimber understood their fear but was impatient. Unable to restrain himself any longer, he unsheathed his sword and slammed the flat side of the blade sharply on the back of the chair in front of him, creating a loud cracking sound. The assembled men stopped talking and stared at him, their eyes wide.

"Gentlemen, we must have a plan," proclaimed Chimber. "That's why we're here. I understand the need to vent one's worries, but Jern is right. All this fretting is getting us nowhere."

"Well, I was getting to that part..." offered Rackley.

Chimber re-sheathed his sword. "Where to hide our food supplies, and in particular, your apple harvest, is not the kind of plan I had in mind. We have to prepare for action. We have to prepare to fight."

"But that's the problem," whined Elder Lumm. "We have no means of putting up a capable defense. We have no walls

138

and too few men."

"So if they come, we stash our belongings and hope for the best?" asked Jern. "Is that a plan?"

"Well...I don't see..." stammered Elder Lumm.

"I have a plan," announced Chimber. He proceeded to the podium and looked over the assemblage of frightened faces. Old Man Rackley meekly returned to his seat. "We have about forty men capable of fighting. Elder Lumm is correct—that's too few to defend the town. However, this cadaver army is outside of Keeman, hence on the other side of the mountains. Should they attack Math, they must go through Bie Pass."

"Unless the army returns to their ships after sacking Keeman and comes at us by sea," protested Elder Lumm.

"That's possible," said Chimber, "but it doesn't seem likely. They would need to ferry troops back and forth several times to muster their army here. And unlike Keeman, Math has no open area upon which they could assemble. And, well, to put it bluntly, Math is not that important. I see them continuing down the coastal road to Gretly, should they take Keeman. And if they come at us at all, it would be a quick strike through the pass, probably with a small force."

"Forty men could defend the pass," said Jern. "It narrows to a mere ten paces at its highest point, with impassible ridges on either side."

"I know that place," said Rackley. "It's just above Keeman. But then, couldn't the enemy troops look up and see you? You might provoke them into attacking. Perhaps we should lie low and just hope—"

"No," asserted Chimber. "We can't just hope the evil will go away. We must be prepared. And we can defend the pass with forty good men. But I take your point, Mr. Rackley; we should stay out of sight."

"I don't see any better plan," agreed Elder Lumm.

"Okay," added Rackley. "You men secure the pass. The rest of us will assemble our goods and hide them away, just in case."

Chimber faked a smile. "I appreciate your confidence, Mr. Rackley. Now, I need volunteers."

The Fall of the Marshal of Cegril

The road to Bie Pass was steep and winding. Halfway up, it followed the edge of a plateau and then tilted upward between narrow, stony cliffs almost straight uphill. It then crested the shoulder of the mountain at Bie Pass, a thin ridge with steep slopes descending on either side, and switchbacked down the other side of the mountain range before reaching the outskirts of Keeman. It was the only land road to Keeman from Math, and the profits had to be hefty before any Math merchant would undertake the arduous route.

Chimber, Jern, and thirty-four volunteers from Math slogged up the path, peering about them for any sign of an ambush. It was a grave, rather quiet group, considering they were all townsmen who had known each other their entire lives.

Every man carried a makeshift shield, and most had a serviceable sword sheathed at their side. The others carried crude lances. A few wore rusted vests of homemade mail. While Chimber was proud of these brave volunteers and, now, comrades-in-arms, they weren't a formidable bunch.

Leading the way was Curl, a damn good blacksmith and the strongest man he knew, but he was no soldier. And a few steps behind him was Thomas, owner of the mercantile and a fine businessman. But he was of slight build and better suited to the ledger book than fighting. He looked tentative now, not at all in his element. Chimber would stick close to him just in case.

He couldn't help but wonder how much help he would receive from his compatriots. And what if things got really bad? A real fight? He worried that few, if any, would return.

But they all knew the possibilities and were suffering under no delusions. They were headed to Bie Pass to defend their town, and if the entire army attempted to force their way through the pass, their small force would not hold them for long. They banked on the hope that a raiding party searching for supplies would be the worst they would face.

Chimber thought over the events he had witnessed at Bewel City a few days before—the awkward movement of the cadaver they found in the warehouse and how oblivious they were to the gravediggers who tried to communicate with them.

How well can they fight? Maybe all this concern is misplaced.

It was late afternoon when they reached the pass. There was no room to make camp, so they went down one switchback to where several large boulders just off the road shielded them from view. They climbed up one of the boulders and looked down at the scene many feet below. They saw the switchbacks zigzagging down the mountainside. Just beyond the foot of the mountain stood Keeman and its nearby plain. To the east, the sea was several miles distant. Opposite them, on the far side of Keeman, they could see the short road to Keeman's port to the north of town. A dark strand of stragglers made their way down the coast road toward Gretly.

They had a good view into the interior of the wooden palisade and could see the meager forces of the city congregated along the wall facing the plain. As their eyes veered toward the east, they saw the dark cluster of animated corpses gathering before the city and a stream of reinforcements flowing from the eastern coast.

"Why, they're just a mob!" exclaimed Jern. "Unorganized. Surely, a disciplined army would wipe them out."

"They might," replied Chimber. "But remember, these aren't normal soldiers."

"I know. They're the animated corpses of the dead citizens of Bewel Island. It sounds disturbing, but it doesn't mean they form an effective fighting force."

"Well, we have no idea how well they fight," said Chimber, gazing at the gate on the eastern wall of the city. "But we may soon find out. Look!"

He pointed to a small group of riders streaming out of the gate toward the gathered mob, about twenty-five in total. They galloped quickly and gathered at the right flank of the dark cluster of cadavers, a mere hundred paces distant. Chimber studied the mob as the developments played out and saw no change in their swarming mass. They didn't even change their facing. In fact, they seemed entirely uninterested in the mounted force. Chimber's heart beat with a new hope. Perhaps these cadavers were an empty threat. If they didn't possess at least a rudimentary sense of military tactics, then the army could be destroyed.

"They're getting ready to charge," cried Jern.

Chimber watched the mounted force form into a loose wedge. It would normally be risky for such a small force of mounted men to charge into an infantry army of several thousand, but Chimber thought it made sense. Because the cadavers were slow-moving and apparently unaware of their existence, the attacking cavalry should be able to disengage after the first exploratory assault.

"That's a woman leading the charge!" exclaimed one of the men peering over the boulder.

It was true. Chimber saw her long hair flowing back in the wind, and made out her tall, shapely form. He was struck by her brave posture and admired her immediately.

As the thirty-six men of Math watched, perched high above the Keeman plain, the wedge of mounted cavalry charged the mob and plunged viciously into its flank. Chimber saw many of the cadavers fall from the force of the impact. He could make out the arms of the mounted troops brandishing swords and hacking downward again and again as the mob surrounded them.

"They don't seem to be causing much damage," said Chimber, intently watching the enemy troops near the mounted attack. "They knock them down or hack into them, but the cadavers keep coming."

"Maybe they should disengage and charge again," suggested Jern. "They're becoming encircled."

"There go two riders!" exclaimed Chimber, watching the cadavers pull two men off their mounts. "And there goes another one."

"They'd better hurry and disengage!" cried Jern. "They're being engulfed by that mob."

"They can't," said Chimber. "Look. The cadavers grab the riders' legs and hang on even while they are being struck by swords. The riders can't get free."

They watched in horror as, one by one, the cadaver soldiers pulled the riders from their mounts and hacked them to pieces. The remaining mounted troops panicked as they struggled to break away from the crowd. More fell, but the remaining few fought their way near the outer edge of the mob. Chimber saw the woman warrior, still alive and viciously wielding her sword, a blur of controlled fury. But no one could keep that up for long. If they didn't disentangle themselves, they would be lost.

As more riders got taken down and hacked to death, their awful screams reached the men of Math as they looked down from their mountain perch. Neither were their mounts spared as the cadavers turned them into bloody brown piles. The woman and four others broke free and bolted back toward the gate. A small group of cadavers followed on foot, ungainly and slow, but apparently determined.

"They'll never catch them," thought Chimber. "Unless the riders fall from their mounts."

It was at that exact moment he saw a rider, obviously wounded, slide off his horse and tumble to the ground. The woman warrior heeled her horse and headed back to the aid of her fallen comrade. The other riders sped onward with barely a glance.

"Cowards!" Jern yelled at the retreating riders, though they were too far away to hear. He then turned to Chimber. "It'll be a close thing."

Chimber's eyes were wide. "We should help."

"But how? We would never reach them in time."

"We could, if we go that way." Chimber pointed over the boulder. Jern pulled himself over the edge and peered down. It was a long, steep slope covered with mountain scree.

"What! Go down there?" asked Jern. But then, he looked out at the woman dismounting her horse as the cadavers approached. "Do we have time?"

"You've seen that woman in action," said Chimber. "They won't be able to kill her immediately. She will fight rather than let her comrade die."

"Okay, Chimber! Let's go," blurted Jern. "I'm with you."

Chimber hesitated. They would have to scurry down the slope to the plain and then run several hundred paces to come to her aid. Not only would they be open to attack, their presence would be revealed.

"We would be vulnerable..." Chimber pondered aloud, re-considering.

"They are tough but slow. We would have plenty of chance to escape back up the slope."

"But what if they follow us? What if we're putting Math in danger?"

"Damn, Chimber! Do you want to help her or not?"

Then Jern, not waiting for an answer, grabbed Chimber by the shirt sleeve and slid off the back side of the boulder, pulling Chimber after him. They both began their descent. To their surprise, they managed to keep their feet on the steep slope as they slid down the loose gravel at great speed. They reached the bottom of the slope much more quickly than they would have expected.

"You will get it for this," shouted Chimber as they took off in a run toward the woman.

"You'll get your turn," replied Jern between puffs. "But first, I have a date with some walking cadavers."

As they approached, the woman was busy pulling at the body of her fallen comrade, attempting to get him up on her horse. But, the group of cadavers approaching her came upon her, swinging their swords. She let the body fall to the ground in time to parry a crude killing stroke from the nearest one. Another one swung at her mount, piercing its haunches. The horse squealed in pain and hobbled away. She stood her ground, fighting desperately over her comrade's fallen body, protecting him the best she could. Although her strikes often found their mark, they seemed to do little to deter the animated corpses.

Suddenly, she howled in pain. Chimber saw the cadaver of a small girl standing behind her holding a dagger. The strike of the child-cadaver's blade had found the flesh of the woman's leg in the seam between her chain mail and leather leggings. She kicked the corpse aside, trying to maintain her footing, but just as Chimber and Jern approached, a blade struck the woman across her helmeted head and she collapsed. At that moment, the cadavers wheeled to face the newcomers, who had hesitated, catching their breath.

Jern looked at Chimber and smiled weakly. "You know you should never listen to me, right?"

Chimber shook his head and watched gravely as the cadavers came nearer, but then they heard approaching footsteps behind them. It was the rest of their party, who, after a moment's hesitation, had followed them down the scree slope. Chimber took charge.

"Men, engage these corpses. Jern and I will slip around and see about those two," he shouted, pointing to the two downed riders.

The men of Math, thirty-four stout souls, surrounded the small cadaver group and thrust their spears and swung their swords. They were not particularly adept at it, but the cadavers were slow, and although they did no noticeable damage, they found they could swing and fend off a counter strike with their shields, at least most of the time.

Chimber checked the downed rider—the male who had fallen from his horse. He was lifeless.

"She's still alive," said Jern, who was standing over the woman warrior.

"Let's pick her up and carry her back up the slope," said Chimber. "Quickly!" The woman's body was long and muscular and clad in armor, so no lightweight burden. Chimber grasped her under her arms, and Jern grabbed her legs.

"Disengage and follow us," shouted Chimber. The men of Math broke free, leaving two of their number dead on the ground. The skirmish had exhausted all of them, but they found that they could easily outdistance the awkward cadavers. They were halfway up the scree-covered slope before the cadaver party reached its base. Chimber looked back and was relieved to see their pursuers had stopped at the edge of the slope and returned to the rest of the mob.

Someone in their group screamed. Chimber looked over to see Jymin, the baker's son, wildly hacking at a severed arm still clinging to his ankle.

"It won't let go," he shouted. "Get that thing off of me!"

The arm was hacked off at the wrist, yet the hand refused to release its grip. Two men, using both of their hands, pried the hand off. They all continued climbing up the slope.

They made it back to the ridge of boulders whence they had come and slipped behind them, breathing heavily and looking down on the plain. The cadaver army gave no indication of following. Chimber and Jern gently laid the woman's armor-clad body on the lush grass just on the other side of the line of boulders.

"Chimber, will you look at this?" asked Jymin, pointing down the slope.

Chimber came over and peered down. There, just a few feet from the ridgeline, was the severed hand they had pried loose. Using its fingers, it was clawing its way up the slope, still on the attack. Disgusted, Chimber took a spear from the man next to him and pierced it, pinning the hand in the dirt.

The Destruction of Keeman

The men of Math set up camp in a grassy enclave just on the Keeman side of Bie Pass. Chimber and Jern attended to their patient as best they could. They cleansed the assortment of wounds on her body, including the large gash on her thigh, which they stitched up. These were nasty wounds, but it was the blow to her head that had them especially concerned. For that, there was nothing they could do other than keep her comfortable and hope she came out of her coma.

From their vantage point high above Keeman, there was no possibility that the cadaver force could surprise them during the day. But nighttime was another matter. They had little concern about an attack up the scree slope. It was steep and, as they well knew, covered with a layer of loose gravel. They doubted the awkwardly moving cadavers could manage it. The much longer road, following switchbacks up the mountain, was another matter, and so that evening they posted a series of sentries at intervals down the road. Should the enemy make a foray against them, these men would run back up the road to alert the rest of the small force.

But the night passed without incident, and when the party awoke the next morning, little had changed out on the Keeman plain, except that now the horde of cadavers had increased in size.

Chimber examined their wounded warrior. The previous evening, he had removed her armor and swaddled her in his and Jern's coats to protect her from the night chill. Although she was still unconscious, he was encouraged by her even and regular breathing. He joined the group of men peering over the ridge of rocks.

Jern gestured toward the black horde. "It looks like they're making their move."

The swarm of cadavers was fanning out into a large crescent. Motion was evident within the city walls below, and Chimber watched in dismay as many of the small force manning the walls broke away, heading for the gate at the far side of the city. Perhaps a hundred of the garrison remained.

"Why are they staying?" wondered Jern aloud. "It's hopeless."

"They don't want to give up their home," suggested Chimber.

As the massive crescent of walking dead advanced on the wall, more of the city's defenders fell away. Those who remained gathered up the discarded bows and arrows and fired away at the approaching mob.

"Just how do they plan to broach the wall?" asked Chimber.

The cadaver host halted in front of the wooden palisade and began using their swords to hack the wood. Oblivious to the arrows or any other objects the defenders flung at them, the animated corpses patiently swung their swords. For two hours, they kept it up. Eventually, the relentless efforts of the cadavers created gaps in the wooden barrier. Through these gaps, the cadaver army stumbled through, sending the remainder of the defenders scurrying away from the wall *en masse*, outrunning the slow-moving cadavers. A few hardy men attempted hand-to-hand combat with some of the corpses, and occasionally, by dismembering them, demobilized them. But, there was no killing them, no stopping their motion. Slashed, hacked, pierced, or burned, the cadavers fought on, oblivious to the damage done to them. Soon, the entire city was swarming with the lurching cadavers, and every human defender had either taken flight or perished.

The men of Math watched in horror as the army destroyed the buildings of Keeman, setting them ablaze. High above the forlorn city, they felt the heat of the flames as they reared up several stories high. As night approached, the cadavers amassed on the far side of the town, along the road to Gretly, their ghastly forms visible from the light of the still-raging fires.

The next morning was a sorrowful sight. The city, which every one of the Math volunteers had visited countless times, appeared as a large saucer of charred ash and stone foundations. Smoke plumes wafted upward, bringing the smell of wood ash to the nostrils of the small troop. The scent was laced with the unmistakable overtones of charred flesh.

"I hope Corina got out okay," said Jern, referring to a young lady Chimber had once fancied.

"Yeah," said Chimber not averting his eyes from the dismal scene before them, "I'm sure her brother saw to that." Chimber shuddered at the smell and thought about the citizens of Keeman he knew.

"Incredible!" blurted Jern. "The whole damned town—up in smoke!"

Chimber turned to Jern. "They're cadavers! Can't kill 'em. How do we fight 'em?"

Jern shrugged and slowly shook his head. "I have no idea."

Chimber scanned the scene below him. In the bright morning light, he could easily see as far as the loading docks. But the cadaver army was nowhere in sight.

Several men went down to the plain to see if they could locate the bodies of their fallen comrades. Chimber stood by Curl, watching the men below from the line of boulders.

Jern came up and peered over the boulders with them. "Why destroy the city? What advantage does it serve?"

"Because they are a bunch of evil assholes," suggested Curl.

"They want to break our spirit," said Chimber. "Let's make sure they won't succeed."

Jern scratched the back of his neck. "If we assume they're heading for Gretly, I figure it would take them at least a week to get there, given their pace of movement."

"Maybe not," said Chimber. "They don't sleep, they don't rest. If they take no breaks, I would guess they would reach Gretly in three or four days."

"Do you think there's any chance they'll double back and attempt the pass?" asked Curl.

"It wouldn't make sense," said Chimber. "Unless their departure was a subterfuge. And I don't see this army using much subterfuge."

"Yeah, why would they need to?" said Jern. "They could've overwhelmed us, had they a mind to."

"Even so, we'd better leave a couple of men here to keep a watch on things," suggested Chimber. "And while we wait for the others to return from below, let's build a few stretchers to carry the bodies back to Math, including our patient."

"Do you think she will survive the journey?" asked Jern.

"I do now, since I noticed the Tear of Life dangling from her neck this morning."

"Well, I would hate to lose her after all we went through. We lost two good men down there."

Chimber looked down at the plain below them and somberly nodded his head. He then turned his attention back to his ward. "I think it's already made a difference. She's breathing regularly, and I've noticed her moving her limbs."

"Let's get her home," said Jern. "We'd better report back to the Council and then reconnoiter the movements of the enemy. We can't rule out the possibility that Math might be next."

Chimber's Patient

The first thing of which Brechlin was aware was a piercing pain inside her skull. Awareness of other, lesser pains soon followed. Her eyes didn't focus at first, but she was undressed and in a comfortable bed. Although her vision was blurry, she groped around for her sword, seeking its comfortable hilt, but not finding it. After a moment, her vision resolved, and she discovered she was in a rustic room, simply furnished, with a fine fire blazing in a corner. No one was to be seen.

She attempted to sit up but opted to abandon that course of action when the pain in her head ratcheted up several notches. She stared at the ceiling and, once the surge of pain subsided, tried to reconstruct the events that had brought her here. She remembered the sortie against the cadaver mob and their subsequent retreat. Then going back to help the fallen rider and fighting the group of cadavers that attacked her. After that, all was dark. Could she now be a prisoner?

Her fears were allayed, however, when Chimber's handsome, friendly face entered the room. He sat down beside her with a smile.

"Glad to see you're awake," he said. "You had us worried there for a while."

"You took care of me?" she asked.

"Well me, Jern, and a few others."

"Where am I? What happened?"

"You're in Math, and this is my cottage. Our little group was watching your attack from Bie Pass when you were set upon. We came down to help and brought you to safety after you were knocked unconscious."

"And Keeman?" asked Brechlin suddenly. "The defenses? I must go..."

She sat up and looked around for her clothes.

"Please, where are my things? I must go," she said, grimacing with the sharp pain that once again overwhelmed her.

"Please lie back down," said Chimber. He firmly pushed her down by her shoulder. She could not resist.

"There is nothing you can do," he added. "Keeman is lost. The citizens have fled."

"Lost?" she managed after the intense waves of pain subsided. "How long have I been out?"

"You've been unconscious for several days."

"And the enemy? Where is the cadaver host?"

"I don't know, exactly. They left Keeman heading west along the coastal road. Fortunately, they didn't seem interested in our small town."

Brechlin pressed her lips together. "They'll attack Gretly next. And then strike at Capital Island. I have got to get back to Cegril."

"Try to relax," soothed Chimber. "You will get home. Just not right away."

Brechlin forced her tense body to relax. There was nothing she could do about it right now. She couldn't stand up if her life depended on it.

"Can you send somebody to find out what's going on?"

asked Brechlin. "It's important that I know."

"We already have," said Chimber. "I sent two men along a minor road that follows the southern coast. They can head up into the mountains at the western end of the island and look down on Gretly. They'll be able to see what the cadaver army is doing. Better give them a couple more days. In the meantime, your wounds need attending. And then we'll try solid food." Chimber pulled out a container of ill-smelling ointment.

Brechlin's nose crinkled. "Are you planning on putting that vile stuff on my wounds?"

"This is Frakar's Ointment. An old family recipe, and yes, I've been putting this stuff on your wounds for days already. That is part of the reason you are healing so nicely."

"And explains why I smell funny," managed Brechlin, smiling weakly.

"Ah, a smile! A superb sign. Now, let's pull down your covers."

Chimber reached for the sheets and began drawing them down, but Brechlin resisted, gripping the coverings. She wasn't used to being vulnerable and naked with men. She was too weak, however, and Chimber easily tugged them away. He gently pulled them down to her feet but avoided looking directly at her body, nude now except for bandages.

"We have to continue dressing your wounds regularly. I'm sure its uncomfortable for you and I'm sorry. Just a few minutes, and I'll be done."

It surprised Brechlin that she felt shy about her body being exposed to Chimber's view. But he put her at ease with his tender professionalism. She watched the young man intently and with modest pleasure as he went about his work. It was a change having someone attend to her. She wasn't used to such fuss.

A pendant dangling around her neck caught her attention and she held it up. "What is this bauble I'm wearing?" she asked.

"It's called the Tear of Life. It aids your healing. I suspect it to be a piece of the White Mountain."

Brechlin studied the white piece of crystal with wonder as Chimber put the ointment away.

"Well, thank you," she said. "It seems to be working. May I cover up now?"

"Not right now," he replied. "The ointment needs to dry for a minute or two. But if you're uncomfortable, I'll leave the room."

"No, it's okay," said Brechlin.

Chimber shrugged. "I looked you over carefully for wounds. Your body has quite a few scars. Have you been in many battles?"

"I've seen my share of blood. It goes with the job."

"Ah, yes. The life of a public servant."

"You don't know who I am, do you?"

"I assumed you were an officer in Keeman's police force—I saw the insignia on the horse you were riding. But I didn't know they hired women."

"They don't. But Cegril's army does. Me and three other officers. All daughters of officers."

"I know the marshal is a woman. Quite a leader, from what I hear."

"Thank you for the compliment."

"You? Are you saying you're the marshal?"

Brechlin bowed her head. "She is I."

"But, how did you end up..."

"I was leading a force intended to delay the attacking army while the citizens escaped. We were probing the defensive capabilities of the enemy host when I fell, and you saved me. Who, may I ask, are you?"

"Chimber's the name," he replied. "Master gravedigger and xebec captain."

"Glad to meet you," she said sincerely. "And thank you for saving my life."

"Well, that's the least I could do for the queen's right-hand man—er, woman. Now, cover up while I bring you some soup."

"Not, I hope, another family recipe devised by old Frakar," she said.

Chimber laughed. A deep, free roll of mirth. Brechlin's eyes lit up with pleasure. She liked this man.

"A soup of my own design, I assure you," Chimber said as he left the room.

* * *

The next morning, Chimber entered Brechlin's room with ointment in hand. But, she surprised him when he found her sitting up on her bed, fully dressed.

"Surely you're not planning on getting up?" asked Chimber.

"I've already tried it, and I didn't get very far. Can you help me?"

"I don't think it's a good idea."

"Look, my wounds are just fine," said Brechlin. "Thanks, no doubt, to your kind care and this necklace. The pain in my head, however, is still severe. But I would like to make it to the breakfast table, if you please, and dine sitting up."

Before Chimber could respond, Brechlin was attempting to stand. He saw her waver and put his arm around her waist to support her. Together, they made it to the half-log bench placed alongside Chimber's table. Brechlin plopped down, rested her head in her hands, and frowned. Chimber sat beside her, concerned.

"Is there anything I can do?" he asked.

"Just give me a minute," she said. After waiting a few moments, she sat upright. She looked up at Chimber's concerned face and smiled. "So, what's for breakfast, my dear Chimber?"

"An appetite is a good sign. You're recovering quickly. Can you handle a seared beefsteak and a piece of yesterday's goose pie?"

"A breakfast a woman can sink her teeth into. By all means," she said with warm enthusiasm. All she'd had over the last few days was Chimber's soup.

As Chimber bustled around the room preparing breakfast, Brechlin looked around her, taking in the details of the humble abode. Soon she heard the sharp sizzle of meat, and an enticing smell woke up her belly.

"Smells good. Do you live here alone?" she asked.

"I do." Then after an awkward silence, he added, "It's modest, a starter place while I save and search for something better. In my line of work, I can live just about anywhere. Although, I don't like being too far from the sea."

"Ah yes, she gets in your blood, doesn't she?" Brechlin replied weakly.

Chimber sat the better part of a goose pie on the table with utensils and two cups of warm mead. "And you? Where do you live? I assume in Cegril." He pushed the goose pie toward her. "Go ahead and help yourself, Brechlin." He looked at her and smiled. "May I call you Brechlin?"

Without waiting for an answer, he returned to his skillet. With his back to her, tending to the steaks, she studied him. *Brazen or ignorant?* She decided neither. And she liked the sound of her name rolling off his tongue so comfortably.

"Yes. I have personal quarters overlooking the harbor. And it's small as well, but comfortable. All I need. I don't spend much time there, really." Her voice was trailing and growing weaker.

Chimber brought the meat over to the table and sat down, looking her over. "Let's get some food in you and then back to bed."

As they sat congenially dining on their morning fare, they heard a knock. Chimber opened the door to find Jern standing there, covered in the grime of travel.

"Jern!" cried Chimber. "Back already?"

Jern walked into the room and candidly leered at Brechlin.

"Sorry to put a pike into your plans," he said with a smirk.

"Jern," exclaimed Chimber, somewhat aghast. "This is Marshal Brechlin. Please!"

"Pleased to make your acquaintance," said Jern, continuing to leer and apparently unaffected by her title. "I've heard good things about you. I'm Jern, Chimber's faithful sidekick and ever-present conscience." He bowed as he said this, smiling at Chimber.

Brechlin bowed slightly in return. "Well, Jern, pleased to meet you. And I understand you played a part in my rescue."

"Yeah, I did my best," he said, but then his smirk turned into a genuine smile. "And I'm glad to see you're doing better."

"Thank you, Jern. It's good to be sitting up again."

Jern nodded. "I have news. I suppose it's good news for us.

Not, perhaps, for the people of Capital Island."

"What is it, Jern?" asked Chimber.

Jern sat down in a chair and began nibbling on a piece of discarded goose pie crust. "Those cadavers made it to Gretly, but from what I gathered, the townspeople mostly got away. They all sailed across Ger Strait to Cegril or scattered into the mountains if they couldn't get a boat. Every craft capable of floating on water was taken. A couple of shepherds we spoke with said the cadavers started tearing up the wooden houses of the town and building boats, presumably for crossing the strait. At least they're not burning the town."

"Was there no army to meet them outside Gretly?" asked Brechlin.

"None. Just Gretly's militia."

"Damn Tarmot!" she cried and then nearly swooned as her face scowled in agony. After a minute, she looked up at Jern and Chimber. "Cegril is in danger."

"I agree," said Jern. "They seem to have no interest in the smaller towns of our island. But you have time. Boat-building must difficult for an animated cadaver, and they have to make quite a few. It'll be some time before they can attempt the strait. Weeks, I would think."

"And I doubt they would risk a piecemeal landing with Cegril's army so close at hand," pondered Chimber. "They must wait until the entire transport fleet is ready."

Brechlin nodded. "Sounds right."

"So relax, Marshal Brechlin," said Chimber. "I own a small xebec, and with a decent breeze, I could get you home in less than a day. Rest up for a day or two, and we'll get you there in plenty of time."

"Will do, Master Gravedigger," said Brechlin. "I couldn't

manage it today."

"Hey, you got any more of that pie?" asked Jern. "Not much time to eat on the road." He looked up at Brechlin while stuffing the last piece of the goose pie into his mouth. "Marshal Brechlin—"

"Just Brechlin, please. To my friends."

"Brechlin, what can you tell us about this army? What's this all about?"

She looked down at the crumbs on her plate. "As far as we can make out, it's a power play by the new Krakul Gat. His name is Dran."

"The Medium of the Gray Mountain is behind this?" asked Chimber with surprise.

"That's right. Grael was a reliable Medium, but this Dran is a different story. Apparently, he and his adviser devised a way to pulverize part of the Gray Mountain into powder and sent it in the form of a poisonous cloud to Bewel Island. The poison killed the citizens of the island while the gray powder coated their bodies. Now, Dran can control them from afar, just as his peaceful father controlled the animated corpses that work the mines underneath Kromul Island."

Jern brushed the crumbs off his palms. "An army of animated cadavers. It ain't natural. The Mediums are a scary lot, playing with magic."

"They're not all bad," said Chimber. "The Medium of Mount Krin heals people."

"If only we could find him," said Brechlin. "I wouldn't be surprised if Dran had something to do with his disappearance."

"Do you think he's dead?" asked Jern.

"No. If he were dead, all the Gludemic Mountains would

gradually become dormant. It's how the Covenant is set up. Dran would have to keep Ferrin alive to preserve his own power."

"Wouldn't a good rainstorm wash away the gray powder?" asked Chimber.

"Yes, the powder on their skin," said Brechlin, "but the unfortunate citizens of Bewel Island have breathed the powder into their lungs. And, that's all Dran needs to continue his control."

Jern walked over to the hearth and poked the low flames. "I've always been told there's another Gludemic Mountain. A blue one. Way north somewhere on the Rolucca Peninsula. Doesn't it have a Medium, too?"

"That would be Er Lomith, the Medium of the Blue Mountain," said Brechlin. "I have no reason to believe she is involved in any of this."

"I've heard that name," said Jern. "She's one of the Lomitheri."

"I don't believe Lomitheri exist," said Chimber. "I've never seen a person with wings and blue skin. I'm not sure anybody has."

"No, they exist," said Brechlin. "And they have wings, but their skin isn't really blue. Just bluish highlights here and there. But, they are very secretive. And sensitive to heat. So, they have to live where it's cold."

"Can they really fly?" asked Jern enthusiastically.

"Well, as I understand it, they can fly, but only for short spurts," explained Brechlin. "And even then, only if they are in decent physical shape. Sort of like you or I running at full speed."

"I would love to see that," said Jern. He hung the fire poker on its mantel hook and came back to the table, shaking his head. "This is all so disturbing. A cadaver army!"

"Very disturbing," said Chimber. "Can Cegril's army defeat them?"

Brechlin slowly stood up from her chair. Chimber came to her to help, but she motioned him away. She made her own way back to her bed and sat down on its edge, resting her face in her palms.

"How do you stop a cadaver?" she asked. "I hacked them and stabbed them, and they kept on coming. They aren't alive, so it doesn't matter what you do to their bodies. They keep on coming."

"What can be done?" asked Chimber.

Brechlin shook her head. "I don't know. I hope Cegril's walls will hold."

"Isn't the Covenant supposed to protect us from this sort of thing?" asked Jern.

"That's the legend," said Brechlin. "That the power of two Mediums is always greater than the power of one."

"Wouldn't the power of one Medium, therefore, be approximately the same as another?" asked Jern. "Shouldn't we get the Blue Medium involved?"

"Interesting idea," said Brechlin, "but I don't know much about the Lomitheri or the power of the Blue Mountain. I've heard things, but it's hard to separate myth from reality."

"Do you know where they are?" asked Jern.

"They live in the Ice Shard Mountains, north of Wolfglen Forest, not far from the edge of the frozen wastes."

Jern threw a fist into the air. "Well, let's go find them! I bet they don't even know what's going on. With the Marshal of Cegril's army with us, they would have to give us an audience."

Chimber shook his head. "Jern, you're so full of yourself. You just want to see the flying Lomitheri. There is no way in hell we're going to make a trek into the northern reaches of the Rolucca Peninsula."

Brechlin sat up straight and looked at Jern and Chimber. "There might be something to what he's saying."

"What?" asked Chimber. "You can't be serious."

"We have some time before the enemy can cross the strait. If we recruit Er Lomith, we can pit Medium against Medium. It would be a great advantage. We just have to get back before the attack, Blue Medium or no Blue Medium."

"But..." said Chimber, opening his hands wide. "You can hardly walk."

Brechlin lay back on her bed, looking up into the timber rafters of Chimber's cottage.

"You have a xebec, right? If we leave tomorrow, and I rest during the trip, I should be okay. It's not my body that's hurting. It's my head."

"Yes!" said Jern, jumping up from his chair. "Let's do it."

Jern and Brechlin looked at Chimber. It was his turn to walk to the hearth. He tossed another fagot on the fire and contemplated the flames. "Seeking help from Er Lomith seems reasonable on some level, but it's a long shot. An arduous trip with freezing temperatures and hungry wolves with the possibility of no payout—I'm not sure it's the best use of our dwindling time."

He turned back to Brechlin and Jern. "And what if Dran has imprisoned Er Lomith, too? We don't know."

"True," said Brechlin. "Then the trip will have been point-less. But, only time would be lost."

"And she *might* be there!" piped Jern.

"I don't know," said Chimber, slowly shaking his head. "It's a lot to ask. Sailing to Rolucca Peninsula and then trekking to its far north. And what about the wolves of Wolfglen Forest? They have a reputation."

"The trip would be a challenge," replied Brechlin.

Chimber poked some more at the fire and then looked at Brechlin. "Isn't this the queen's concern?"

"Chimber, what do you think Dran will do after he has taken the big cities?" asked Brechlin. "Do you think he will leave Math alone?"

"No. Probably not," replied Chimber, speaking quietly.

"Then we have to go, buddy," said Jern. "It's time to act."

Chimber stared into the red coals. He sighed, smiled weakly at Jern, and then turned to Brechlin. "Okay, Marshal Brechlin. If we need to do this to help preserve our lands, then sure, I'll do it."

"Thank you, Chimber," she said, "for your care *and* your courage."

Chimber sighed again and put his hands on his waist. "But if we are to leave tomorrow, we should leave on the morning's tide. We have to get up early. I hope you're up for it."

A Time of Tension

When Queen Cirmar awoke, an array of narrow sunbeams were making their way into the far corner of her room. She studied their glowing display for a few moments, lost in thought, and then looked over at Tarmot in the bed beside her. He was sound asleep. She eased out of bed, put on her morning gown, and quietly walked through the double doors that led to the balcony. The clean morning air and the early light enveloped her, cooling and waking her senses.

It was too early for attendants and advisers, too early even for Tarmot's attentions. She was grateful, for she needed a quiet moment to herself.

She surveyed the balustrade, already adorned with blooming roses, and took in the young but manicured gardens below and the tidy outbuildings. Tarmot and she had moved into the new palace only two days earlier, and the newness was still overwhelming. She felt out of place. Her former abode had a history. Many generations of her ancestors had lived there and, on the whole, had done a decent job of ruling their lands. True, it wasn't so ornate and large as the new palace, but she missed it more than she had expected.

It all seemed so trivial now. Tarmot had moved mountains to keep the construction schedule on pace and had diverted vast sums from the royal coffers to fund the palace's creation. He had made his case that a royal line as noble as hers deserved a noble palace, a home in line with her great heritage. She watched it grow and enjoyed Tarmot's enthusiasm as it materialized. Secretly, she thought it all a tad vulgar, but she did it for him. She wanted him happy. She wanted him near her.

And now, an unstoppable army of animated corpses was preparing to cross Ger Strait and would soon attack Cegril. The fine palace, the generations of wise guardianship, all swept away in a matter of days unless some way could be devised to save the city and its people.

How she regretted allowing Tarmot to bully Brechlin into going to Keeman. The defense of the city should have been Brechlin's responsibility, a proven warrior and wise general. Tarmot's arrogance and insecurity—mild annoyances in peacetime—could prove disastrous in a time of war. She was not sure she had the strength to reel him in and turn the role over to someone with more experience, and with less unfounded self-confidence.

Cegril's bay was visible from the north end of the long balcony. She walked to the end and stepped up on an overturned urn for a better look. The bay was clear of returning ships.

"Be careful, my Queen," said Tarmot behind her. "I would hate for you to tumble over the rail." She looked down at him and smiled. "And what, pray tell, would drive the queen of all the land onto her balcony at such an early hour?"

"Oh, just looking out at our lovely bay," she said. "Hoping that Brechlin was returning."

She noticed Tarmot's cheerful face darken.

"I fear the Marshal is lost, my dear," he said. "We'll miss

her talents, no doubt. But do not overly concern yourself. I assure you the city is in good hands."

She stepped down from the urn and gave him a hug.

"Your confidence is comforting," she said as she laid her head on his broad chest.

"Oh, it's not such a complicated thing, my darling," returned Tarmot, caressing her head. "The enemy is out there, and we are in here behind our stout walls. We merely have to keep them outside. And we have the full force of the army at hand to help ensure that outside is where they stay."

"Yes, it is simple," she said. Then she looked up at his face. "I have scheduled a meeting with our city advisers this afternoon."

"Really, my dear!" exclaimed Tarmot. "Is that necessary? I have my hands full already with a slew of preparations. I have no time for those tired old men to prattle on about their petty worries."

"If, for no other reason, Tarmot, than to hear them out," said Queen Cirmar. "Just hear what they have to say. What would it hurt?"

"If I must," he said rather coldly. "In the meantime, I had best get my morning started. Now I have even less time than before."

He pulled away from Queen Cirmar's embrace and walked off. She watched him stride away, and more afraid than ever, she stepped back up on the overturned urn for one last look out at the bay.

* * *

That afternoon, as Queen Cirmar entered the new Hall of Sages at the appointed time, the smell of fresh paint was strong. It was a vague replica of the historic room in the old palace, where for centuries the wise men of the Dalmeer Islands had advised her ancestors. She was annoyed to find Tarmot and her advisers already in debate.

"My dear Queen," said Tarmot as she entered. "I hope you don't mind we began our discussion of some minor military details before you arrived. Petty things you needn't worry yourself about. And we would have resolved them if it weren't for Alipharem's ramblings."

"Please allow me to judge for myself which details are petty and which are not, Counselor General," she said curtly. "As queen of this land, there is little I shouldn't worry myself about."

The edge to Queen Cirmar's voice caught everyone's attention. As she looked around the group of men, her face was stern.

"We were discussing Tarmot's proposal to prepare our city for the enemy host," said Alipharem. "One you might find interesting."

At that point, the handful of men who formed the core of Queen Cirmar's advisers spoke all at once, and all at her. She thought of leaving the room, of running away from all this fear and chaos. She was thankful when Tarmot intervened.

"Please, men," he said with forceful authority. "The queen cannot be expected to hear all of you at once! Come to order!"

The men quieted themselves.

"We are sorry," said Menom, the scoutmaster in charge of reconnoitering the enemy. "There is so much to be concerned about."

"Yes," agreed Alipharem, "and Tarmot's tactics are adding

to those concerns."

"Alipharem!" said Queen Cirmar, still irritated and over-whelmed. "You are my most senior adviser, but I must ask that you show a little more respect to the Counselor General."

"Yes, my Queen," said Alipharem, long used to Queen Cirmar's unconsidered outbursts. "My apologies, but perhaps you will hear the Counselor General's proposal."

"There is nothing so novel about my idea," said Tarmot. "We load up all the supplies that we can from the surrounding countryside and then burn everything—crops, homes, work-shops. Everything that an invading army could put to use. Without supplies, they would soon lose interest in our walled city and go home."

"Have we received any reports about their means of convey-ing supplies?" she asked, turning to Menom.

"They carry none, my Queen," he said.

"Then perhaps Tarmot's proposal, though drastic, would be a necessary step to ensure victory."

"Well, then," began Tarmot, "do we need to discuss it further? We must attend to the details."

"If I may..." said Alipharem, looking at Queen Cirmar.

Queen Cirmar glanced at Tarmot, who was scowling at Alipharem, but she gave Alipharem a nod.

"Tarmot's proposal would have us destroy the land around Cegril for miles, including the means of sustaining ourselves, not to mention providing a livelihood for many of your sub-jects, all to deny food for the enemy host. Set aside the obvious fact that they could supply themselves by ferrying goods across Ger Strait from Gretly, and recall the more important fact that this army is made of animated cadavers. Dran is controlling the corpses of the deceased citizens of Bewel Island.

There are no officers in the field, no horses to be fed. It is unlikely that they would need *any* supplies. We would destroy our countryside for no purpose."

"How can we be sure of that?" replied Tarmot. "Should we throw away a possible advantage on the basis of conjecture?"

"I say there is little chance your suggestion would aid us in the slightest," said Alipharem emphatically. "It would destroy the economy of the region for years. So, even though we survive the attack, we would have to contend with widespread starvation."

"If that is true, if these soldiers need no supplies, then why wouldn't they raze the land themselves?" asked Tarmot. "Why wouldn't they destroy our crops and livestock to force starvation upon us?"

Alipharem rubbed his forehead while shaking his head. "If Dran chooses to do that, then there is nothing we can do about it, but that doesn't mean we should do it for him! It seems you are giving this army too much credit. So far, they have attacked two cities and have not pursued strategic options such as forcing starvation upon their victims during a long siege. They just attack and kill. Why should their attack on Cegril be any different? Probably a straightforward frontal assault. We either stop them or we don't."

"Queen Cirmar," began Tarmot, "surely you see the value—"

"I don't know, Counselor General," mulled Queen Cirmar. "To destroy the livelihoods of so many of our people..." She felt overwhelmed once again. "Allow me time to consider it," she managed. She turned to Menom. "What is the latest status of the host?"

"As of early this morning, they are still collecting timber, both from surrounding forests and from dismantled buildings in Gretly," he replied. "My scouts said that a few small construction parties were already at work building boats. With such a large workforce at their disposal, I would estimate it would take them less than two weeks before they attempt the crossing."

Queen Cirmar bit on a nail. "I find it incredible that Dran exercises such precise control over his cadavers."

"A crossing of the strait could be accomplished with the crudest of craft," suggested Alipharem. "Perhaps rafts with a single sail and a crude rudder, but they would have to be careful about the weather."

"Wouldn't they be vulnerable as they attempt to land their craft on our shore?" asked Queen Cirmar. "Shouldn't we attack at that moment?"

"Well, no, my Queen," said Tarmot. "We would be unnecessarily exposed. The best option is to remain behind our stout walls."

Alipharem scratched the back of his neck. "Tarmot and I are in agreement on this matter. These are not like human soldiers who could be drowned once their boats overturn. As they near the shore, no longer subject to the strong undercurrents that dominate the central regions of the strait, they could step off their craft and walk to shore with no concerns of drowning. Our men, however, with their heavy armor, are disadvantaged on that count."

"So, we defend our city from behind our walls," said Tarmot. "There seems to be no obvious means for them to breach the walls unless they build siege equipment."

"Well, that sounds positive," said Queen Cirmar. "But they did breach the walls of Keeman and Gretly without equipment."

Tarmot sneered. "Bah! Mere wooden palisades. Nothing like the thick stone walls surrounding our city."

"True," said Alipharem, "but I have known Ginthar for years, and you can wager your life he and Dran have a plan. And speaking of Dran, there is another option we should consider."

Queen Cirmar opened her hands. "Please, Alipharem. Speak your mind."

Alipharem rubbed the bristly stubble on his chin with his thumb and forefinger. "Dran is behind this army. While we are preparing to defend Capital Island from it, we should consider striking at its source. I propose we send an assault force to Kromul Island and attempt to take Dran."

"Assault Kromul Island?" asked Queen Cirmar. "Isn't it impregnable?"

"It certainly is, my Queen," said Tarmot. "It is ringed with cliffs. There is no place to disembark troops except at the harbor, which is extremely narrow. It's impossible."

"It would be difficult," agreed Alipharem, "but worth the attempt. If we brought several hundred troops, it should be sufficient to overwhelm Dran's harbor forces."

"Several hundred men!" bellowed Tarmot. "Are you serious? We number barely a thousand as it is. What if the endeavor fails, and all of them are lost? How do we defend our city?"

"Our chances there are better than confronting the cadaver host head on. The assault should be attempted."

All eyes turned toward Queen Cirmar. "It seems such a gamble," she said quietly.

"It is a gamble," echoed Tarmot, "and we could potentially lose everything. A steadfast defense of our city, with all of our forces at our disposal, is our best strategy."

"Yes, but—" began Alipharem.

"No!" interjected Tarmot. "I have been given sole authority over the defense of our city. We will not disperse our forces. Is that understood?"

Tarmot's comment precipitated another chaotic outburst of voices, everyone speaking at once. This time it was Queen Cirmar who silenced them.

"Silence!" she cried, her voice piercing the lower register of the male voices in the room. "Order and silence! Tarmot is right! He is our leader, and his decisions are final. At times like this, it is best to have a single individual in charge, for there is often a need for quick and decisive action."

"But he has no experience," complained Menom.

"Perhaps slow but deliberate decision-making is to be preferred over quick but wrong-headed action," suggested Alipharem. "If we don't have Marshal Brechlin, then perhaps one of her senior officers..."

Tarmot slammed the flat blade of his sword down on his podium with a dramatic, sharp sound. "Brechlin! I am tired of hearing Brechlin's name! She is not here. And I'm not about to put the welfare of this kingdom into the hands of a lower-ranking officer. The queen has put me in charge, and I will decide on the best means of defense.

"In fact," he continued, re-sheathing his sword, "I find these meetings tiresome and a waste of our precious time. I hereby proclaim them defunct. Now, gentlemen," he said, looking at the men with arrogant contempt, "this meeting is adjourned. I have a city to save."

As he stomped out of the Hall of Sages, Queen Cirmar called after him, but he paid her no heed, slamming the door behind him. She started after him, but as she reached the door, she hesitated and, almost apologetically, looked back at the group of concerned advisers.

"I'll talk to him," she said and vanished through the door.

Northward Bound

The rays of the sun had not yet pierced the sky by the time Chimber had launched his xebec from its mooring. He set sail to the east with Jern and Brechlin sitting on the deck, leaning back on their supply packs. In minutes, they left the smooth water of Math's sheltered bay and hit the choppier swells of the open sea, the moonlight flickering on the waves. Chimber turned the craft toward the northeast, a few points closer to the wind, which calmed the motion of the ship. He strapped the rudder wheel in place and set up a pallet with a pillow along a wide ledge near his tiller post and offered it to Brechlin.

"Even Cegril's Marshal needs to rest," he said. "I've perched you high enough so you may see anything of interest."

Brechlin smiled at Chimber and again felt a pleasant surge of warmth. His attention to the details of her comfort pleased her, and she was surprised by her reaction. In her powerful position as Marshal of Cegril, she held the careers and even the lives of hundreds of men in the palm of her hand. She was used to respect and obeisance. Yet Chimber was not under her command and had no ulterior motive for being kind to her, except that he was.

She had long grown accustomed to being treated as if she was callous inside. Indeed, she behaved that way. It was the way one must behave in her position. She had been careful never to show tenderness. Yet there it was. And this man unwittingly unveiled it time and time again.

"I feel strong," she said, "but it is comforting to know that I have somewhere to retreat should my strength fail me." Indeed, the fresh breezes and salty spray seemed to have rinsed away the throbbing in her skull. She was becoming her old self again.

Brechlin leaned back on the gunnels and watched Chimber handle the ship with pleasure. She admired his athletic form as he occasionally scampered up the stays to the crosstrees or secured a dangling rope. He impressed her with his skill in keeping the craft on course, for Jern was of little help in maneuvering the ship.

They made good time throughout the morning, glimpsing Narth Geyser in the distance a few hours after departure. Around noontime, they made out the coastline of the southern shore of Bewel Island. They looked on with solemn silence. All three of them had known many of the former inhabitants, now unwitting participants in Dran's cadaver army. The island was now a wasteland of deserted homes and farmlands, perhaps still tainted by Dran's poisonous cloud.

"It's hard to comprehend," said Jern. "The entire island emptied of life."

Chimber watched the wind fill a momentarily slack sail. "I try not to think about it. I knew lots of folks on Bewel, and my aunt's family lived in Trimlin."

"Just remember you're doing your part to make it right," said Brechlin. "If Dran is behind this, then once his army is defeated, he will pay for his crimes."

Chimber nodded, looking down at the boat deck. "I hope

you're right, but justice will not bring those people back."

The wind shifted to the east in the afternoon, but their progress remained steady. They reached Rolucca Bay, the only settlement on the Rolucca Peninsula, just before dusk.

They had felt the increasing chill of the northerly winds for the last hour and were compelled to bundle up. They moored the xebec, stepped up on the pier, and entered the community. An expanse of pristine alpine forest began just beyond the small huddle of log dwellings, washing them with the bright scent of evergreens. A few miles in the distance and to the northeast, they made out the knobs forming the Lonely Hills in the fading light, their caps dusted with a light snow and glowing in the setting sun. The land looked rough and wild.

They walked around the village and found few roads heading out of town, and none in a northerly direction. It appeared that bushwhacking cross-country was their only option. They would need help if they were to have any chance of locating the home of the Lomitheri.

They entered a tavern on the town square and found an early crowd gathered around a large ale barrel mounted sideways on a wooden stand. The rustic townsmen in the tavern were cheerful and friendly, and most knew the general whereabouts of the Ice Shard Mountains. A few even claimed to have met the Lomitheri in their rare travels away from their secluded homeland, but no one would act as their guide. Although they had heard the news about a war, it didn't concern them. Rarely did the events on Capital Island affect them. Besides, the trek was treacherous. The land was wild and cold, and everyone knew that Wolfglen Forest harbored packs of vicious wolves. Few traveled to the far north, and even fewer returned.

Somewhat dejected, Chimber, Brechlin, and Jern sat down

and enjoyed a couple of rounds with the friendly townsmen.

By this time, Brechlin's head was pounding again, and they had a big day ahead of them, so they rented lodging and retired early. The next morning, the three of them took to the streets of the village, chatting with anyone they encountered. They spotted a group of men on the outskirts of the community at work repairing the dry stone fence that encircled the town. They strolled over and engaged the workers in conversation, but these men were as reluctant to help as the men in the tavern. None of them had ventured very far to the north, preferring to make their living along the coastal areas of the peninsula. And, even if they had, they would not be willing to risk the dangers.

As they stood around, unsure what to do next, a tall man in chains caught Brechlin's attention. His chains were attached to a spike driven into the ground, and he was busy stacking large stones on the fence. Brechlin thought that there was something familiar about him.

"Who is that man?" she asked of one townsman.

"Oh, that's Flackard," the townsman replied. "He had been raiding our village for months before we caught him last week."

"He's a prisoner?"

"Yeah, until we figure out what to do with him. We can't just let him go back into the woods and resume raiding our stores."

"I think I know him," she said, half to herself. She walked over to where the man was working, picking up flat rocks and placing them in gaps in the fence. Despite the chill, he was shirtless and covered with sweat. She studied the tall man's face. He ignored her at first, but after a moment, he stopped his labors and smiled at her.

"Marshal Brechlin, I presume," he said and offered a vague salute.

"Yes, I'm Brechlin. And you are familiar, although I can't place you."

"I am—was—Captain Flackard."

"Captain Flackard! You were sent out after Desmondi," Brechlin said with surprise. "But that was over a year ago. You and your men never returned, so we assumed you were dead."

"As you see, I live," said Flackard, bowing.

"And your men? Are they still with you?"

"They are," said Flackard, nodding toward one of the knobs forming the Lonely Hills. "Up there, near the crest of that hill."

"I don't understand. Do they live up there?"

"They are dead. Ambushed," said Flackard. "They are all buried up there. I couldn't leave them." He took a quick glance up to the hills and quietly returned to building the wall.

Brechlin remembered Flackard's fierce loyalty and reputation as a warrior. Like her, he knew his priorities and lived by them, even in less pleasant times. As she pondered his current predicament, she decided that fidelity deserved reward. Besides, she needed him.

She walked over to the man in charge of the work party. "Do you know who I am?"

The man stood up a little straighter. "Yes, you are Brechlin, the Marshal of Cegril."

"This man, your prisoner, is a captain in the Queen's Guard. He has deserted his post, and I will take him into custody." She looked back at Flackard with some uncertainty. "Perhaps for just a few minutes, or perhaps permanently."

"Well, that's fine," said the man, "but it's Cegril's responsibility if he gets free and begins raiding our town again."

"I understand." She turned to Chimber and Jern. "Remove his chains."

They hammered loose the metal cuffs.

Flackard rubbed his raw ankles and looked at Brechlin. "You have freed me. Now what?"

Brechlin gestured toward the town. "Follow me." They escorted him to the rustic tavern on the village square they had drank at the night before, sat him down, and handed the man an ale. While he savored his drink, Brechlin looked him over. He was in excellent health and even taller than Chimber, with a robust frame that displayed well-defined muscles and spoke of quiet strength. A recent scar gashed his forehead, reaching into his thick mop of dark brown hair, leaving a gap several inches long.

Brechlin slid him a second round. "Okay, Captain Flackard, what happened? Why have you been raiding this town for the last year?"

Flackard took several big gulps and then stopped to stare into the foamy recesses of his mug. "Desmondi discovered we were pursing him, so he and his pirate band left the Southern Cays." He wiped foam off his lips. "We followed him here. Their trail led up into the Lonely Hills. We were told they had camped inside a small canyon on the far side of the main ridge, so we thought we would take them by surprise."

He paused for a moment, taking another full swallow.

"It was they who surprised us. They ambushed us on the trail leading up to the ridge. Maybe they were tipped off, I'm not sure. But they wiped out my entire team and left us to rot.

Fortunately, I was merely unconscious. I awoke and stitched myself up."

He pointed to the gash on his forehead.

Brechlin glanced at the gash and nodded. "Why didn't you return?"

"I had unfinished business with Desmondi." He paused for a moment, again looking deeply into the depths of his tankard. "They were still camped in their box canyon. I had to do it one by one, living in the bush. But I got every damn one of them, except for Desmondi himself. Probably back in the Southern Cays, enjoying the warm sun."

"But why didn't you return then?" asked Brechlin. "You had completed your mission as well as circumstances would allow. You had a duty to the crown."

"I acknowledge that duty," said Flackard, "but it was my duty to my men that mattered most. And I let them down. I wasn't ready to leave them. I lived at their side at the top of that mountain but had to raid this town for food, especially in the colder months."

It was Brechlin's turn to swallow a thoughtful draught of her ale. "So, you've lived in this wild land for nearly a year. I suspect you know the area."

Flackard shrugged. "Yeah, I get around."

"Captain Flackard, you said you still acknowledge your loyalty to the queen."

"Yes, I do."

"Well, the queen needs your services again. We need a guide to the village of the Lomitheri in the Ice Shard Mountains."

"The Ice Shard Mountains!" exclaimed Flackard. He shook his head. "I would help, but I don't know the lands north of here. No one does. It's cold and full of wolves. Dangerous."

"Have you never ventured toward the north?" asked Chimber.

"I've been to the lakes north of here but otherwise stayed close to my men," replied Flackard. He set his tankard down and leaned back, looking them over and absentmindedly rubbing the scar on his forehead. "I don't know. Maybe I can be of help. Months before I was captured, I encountered one of the Lomitheri near the shores of Freel Lake. She was wounded and laid low from the heat, though there was snow on the ground. I fed her for a few days and escorted her to the southern shore of Sleet Lake, even further to the north. Before she departed, she told me that River Muoki empties into Sleet Lake on its northern end, and that should I ever wish to visit her and her people, she would value the opportunity to reciprocate my hospitality. I was told to follow the river to its source, and that her village would be nearby."

"That sounds simple," said Chimber. "We find this river, and it takes us to the Lomitheri."

"Yeah!" said Jern. "Who needs roads?"

"And the wolves?" asked Flackard.

"We'll think of something," replied Brechlin. "We must find the Lomitheri without delay." Contemplating Flackard, she added: "So, we could use your services—on behalf of the queen."

Flackard nodded and stood, looking to the Lonely Hills. "It's for the queen, men." He held his tankard in the air toward them, took one last swig, and sat back down. "I'm at your service. My men will have to understand."

Into the Cold

Early the next morning, Brechlin, Chimber, Jern, and Flackard started out on their cross country journey. Their knapsacks were full of supplies, and they wore thick garments to protect them from the frigid temperatures they would encounter farther north, though they were too heavy for the relatively lower temperatures of the peninsula's coast. They followed a faint and infrequently used trail north toward Freel Lake, and soon they were all in a heavy sweat.

"This coat weighs a ton," complained Jern. "Is this heavy gear necessary?"

Flackard chuckled. "Just enjoy the sweat while you can. Soon, it'll be a distant memory."

They made steady progress throughout the day, passing through a wet, lush evergreen forest rife with the scent of pine. Smooth moss and lichen-covered rocks littered the slippery trail. The steady hum of mosquitoes and other insects kept them swiping at their ears. That night, they camped near a small brook.

As Brechlin, Jern, and Flackard were attending to their campsite tasks, they were all struck with a peculiar odor. They looked up to see Chimber applying an ointment to his face.

"I know that smell!" cried Brechlin. "Another awful

concoction by the infamous Frakar, no doubt."

Chimber offered the container. "It smells a bit peculiar, but it works. Rub it on and mosquitoes stay away."

"Old Frakar," said Jern. "He was a genius."

Flackard wrinkled his nose. "I can see why the mosquitoes stay away. That's a strange odor."

"You get used to it," replied Chimber. The insect buzz was overwhelming, so they all begrudgingly applied the greenish ointment to their skin and settled down for the evening.

The next morning, the trail led them to the shores of Freel Lake, the more southerly of a pair of cold and isolated lakes. As they stepped upon the barren, driftwood-littered beach, the turquoise waters, with its brilliant border of evergreens, impressed them all. Two eagles flew overhead, calling to one another and playing on the gusty breeze.

And then a frigid blast of wind from the north came rolling across the lake's expansive surface. They forgot all about their perspiration.

The company followed the shoreline for two days, camping on its sandy beach. On the third day, they reached the northern extreme of Freel Lake and followed a small connector stream to Sleet Lake, the more northerly member of the pair. It lacked none of the beauty of its southern neighbor, but the air had a sharp, brittle quality, and the water was a deeper color of blue.

Since there were no trails this far north of Rolucca Bay, they continued their strategy of following the shoreline. The Sleet Lake's beach was rocky and often covered in reeds, so for two days they hacked through thick rushes and scampered over boulders, but otherwise their days were uneventful.

Their loads were heavy and chafed their shoulders and strained their backs. Even so, they were becoming accustomed to the exertion. Their muscles grew steadily stronger, and calluses formed on their feet and shoulders. Their tolerance of the decreasing temperatures improved. By the time they rounded the northern point of Sleet Lake's shore, they hardly noticed the growing cold.

They set up camp that night near a confluence of the lake with a large river. Flackard told the group he was confident they had reached the River Muoki. All they had to do was follow it to its source, and they should find the Lomitheri village. He also suggested that north of the lake was where the wolves of Wolfglen Forest gained their reputation, so their passage might soon become interesting.

The weather had treated them kindly so far, but that evening, they learned firsthand how Sleet Lake got its name. By morning, their unsheltered sleeping bundles were wet, ice-encrusted cocoons from an all-night sleet storm. As they arose and looked around them, they saw that the branches of the trees drooped heavily from accumulated ice. Even their small woodpile required vigorous hammering before they could free pieces of wood. They decided the effort wasn't worth it and nibbled on dried beef strips for their breakfast.

They gathered up their frozen knapsacks and gear, breaking them free of ice, and headed due north along the edge of the river. The riverbank was too cluttered with ice-encrusted growth to allow them to follow along the shore, so they walked through the open woods, keeping the river close to the left. They had gone just far enough to bring warmth to their chilled wet limbs when they heard the first distant howls of wolves. Although they were quite a distance away, the sound made the neck hairs of all four travelers stand erect.

At high sun, the party relaxed on a rare stretch of sandy

beach and dug into their dwindling knapsacks for a quick meal. It was then they caught their first glimpse of the famous wolves of Wolfglen Forest. A large male left the cover of the river brush about fifty yards downstream and watched them from the beach. Flackard and Chimber drew their swords, but the wolf didn't approach. He seemed content to stand there observing them. As they gathered up to leave, the wolf dashed back into the cover of the forest.

It wasn't long before they caught more glimpses of the wolf. He became their new traveling companion, seen through gaps in the river brush, or deeper in the forest. A knot formed in Chimber's stomach. He had heard many unhappy tales of wolf attacks in the mountains near Math, but the wolves of Wolfglen Forest were of a different ilk. They were notorious throughout the Dalmeer Islands as being especially aggressive and bold.

"We have new companions," said Brechlin, peering through an opening in the thick trees. "Two more."

"There will be others before we're through this wood," added Flackard. "We need to prepare or we will die."

"Pick up firewood along the way," suggested Chimber. "We'll want a nice big fire tonight."

That evening, the four travelers made camp near a large boulder and settled around their roaring fire with a sizable stack of wood close at hand. They could hear rustling just beyond the rim of firelight and spotted several pairs of red eyes in the dark brush.

"If they rush us, there would be little we could do," mused Jern, studying the closest pair of angry eyes.

"They won't go near the fire," said Flackard. "At least, as long as severe hunger doesn't drive them to overcome their fear."

"Well, how hungry are they?" asked Jern.

Flackard shrugged.

Chimber's brows drew together. "Do you think they'll stay there the whole evening? How will we get our rest?"

Brechlin pursed her lips. "Somebody will have to stay awake at all times. There are four of us, so if everyone takes a two-hour shift, that should get us through the night."

"Sounds like a plan. I'll take the first shift," offered Chimber.

"Hell, who can sleep with our wolf friends close at hand?" wondered Jern.

"You'd better get used to it," replied Flackard. "Learn to sleep with their presence. Otherwise, you'll become exhausted before we reach the Ice Shard Mountains."

Jern watched the sparks from the fire twirl in the air high overhead. "The Ice Shard Mountains. I can't believe we'll meet the Lomitheri."

"Flackard, why don't you tell us what you know of them?" asked Brechlin as she settled back against her pack. "Do you think they'll be friendly?"

"The one I met was friendly enough. But she was in a sore way and needed help. Who knows what our reception will be like at their village?"

"We should be prepared for a hostile reception," mused Brechlin. "Yet somehow make it obvious we come as friends."

"They must like their privacy," observed Chimber. "The Ice Shard Mountains are far out of the way."

Flackard added another branch to the already robust fire. "Perhaps, but I would say it also has to do with being where the temperatures are cold enough. They love the cold."

"So, it was a female Lomitheri you helped out," said Jern. "Do their women often travel alone through these wilds?"

"She never told me why she was in my vicinity," said Flackard. "But as for a woman alone, that is nothing out of the ordinary. Didn't you know they are all women?"

"No men!" exclaimed Jern. "How do they multiply?"

"From what I understand, there are men. But young men. When they reach a certain age, they claim a wife. And then, after much ceremony, he and his bride enter a special chamber where they couple. The heat of the erotic encounter destroys the male. The women, made of hardier stuff, usually survive. It is they who raise the young and lead the village."

"Wow, that sheds a whole new light on commitment, doesn't it, men?" asked Brechlin, smiling at them.

Jern shook his head. "It's crazy. Why would you give away your life?"

"They do it for their kind," suggested Chimber. "They sacrifice their life to perpetuate their race."

"If they are all women, why should we be that worried? Surely we can handle..." began Jern, but as he spoke, he noticed the awkward looks he was getting from Chimber and Flackard. He turned to Brechlin. "Sorry, Marshal Brechlin. I know there are plenty of formidable female warriors, but a whole tribe of them?"

"Jern," began Flackard, "if they wish to be done with us, then our goose is cooked. They are fierce warriors, and don't forget, they have the power of the Blue Mountain at their disposal."

"I heard they can send out blasts of cold energy," said Chimber.

"So have I," added Brechlin.

"I believe that is correct," said Flackard. "Although, I know they use the mountain's power for many other things."

Jern settled back on his back. "I hope they're friendly. Just think, a band full of women with no men around."

"And they are naked, too," added Flackard.

Jern jolted upright. "Naked!"

"Yeah. They stay cooler that way. But don't get too excited about your prospects. Their body parts would give you frostbite."

"Well, on that note, I think we should retire," said Brechlin. "It seems our companions have settled down for the night."

As they peered around them, the red eyes were still there but in smaller numbers, and they were no longer pacing about.

"To sleep it is," said Jern. "Wake me up in a couple of hours, and I'll take the second watch."

The Wolves of Wolfglen Forest

The evening was uneventful, but their unfriendly company was in evidence the next morning as they gathered up camp and began on their way. They heard rustling in the surrounding woods, and flashes of gray fur in the evergreen foliage were not uncommon.

The group stayed as close to the river's edge as possible as they made their way north. Not only did this ensure that they never lost their way, but it made for a greater sense of security—if the wolves launched an attack, it must come from their right flank, since the river protected their left, and it was easier to be on the lookout in one direction.

During the day, the wolves kept their distance, but the travelers noticed that the group continued to acquire new members. Two wolves joined about midday, and two more toward the day's end. Glimpses of gray fur through the dark trees were common enough now to no longer merit comment. The group stayed alert, picking up occasional pieces of firewood along the way, and doggedly trod onward.

As the long day neared its end and fading light limited visibility, they looked out for a suitable campsite. They preferred one as close as possible to the river. Ideally, they would camp on a sand bar or a point that protruded into the watercourse itself, which allowed for even greater security, providing a water barrier on multiple sides. But, such sites were uncommon, so on this day, with daylight waning, they set up camp close to the river's edge. They had a good supply of firewood from the day's collection, so they felt reasonably secure.

They went through their routine of settling in a new campsite, getting a blazing fire going, setting out bedding, and preparing their main meal of the day. They had just finished up their ration of smoked fish and cheese and were putting away their utensils when they heard a low, rolling growl and looked up to see a pair of angry red eyes peering at them from surprisingly close range. Although the fire was burning with a healthy glow, Chimber instinctively stepped over to the woodpile for another piece of wood. As he did so, he was startled to see two large wolves approaching them from behind the woodpile.

"Look out!" he shouted and unsheathed his sword just as the first wolf leapt for his throat. With a mighty swing, he buried the blade deep into the shoulder of his attacker, killing the wolf but lodging the sword in solid bone. As he vigorously tugged at the stubborn blade, the wolf's partner closed in to make its move. But as the wolf lunged for Chimber's thigh, he saw Brechlin's lithe frame, as quick as light, leap in front of him. Her sword whirled through the air, and he heard a yelp from the wolf as her weapon pierced deeply into the animal's gut.

The two animals lay dead at their feet. The others remained at a distance. Chimber finally dislodged his blade from the carcass of his slain wolf. The body was still convulsing, and blood poured from his open jaws.

"These are exceptionally large wolves," observed Brechlin.

"And fast, too." He put a hand on her shoulder. "Thanks for your help." They exchanged a quick glance.

Jern walked over and kicked at one carcass. "It's almost as if they had planned their attack."

"What do you mean?" asked Flackard.

"Well, the first wolf was a distraction. He got our attention while the other two came at us from behind the woodpile."

Flackard studied the two carcasses. "I don't like it. They seem unusually bold." He motioned to Chimber to grasp the paws of the nearest one, and together they swung it beyond the fire's ring of light. Immediately, they heard chaotic motion and growling from many sources as the ravenous wolves tore the carcass apart.

"Better feed them both," said Brechlin. "Maybe with their hunger sated, they'll ease off some."

"Whatever happened to their fear of fire?" pondered Chimber.

Flackard frowned. "Their hunger is making them brave. We had better keep the fire burning large."

They flung the second carcass into the darkness.

"How many would you say are out there?" asked Jern.

"It sounds like a lot," said Brechlin. "More each day. You would think there would be something else besides us to eat in this forest."

They threw a few more sticks on the fire and listened to the savage sounds of the wolves consuming their fallen comrades.

Flackard stroked his beard as he stared into the darkness. "If they attack as a group, we would not survive."

"Let's hope they're not that smart," said Brechlin.

"Or that brave," added Jern.

"How many more days do you reckon we have left?" asked Chimber.

"I'm not sure," replied Flackard. "A few more days, at least, of steady walking."

"I hope we make it," said Jern as he eyed the surrounding forest.

No one got much sleep that evening, and the first cold light of the morning found the group on the move. They decided to stick close to the river. As they hacked their way along the riverbank, the growls and calls of their canine companions continued. Movement filled the nearby brush.

"This is getting serious," said Brechlin.

"Everyone stay alert with sword in hand," suggested Chimber. "I wouldn't be surprised if they tried to make an attack while we're on the move."

"They're closer today," observed Flackard.

"There's one now." exclaimed Jern, pointing his sword at a patch of gray fur barely ten feet away. "And there's another one! Man, they're swarming."

"Just keep moving," said Brechlin. "If they come at us, we'll just have to fend them off."

"Hmm, I don't know," said Chimber. "I may have a better idea." He moved over to the edge of the river and motioned for the group to stop. "The river will get smaller the closer we get to its source. So, I think we should make for the far bank while it's still fairly wide."

Brechlin stepped to the riverbank and stuck her hand in. "That water is near freezing! We wouldn't make it across. Besides, there are wolves on that side, too."

"True," he responded, "but they are not concentrated on our trail like our friends here."

"Marshal Brechlin is right," said Flackard. "Our muscles would stiffen up in that cold water, and we would drown."

"Yes, but..." said Chimber as he dug into his knapsack and pulled out a rope. "Jern, I will need your rope, too."

Chimber tied the two sections of rope together and then fastened it around a large stone on one end. "Do you see that tree jutting out on the opposite bank? If I can loop this rope around the trunk of that tree a couple times, then we can use it to help us get across."

"But you will still need your muscles to pull you across," cautioned Flackard. "As the cold numbs your flesh, you won't be able to hold on, much less pull yourself across."

"Ah, but you don't have to pull yourself across," said Chimber. "Since that tree is on the other side of the river, if I tie the rope around my waist and ease out into the water, the current will carry me to the other side. I just have to keep my head above water."

"You can use this," said Brechlin, pulling out her pigskin water bladder and blowing air into it. "Tie this around your neck to help."

"Thanks." Chimber twirled the stone in the air and, with a mighty heave, sent the rope flying. The stone splashed in the water about three quarters of the way across.

"You need a bigger stone," offered Flackard. Jern eyed the proceedings pensively as Chimber pulled in the wet rope and began swinging the stone again.

"I don't think so," Chimber said. "Just need to time it better."

He swung again, and although it landed closer, it was still disappointingly short. He pulled in the rope once again.

"Men!" announced Brechlin as she peered into the surrounding brush. "We can't remain stationary like this. If we don't get moving, the pack will close in. I can already hear their panting."

"Chimber," said Jern, "I know you're a big strong guy and all, but may I take a shot?"

"Not now, Jern," responded Chimber. "We've got to—"

"Just give me the goddamned rope!" barked Jern. Chimber gave him a surprised look but handed over the soggy rope coil.

Jern eyed the opposite bank. "It is not about strength, but about timing and practice."

He twirled the rope over his head with surprising confidence, motioned everyone to move back two steps, and increased the length of the rope swinging over his head before finally releasing the stone with a grunt. It gracefully arced over the frigid river and wound around the extended tree trunk on the first try.

He smiled at Chimber. "You forget I work with horses. A horse trainer without a good lasso arm is not worth a jot."

"You were just lucky," said Chimber. "Plus, I was gaining on it."

"Can we get moving, men?" pressed Brechlin, sword in hand and heeding the nearby brush.

Chimber tied the rope just under his armpits and secured the inflated pigskin around his neck. He then took a cautious step into the water and took a deep breath.

"Damn, this water is cold!" he exclaimed.

"Ah, don't be such a girl...er, sissy," chided Jern, looking quickly at Brechlin.

"Well, here goes nothing," said Chimber as he plunged into the water. He took quick short breaths but regained his composure and began kicking himself out to midstream.

Flackard held on to the other end of the rope and fed it out. Slowly, the current swept Chimber to the far side of the river. The remaining group watched as Chimber weakly climbed up the bank. He rested on his knees and began painfully moving about. He then waved them on.

"I'm okay! Let the next person come on. I can help them up."

He secured the knot on the tree truck, tied the bladder to the rope, and gestured for Flackard, who still held the far end of the rope, to pull it back across the water. One by one, the remaining members of the party reluctantly eased into the frigid river and allowed the current to pull them over to the far side. All made it safely but with their limbs numb, needed help climbing up the bank. Wet and shivering, they huddled around a blazing fire Chimber had started with his flint and stone.

"My God, that took my breath away," commented Jern as the fire brought life back to his limbs.

"I could barely climb up the bank," added Flackard. "Oh, joyous fire."

Brechlin jerked her head toward the river. "Look across." They turned to see a pack of large wolves swarming the bank they had just left. Occasionally, one would gingerly put its paws into the water. Then one particularly brave wolf plunged into the water and swam, but the current rapidly moved it downstream. It lost its nerve and, thirty feet downstream, swam back to the bank from which it came. None of the others attempted the river.

"I think it worked," said Brechlin. "They can't get across."

"That's a lot of wolves," said Flackard.

"I count twenty-two of them," added Jern.

"Good riddance," said Chimber.

Brechlin stood. "Well, it won't take long before more join us on this side. We had better continue onward. Steady exertion will warm up our muscles faster than this fire."

Ambivalent Refuge

Over the next two days, the land began to rise. The width of the river narrowed, but its flow became rapid, more turbulent. It didn't take long for the party to pick up several new wolf companions. They trailed alongside them during the day and circled their fire at night, keeping everyone on edge and near the point of exhaustion.

It was late in the afternoon on the second day after their river crossing when they reached a point where the River Muoki roared through a steep-walled gorge thirty feet below their path. On either side of the gorge, sloping cliffs towered over their heads. Brilliant green moss and cascades of ferns adorned the cliff face closest to them, and a hundred feet up the steep slope from where they stood, a stunning waterfall rumbled.

Flackard halted the group and stared up at the waterfall. It was comprised of two sections—one long cascade and, above it, a shorter waterfall of only eight feet.

"A double waterfall," he said, scanning the slope leading up to it.

Brechlin glanced up. "They're lovely, but perhaps we should move on."

"Yes! I think we can make it," Flackard blurted. "I see a

path."

"Up there? But why?" asked Jern.

Flackard looked at his companions. "My Lomitheri ward spoke of a place of refuge, marked by a double waterfall high above the path. We are all weary and could use a real rest."

"What sort of refuge?" asked Brechlin.

Flackard shrugged. "I might be mistaken, so let's just see if it's there. I wouldn't want to get everyone's hopes up for no reason."

Too haggard for further discussion, the hopeful band followed Flackard up the side of the sloping cliff face along what appeared to be a faint trail, the first they had seen in days. They climbed past the first falls, an elegant veil of thirty feet, and ascended to where the smaller falls dropped into a shallow plunge pool. Flackard looked at the falls for a moment, studying it carefully. Then he waded into the frigid plunge pool and tentatively extended his arm into the falling stream. A second later, he vanished behind the falls.

"Come on in," he yelled from behind the waterfall.

One by one, they entered through the falls into an open space. At the back of the small space was a narrow fissure. Moving single file, they threaded the fissure, and once it widened, they scampered up a boulder-strewn ledge and dropped into a tunnel on the other side. They had to stoop to continue, but after walking several feet they entered a clear area ten feet wide and twice as long. It was open to the sky but enclosed on all sides by natural stone walls. The floor of the enclosed space had a lush carpet of grass, but what got everyone's attention was a spring that bubbled up in the center of the open area, forming a small, steaming pool before the overflow water streamed away and disappeared through the rocks.

"A hot springs!" cried Jern.

"Nice refuge," said Chimber, slapping Flackard on the back.

"I'm glad I was right," he replied. "And, it's wolf-proof. Our friends won't pass through the falls."

"Your Lomitheri ward told you about this place?" asked Brechlin.

"Yes. We had a lot of time on our hands as she convalesced."

"And what of those fruit trees?" asked Chimber, pointing to several stunted trees growing toward the back of the open area. "I've never seen their kind. Are their fruits edible?"

"Well, they nourish the body, but there may be side effects."

"What kind of side effects?" asked Chimber.

"I can't say. Nothing serious, at any rate. There are plenty of ripe ones on the ground. Best chow down."

They sat down under the small trees, shed their packs, and gorged themselves on the strange but tasty fruit that lay about them. Thanks to the hot springs, their protected refuge was steamy and significantly warmer than the air outside. Soon, their thick garments became clammy and overly warm, and they shed them down to their undergarments.

"Gentlemen, if I can have some privacy, I think I will take advantage of this warm pool," said Brechlin. The three men all respectfully shifted their seated positions so they were facing away from the hot springs.

After a moment, Chimber snuck a glance toward the pool. Brechlin had disrobed and was leaning back in the steamy water.

"That looks heavenly," he said.

"Beyond description," she replied. "You'll have your turn before long."

The men continued feasting on the strange fruit. It wasn't

long before Chimber felt something out of the ordinary. He respected Marshal Brechlin, but the thought of her nude body a mere ten feet away began to fire his imagination.

He stared hard at the fruit. "I feel...strange."

"Oh my Gludema, this fruit is an aphrodisiac!" blurted Jern. "I'm filled with lust."

Chimber looked at Flackard. "You should have told us!"

"Well, I didn't exactly know what the side effects were," he said defensively. "I just knew they weren't harmful."

"I wonder if it has affected Marshal Brechlin, too," said Jern as he turned toward the hot springs.

"Front and center, soldier!" cried Chimber.

Jern lowered his head and turned back around. "Damn. This is miserable."

"A refuge this place is," said Flackard, "but I, for one, will not get much sleep tonight."

"Now, you stay away from me, big guy," said Jern. "I know you've been in the woods for some time."

"You do have a cute butt," said Flackard, leering at Jern.

"Flackard!" exclaimed Chimber.

"I'm just kidding, for Gludema's sake!"

"Next!" Brechlin yelled, and they looked around to see her wrapped up in her riding cloak. "There is only room for two, however."

"You two go ahead," suggested Chimber. "I'll wait my turn."

"I bet you will," said a smirking Jern. He and Flackard walked toward the spring, removed their few remaining garments, and eased into the steamy recesses of the pool. Brechlin returned to where Chimber was waiting and sat down next to him. She grabbed a piece of nearby fruit and nibbled on it.

"These aren't too bad, but they make me feel odd. Do they affect you?"

"Well, what sort of effect do you mean?" asked Chimber rather coyly.

"Hmm, I don't know. I feel rather, um, frisky."

"Frisky, huh? What does that mean, exactly?"

"I don't know," she replied, stretching out her body and looking at Chimber with a heavy-lidded stare. "Let's just say that if those two weren't here, you would be in trouble."

"I like the sound of that," said Chimber. Emboldened by her innuendo, he leaned over and kissed Brechlin softly on the lips.

"Hmm, nice," she breathed and closed her eyes. But, after a moment, she opened them and gestured toward the hot pool. "But, like I said, if they weren't here."

* * *

Chimber awoke after hours of restless sleep, burning with the fire of sexual arousal. His dreams had been laced with erotic interludes, most of which involved Brechlin. He shifted his sleeping tunic, freeing his stiff manhood from a wrinkle in the cloth, and sighed in frustration. *I needed a good night's sleep. Damn that fruit.*

Moonlight streamed into their secluded clearing, bathing the newly-found refuge in pale light. Chimber glanced at Jern and Flackard, both snoring loudly. He rolled over to look at Brechlin but was surprised to find her sleeping pallet unoccupied. Then, the sound of softly splashing water got his attention. Brechlin was in the hot springs.

Moving slowly, Chimber positioned himself so he could

observe the spring, not ten feet away, without being noticed. There she was, submerged in the steaming water, damp curling tendrils of hair clinging to her neck. Her eyelids were closed, arms stretched out along the side of the pool. His eyes followed up from her hand to her arm, shining wet in the moonlight, all the way to her armpit and shoulder; there, he lingered. He allowed his mind to imagine the scent of her. She would smell musky, feminine, and earthy—the way a woman should smell. He thought about the feel of her skin next to his, her breasts, the arch of her back, and the sound of her moans raspy and low in his ear.

Now rattled, he stopped himself and tried to shake off his lascivious thoughts. The fruit was having a powerful effect on him, but he had desired Brechlin since tending her damaged body in his cabin. Tonight, secure in their comfortable refuge and knowing she was so close to him—and naked, no less—made him ache with desire. His resistance was useless. He could take it no longer.

Clearing his throat to let her know he was awake, he threw off his makeshift covers and stood up. "I can't sleep," he said, walking over to the springs and quietly sitting down.

"So I see," Brechlin said without even opening her eyes.

Silence.

"That's some weird fruit!" he commented, ever so conscious of his erection.

"It's a strong aphrodisiac," she noted in a matter-of-fact tone. "Very intense." She still hadn't opened her eyes to look at him.

Chimber felt deflated. She clearly was not interested. He sighed, ran his hands through his hair, and stood up. "Guess I'll give sleep another go. We have another long day tomorrow." He went back to the darker confines of his sleeping space and lay back down on his pallet. He turned away from her, feigning sleep. He heard her splashing as she stepped out of the spring, but tried to put her out of his thoughts.

Silence. He sighed.

Then Chimber felt movement on his pallet. He didn't move or speak. Brechlin crawled in under the covers next to him. Her skin was damp and warm. He rolled over to find her facing him. He touched her body. Neither said a word.

She took Chimber's face into her hands and kissed him fully. He responded with enthusiasm. Her lips and mouth were as he had fantasized—soft, warm, and inviting.

Brechlin ran her hands slowly down his chest and torso. When she reached his manhood, he offered an embarrassed explanation. "As you can see, I ate quite a bit of that fruit." She still said nothing.

She slowly worked on him for a long time, kissing and caressing, building up his arousal to even greater heights, only to let it gently subside. He was ready to explode when, finally, she positioned her body over his and guided him into her. He entered easily and let her set the pace. He met her thrust again and again until, quietly, they both climaxed almost at the same time—wave after wave of orgasmic pleasure washing over their bodies.

It had been too long for both of them. And now, sated and basking in the glow of their lovemaking, they slept soundly.

Cool Greeting

The next morning, Jern was the first to wake, followed by Flackard. They stared at Chimber and Brechlin, still embracing on Chimber's sleeping pallet.

"Can't say I blame them," said Jern. "That fruit is pretty potent."

Flackard gently shook Chimber's shoulder, and they all got up and dressed. Jern smirked at Chimber and shook his head, but no comments were made.

No one was in a hurry to return to the Roluccan cold and their hungry traveling companions, so they took their time breaking camp. They exited through the waterfall into the cold, clear day and scampered down the slope. There were no wolves in sight, but within a few miles of resuming their northern trek, the party began glimpsing patches of gray fur in the thinning woods.

"They're back." Jern through a stone at a nearby patch of gray, but missed.

"As long as it is only two or three, I don't think they'll attack," said Flackard. "And the wolf population should thin out the farther north we go. There isn't much to eat up there."

They settled down for lunch near the river, now substantially narrower than when they had made their crossing. From where they sat, they had their first look at the Ice Shard Mountains rising in the distance.

Chimber gazed at the snow-covered peaks. "They don't look far off."

"Yeah, I would say about a half-day's march," replied Brechlin.

Jern pointed toward one of the peaks. "Hey! Isn't that the Blue Mountain?"

All members of the party stared at the mountain range. A thin sliver of blue could be seen protruding beyond the deep shadow of an adjacent towering peak.

Brechlin nodded. "That must be it. The rest of the mountain is still hidden. We'll no doubt see it in its full glory soon enough."

"The Blue Mountain and the Lomitheri," said Jern. "This will be something to tell our youngsters about."

"If we live," added Flackard.

"Well, to die at the hands of a tribe of flying, naked women wouldn't be the worst way to go, now would it?"

"Do you ever think of anything else?" asked Chimber.

Jern shrugged but then sprang up and dug into his knapsack. "I have a nice dessert for us."

But, as he reached into the knapsack's storage cavity, he pulled back his hand full of a reddish gooey pulp.

"Ugh!" he said, scowling at his hand.

"Whatever that is, it sure smells," exclaimed Chimber. "What the hell is it?"

Jern let the ball of pulp fall to the ground. "Well, it *was* fruit from that horny tree. I guess it doesn't travel well."

"It's for the best," said Brechlin. "That fruit in the wrong hands could cause trouble."

Jern gave her a big smile. "Yeah, I would hate to be a little troublemaker."

During the afternoon, the river became smaller each hour of travel. Lichen and exposed rock became as common as forest litter and brush. Permafrost crunched under each step. Toward the end of the day, after crossing several half-frozen feeder creeks, they found the source of the river—a large gurgling spring pouring out gallons of pure water, creating a wide, boggy pool with wisps of steam. They looked up through the sparse trees to the dramatic range of ice-covered mountains—jagged and sharp. Set among them, striking in contrast, they espied a huge blue massif.

"There it is," said Brechlin. "The Lomitheri should be close at hand. Shall we try to make for their village or camp here for the night?"

Just then, they heard a distant howl. There were still wolves roaming the land.

"A nice warm cabin would be a welcome change," said Jern, who valued his comfort.

"I don't know if I would count on that," cautioned Flackard.

"We don't know if they'll welcome us," agreed Brechlin.

"Well, let's find out," said Chimber.

The pool before them was no simple obstacle but stretched for many feet, although it was shallow enough to see its bottom. They tried walking to either side, but on both sides they found muddy bogs that were mushy and deep.

"The warmth from the springs keeps these bogs from freezing," said Flackard, probing the mud with his boot for a dry path. After several minutes of searching, they gave up and walked back to the pool's edge.

Chimber explored the ponds bottom with his walking staff.

"Well, it's only a few inches deep and the bottom seems firm. I'd rather cross it than to get bogged down in the mud."

Brechlin took the first step. "Come on. Time to get our feet wet."

"Great," offered Jern. "I love the outdoors."

They were about halfway across the pool when they noticed, in the fading light, several small beings standing along the pool's far edge. Their sudden presence surprised the four traveling companions. They drew their swords, ready to fight.

"Approach no further," commanded one of the beings in an authoritative but definitely feminine voice.

"Are you members of the Lomitheri?" asked Brechlin as she took several steps forward. "We come as friends."

"I said halt!" barked out the leader of the group. She grasped a blue crystal pendant she wore around her neck and placed it near the water. A soft blue beam of light emanated from the pendant and struck the surface of the water. Her comrades, of which there were five, followed suit. The pool froze solid in a couple of seconds, trapping the feet of the four traveling companions in the ice.

"Yeow! My feet!" cried Jern.

The strange beings calmly walked across the frozen pool and stopped just out of sword's reach of the traveling party. All six were female and nude. They were all under five feet tall and had a distinctive bluish tint to their skin in the creases of their body, such as their underarms, crotch, and neck. Their hair was long and pure white, and translucent wings sprouted from their backs. Each held a sword in one hand and a blue pendant stone in the other.

"Who are you?" demanded the authoritative female in the center.

"I am Brechlin, Marshal of Cegril's army. We mean you no harm. We are here to speak with the Medium of the Blue Mountain."

The leader turned to her companion on the right. "Do you think humans are good to eat?"

"I've never tried their flesh," returned her companion. "But I would give it a go."

"Hey!" exclaimed Jern. "Didn't you hear? We're friends!"

"You have entered the lands of the Lomitheri uninvited. As far as we are concerned, you are enemies."

"Flackard? Is that you?" blurted one of the Lomitheri. She fluttered her wings and flew over toward Flackard to get a better look.

"Delvisha?" asked Flackard. "Well, I've never seen you fly before! You seem to fare well."

Delvisha looked over Flackard with a smile, then at his traveling companions. "Who are the people with you?"

"This is Brechlin, Chimber, and Jern."

"I am Delvisha," she said, now out of breath from the exertion of flying. "And this is...Schmie, the leader...of our party."

"There is a terrible war going on," said Brechlin. "The Krakul Gat is marching an army on Cegril, and we need Er Lomith's help. May we have an audience?"

"I don't know. We will see," said Delvisha. She returned to the other Lomitheri.

"This is the human who nursed me while I was injured in the Southern. He is a friend."

"We are all friends," offered Chimber.

"Friends with very uncomfortable feet," added Jern.

Schmie looked them over for a second. "Okay, we will set

you free and take you to our village. There, you can speak with the village elders. But you may be saving us the effort of carrying our dinner home."

"Can you reverse this ice magic?" asked Brechlin.

"No," replied Schmie, "but we will hack you loose with our swords."

"Great," returned Jern sarcastically. "Just please hurry."

Tireless Maestro

As Ilsher climbed the last few steps approaching Dran's recess in the shoulder of the Gray Mountain, the breeze lifted the white linens from the basket of food she was carrying and nearly blew them away. Her quick hand trapped the cloth just before it cleared the basket.

As always, she became exhilarated as she approached the high perch from which Dran manipulated the Gray Mountain's unique power. It was a combination of the expansive views, the sea-tinged breezes, and the proximity to the mountain's power that made her feel so giddy. She completed the last few steps with abounding energy.

She approached the opening to the tunnel at the back of the recess and called out Dran's name. No one without a crystal collar could safely enter the interior of a Gludemic Mountain. The unchanneled energy would disintegrate any who dared.

A few seconds later, Dran emerged. As usual, he was covered with sweat and haggard in appearance.

It's a shame that refreshing breeze doesn't reach very far into this recess, she thought as she sat on a short bench.

"Lunchtime," she sang. Dran plopped down beside her. Ilsher noticed his gray collar still retained some of its mellow light.

"What do you have?" asked Dran with a weak smile. "I'm famished."

"Mutton stew with watercress and yeast buns," she replied. "Along with small beer, very cold."

"Ah, yes," he said and rummaged through the basket.

Ilsher stared into the dim light of the tunnel. "The thought occurred to me that you are like the maestro of some choir while you control the powers of the mountain, but you wave your mind instead of your hands."

"The analogy is good," Dran said between mouthfuls of food. "Except I have to control thousands of voices at once. And this boat-building, such meticulous work! Try coaxing lumps of dead flesh to build a seaworthy craft! Very tiring."

"Ger Strait is narrow; do they have to be well built?"

"Not so well built, but there may be rough waters. I don't want to lose my army, so I have to make sure the vessels are at least watertight."

Ilsher's brow furrowed. "I worry that the crystal powder will lose its potency. How much longer before the boats are ready?"

"We should cross the strait in a week, and then there is nothing Cegril can do to stop us. I'm not worried about the powder. I just have to get the damn army on the island."

He set the lunch basket aside, stretched out his arms, and slumped down on the bench. Ilsher watched him close his eyes.

"No naps, please, Father. Time is essential—we've got to get those boats built. You can sleep once you're in power."

"I can concentrate better with a little rest. I'll just lie—"

"No, Father!" insisted Ilsher. "We believe in you! Don't let us down! You can sleep at bedtime, not now."

Dran did not respond. He sniffed and fished out another roll from the basket. But after a moment he sat up straight. "Okay, you're right. Back to work."

He hugged his daughter and kissed her forehead before slowly standing and returning to the tunnel. Ilsher watched him disappear inside, grabbed the empty basket, and hurried down the steps. A warm bath would be waiting for her in her room.

The Realm of the Lomitheri

Once the tingling in their feet had subsided, Brechlin, Chimber, Jern, and Flackard followed Schmie, Delvisha, and the rest of the Lomitheri scouting party along a trail up into the mountain range toward the imposing blue massif. Soon, the land changed significantly. Dusty snow and a crust of ice covered most objects, and the temperature dropped even further.

As they rounded a large exposed boulder near the foot of a mountain, they encountered a boardwalk constructed of wooden planks that crossed an ice field and led to a wooden staircase. Looking up to where the staircase led, the travelers saw the edge of a small hanging valley on the shoulder of the mountain. Adjacent to it was the striking outline of Mount Lomith itself, its blue crystal diffracting the setting sun's light and casting an azure tinge across the landscape.

The ascent to the hanging valley was steep, but the wooden steps had been kept clear of ice. After the stairs crested the floor of the valley, a wooden boardwalk led to the head of the valley toward a lone wooden building. Steep ice walls were a mere twenty feet from either side of the path, and there were many openings.

The party followed their Lomitheri guides down the boardwalk toward the wooden structure. They noticed movement at the openings in the ice walls on their left and right, and saw the heads of other Lomitheri peering out at them.

"They live in the ice!" exclaimed Jern.

"And look," said Chimber, pointing to the floor of the valley. Underneath their feet, in the thick layer of clear ice below them, they spotted the vague outlines of other Lomitheri moving around and looking up at them.

"They must have tunnels and homes in the ice," said Brechlin. "That's why they don't need buildings."

"It's hard to believe they don't just freeze solid living in these conditions, naked as they are," mused Chimber.

Several of the Lomitheri crawled out of their small openings and took flight, hovering over them for a closer look. A few smaller males were there, but all the adults were female. They chatted nervously among themselves in their strange dialect, and it was clear that visitors were a rare sight in their little community.

The four travelers were led inside the front doorway of the wooden building, which was constructed in a conventional rectangular design. The first room had a massive stone fireplace in the corner, but it was as cold as the rest of the valley. They passed through the empty room and into a spacious back chamber where three older Lomitheri women sat at a large, rough-hewn table. One woman sat on a tall wooden chair at the table's head. The chair's trim was painted white and blue. Thick, white drapes covered the walls of the room, and in the corner stood two large wooden boxes filled with swords and other armament.

The seated Lomitheri looked up curiously at the group but said nothing.

"This is Kleeum," said Schmie, gesturing toward the woman on the tall chair. "She is the mayor of our village." She turned to Kleeum. "We found this party of humans approaching us through the lower bogs."

"And yet they live," observed Kleeum in a low, gravelly voice.

"Yes. One is the human who aided Delvisha when she was injured in the Southern. They said there was war in those lands and that they desired an audience with Er Lomith."

Kleeum slid down from her chair and walked over to the group of humans, looking up at them pensively. She then looked at Delvisha with a questioning expression. Delvisha pointed at Flackard.

"We are a protective clan," she said, looking at him. "We do not readily welcome visitors. Things were not always so. At one time, we would occasionally receive human officials from the Southern. We welcomed them within this building with a fire roaring in the room through which you passed. But, alas, our experiences with outsiders have taught us caution. In these times, we maintain our isolation with force."

Kleeum reached out her small, wrinkled hand and grasped Flackard's. "Yet, we are sensitive to kindness when it is given, so we thank you for that." She returned to her chair and regarded the two seated Lomitheri. They both shook their heads.

She looked back at her party. "But I am afraid that all we can offer you in return is to provide you with a little food and to wish you well. Er Lomith, the Medium of the Blue Mountain, cannot be disturbed."

"No, no, it is impossible," added one of the seated Lomitheri. "Especially today."

219

"Teppe and Smark are to achieve union in the mating chamber," added the other. "Preparations are made." They all three shook their heads to reinforce the point.

Brechlin stepped forward and bowed before Kleeum. "I am Brechlin, the Marshal of Cegril's army. We have traveled through these inhospitable lands, fighting the wolves of Wolfglen Forest, for a dire reason—the Dalmeer Islands are facing a great peril. The Krakul Gat has turned against Capital Island, and our demise may be imminent. Even as we speak—"

"My dear Marshal," interjected Kleeum, "the affairs of humans no longer concern the Lomitheri. As long as we are left alone, we do not wish you harm. But, we will not get involved."

"You will become involved," insisted Chimber. "After the Krakul Gat has taken the White Mountain, it is only a matter of time before he turns his attention to Mount Er."

"Of what value would Mount Lomith be to a human?" asked Kleeum. "I see no reason..."

Brechlin, who wore an elbow-length leather glove with stitched plates of armor, slammed her fist down in the center of the table with surprising force, startling everyone in the room.

She had lost her patience. The security of the kingdom was at stake, and they had not made this treacherous journey to be dismissed by these village administrators who didn't understand the significance of the occasion. Brechlin needed to speak to the Medium of the Blue Mountain, and she was not leaving until she had done so.

"Enough!" she shouted. "Did not the Medium of the Blue Mountain partake of the Covenant to protect these lands? Have you forgotten the age of the Dark Overlord? No more petty squabbling. I am the representative of Capital Island and the

White Mountain, and I demand an audience with Er Lomith."

The armed Lomitheri in the room recovered from their start and unsheathed their weapons. Brechlin found three sword points inches from her throat.

"We will not tolerate such insolence from humans, not in our meeting house," snarled Schmie as she moved the sword nearer to Brechlin's throat.

"Schmie, please sheathe your sword," said Kleeum, gesturing for the others to do the same. She gravely studied Brechlin's face for a few moments and nodded. "We must discuss this."

She and the two seated Lomitheri stood up and walked through an opening in the thick white drapes. They could be heard whispering among themselves in an adjacent chamber before returning, whereupon Kleeum addressed the group.

"You invoke the Sacred Covenant. In this, my authority has no bearing. Whether our people get involved in your war is a decision for the Medium of the Blue Mountain. We will take you to Er Lomith." She looked at Schmie and Delvisha. "Escort them up Mount Lomith and report back to me what is said. And Schmie, leave your sword in its sheath."

"Yes, Your Honor," replied Schmie, still eying Brechlin suspiciously. She waved to the group to follow her, and the four of them trailed after her and Delvisha. They walked further toward the back of the valley floor, where the base of the Blue Mountain was inset into a wall of ice and rock. A set of steps was carved into the blue crystal leading up to a cleft on the shoulder of the mountain.

"These stairs will take us to Er Lomith," said Schmie, ascending the steps. "She works and lives on that cleft in mountain. I warn you, these steps are many and are ice-covered. Take care if you want to reach the top."

"Pardon me," said Jern, who was immediately behind Schmie, "but I'm curious. Why have stairs at all? Why not just fly to the platform?"

"I could do it," said Schmie, looking up at the cleft, "but many here could not, especially the older ones, such as Er Lomith herself. Flying is difficult and tiring. Only the young or the fit fly often."

"I see," said Jern. "So, if one of us slips, you could save us?"

"It is a bold assumption that I would try," replied Schmie. "It is best you not test my good will."

The steps were many, indeed, but the members of the party took care during the ascent, and no accidents occurred. As they neared the crest over which they would reach the cleft, the height set all hearts racing. Cold, howling wind whipped about them.

They entered the recess and saw a small hut about twenty feet toward its farthest reaches. In front of the hut stood another aged Lomitheri. Her long white hair streamed in the wind. She stood silently watching them as they approached.

Schmie bowed. "Er Lomith, these humans have come for an audience. They invoke the Sacred Covenant."

"It's the Krakul Gat, isn't it?" Er Lomith asked without hesitation. "What has he done?"

"There is war," said Brechlin. "Dran has created a large cadaver army, and they approach Cegril. We need your help."

Er Lomith lowered her head and slowly nodded.

"Of course," she said and looked at Schmie. "Settle them into the meeting house in comfort. They will need a fire, and give them food. And bring out a bottle of jumerlo for them to share. I suspect they will appreciate it. I'll be down shortly."

"But Er Lomith, Teppe and Smark are prepared and await. They are to mate this afternoon."

"I know, Schmie," said Er Lomith. "Their union will have to be postponed."

As they strolled back to the steps, Jern's curiosity once again got the best of him. "Why do they need Er Lomith to mate?" he asked Schmie.

Schmie looked at him with surprise. She answered him, speaking slowly, as if to a child. "The heat of erotic passion is harmful to our kind. But, in the mating chamber, the Medium of the Blue Mountain creates a soothing pocket of cold energy. This allows the act to be completed, but..."

"But what?" persisted Jern.

"The males always die anyway. And, occasionally, the females. It is a sad time, but very meaningful."

"Have you lost mates?"

"Jern!" exclaimed Chimber. "Where are your manners?"

"It's okay," said Schmie. "Yes, I have taken three young men into the mating chambers and have given birth to three children."

"They must have truly loved you," observed Jern.

"Yes, and they loved our people. It is our way. Watch your step," she added, for now they were descending the stairs. "We can speak further in the meeting hall." She turned to Delvisha. "Stay with them. I will make the preparations." She leaped into the air, and as the amazed party watched, she spread her wings and soared in widening circles down to the valley floor.

Er Lomith Listens

It was nearly dark, but they made their way down the icy steps without incident. By the time they had reached the meeting hall, weariness and constant cold had taken a toll on their frames. They were delighted to find a roaring fire in the large hearth. Schmie was laying out food and drink. They noticed she was breathing hard, and her bare skin was coated with sweat beads. She had extended her wings for better cooling.

"Please...make yourself...at home," she managed. "Er Lomith will join you...soon." She nodded at the group and left the heated room.

"You know, it's not that warm in here yet, but Schmie was already suffering," observed Chimber.

"But with all that firewood," began Jern, pointing to a hefty pile of fagots, "it won't take long." He shed his outer garments and plopped down in one of the chairs arranged around the table. "And the victuals don't look bad."

The others looked over the spread. There was a stack of moose steaks, several varieties of berry jams, and a thin, crispy bread to spread it on. A bowl of yogurt was placed in the middle. Everyone took a seat, and by the time they had eaten their fill, the room was genuinely toasty. Chimber felt the warm liquid of sleep pouring over him. He stood up to take a few gulps from his waterskin, which he had hung on a wall nail, and noticed a small unopened bottle at the end of the table. He picked it up to examine it.

"What's this? Some kind of condiment, perhaps?" he wondered as he pulled out the cork and sniffed. "It smells good."

"It's a bottle of jumerlo," said a voice, and they all turned to see Er Lomith walking into the room. "Whew!" she added. "I can't take this heat for long. Let's all go into the back room. And take that bottle with you."

They followed her into the back room where they had previously met Kleeum and the other village elders. The room was empty now and much cooler than the front room, but not as cold as outside.

Er Lomith motioned them to all take a seat at the table. She remained standing.

"Take a sip from that bottle," she said to Chimber, "and then pass it around to the others. It's an ancient mead made from leweming root. It has remarkable properties."

Chimber took a sip, and soothing warmth spread throughout his body. Immediately, he noticed an easing of the aches and pains of the past week of travel.

He beamed a smile at Er Lomith. "That's nice stuff. We could use it back home."

"Unfortunately, the leweming plant is very rare, as it only grows in the silt that accumulates in glacial crevasses. And it takes many roots to make one bottle."

Brechlin took her sip and gazed at the bottle with wonder. "That's unfortunate." She reluctantly passed it on to Flackard.

"So, tell me, what has happened?" asked Er Lomith.

She listened gravely as they described the events of the

previous few weeks—of Dran's poisonous cloud and the genocide of the citizens of Bewel Island, of the animation of their corpses, and of the cadaver army's destruction of Keeman and Gretly. And that they were now preparing for an assault on Capital Island itself once boats were built to transport the army across Ger Strait.

"I doubt that the forces of Cegril can stop them," said Brechlin. "It takes a lot of effort to bring a single cadaver down. Wounds have no effect on them. One has to literally sever limbs from their bodies."

Er Lomith had been quiet through it all, nodding her head somberly.

"Will you help us?" asked Chimber.

Er Lomith began mumbling to herself and shaking her head. She looked up at the group. "I have a confession to make. I believe that Ferrin and I brought this tragedy upon the land."

She surveyed their surprised faces and continued. "Yes, yes, the White Medium and myself. Several years ago, Ferrin and I were summoned to the Covenant Stone to replace the fallen Krakul Gat. There, we allowed a gross breach of protocol by accepting Dran as Grael's replacement. We were both persuaded by the dire needs of our people. Then, as my party was returning to the port at Reador for our ship home, a gang of ruffians attacked us. Fortunately, we were alerted to their presence and took flight before they were upon us. We made it to Reador and ultimately home with no losses. And then, a few weeks later, word came that Ferrin was missing. I have no doubt that Dran's treachery was behind it."

"So Dran has Ferrin?" asked Chimber.

"And, from what I understand, he must be alive," said Jern.

"Yes," said Er Lomith. "He must be kept alive. If one

Medium of the Gludemic Mountains perishes, the power of all the mountains will begin to fade, becoming completely dormant in a few weeks. They cannot reawaken until we meet at the Covenant Stone and initiate a new Medium. Since the Gludemic Mountains are not dormant, Dran is keeping Ferrin alive somewhere. He must be."

"What happened years ago at the Covenant Stone matters little now," said Brechlin. "What matters is stopping Dran. Any suggestions?"

Er Lomith shook her head. "I have none. But the Lomitheri will do what we can to help. Please make yourselves at home here tonight. In the meantime, I will consult with Kleeum and the others. By tomorrow morning, we will know what we can offer."

Allies in Blue

The next morning, Chimber, Jern, Brechlin, and Flackard were served an early breakfast, which they finished off with a swig of jumerlo. They had packed up their knapsacks when they heard a knock at the door. All four of them walked out into the frigid but sunny day to see a crowd of Lomitheri gathered around the porch of their building. It was an amazing sight—two hundred small naked bodies standing barefoot on the icy floor of the valley. Many slowly fluttered their wings, cooling them in the crisp air, and all were chatting among themselves, billowing clouds of condensed breath into the bright air. They all had bluish shadings in their skin, and almost all were female. A few teenage boys were seen among the crowd.

As they stood there on the porch, looking over the faces curiously looking back at them, a haggard Er Lomith came forward and ascended the steps. She nodded a grave good morning to the party and turned to face the Lomitheri.

"A dire morning it is, my people," she stated in a loud voice. "War is unleashed upon the lands of the Southern, and it is our duty to assist them in their time of need. For surely as I stand here, our safety is at risk should the Krakul Gat achieve victory. I have taken the liberty to dislodge thirty war kernels from the mountain."

Chimber heard quiet gasps of surprise from some of the gathered Lomitheri.

"I realize that removing thirty kernels of our sacred mountain is an unprecedented step, but our war party will need them. I have designated thirty Lomitheri warriors to travel to the Southern with Brechlin, the Marshal of Cegril."

She turned to Brechlin. "These war kernels will be worn around the necks of our warriors. Its ambient power will enable them to survive in warmer lands, and through these crystals, I will be able to project the power of the Blue Mountain, just as Dran projects the power of the Gray Mountain through the powder that coated the bodies of the cadavers."

She turned back to the crowd. "Schmie, please come forward."

"She's such a lovely thing," whispered Jern to Chimber.

"Whatever happened to Saffral?" Chimber whispered back.

"Saffral will be mine one day—of that there is no doubt. But that does not change Schmie's loveliness."

As Schmie stood before Er Lomith, the Medium reached into a large fur bag and pulled out a blue crystal twice the size of a man's fist. The crowd uttered notes of awe and concern. It was similar in appearance to the blue pendants worn by several of the Lomitheri, but several times larger.

The crystal was attached to a chain necklace, which Er Lomith placed around Schmie's neck. "This will keep you safe, my dear, in the harsh climate of the Southern. And through me, you will become a powerful weapon."

Twenty-nine other Lomitheri warriors came forward, one after another, and received their own piece of the Blue Mountain.

"Are you not going?" Jern asked of Er Lomith.

"I must stay here," she replied. "At least in body. But I will focus the power of Mount Lomith through the crystal amulets. Although a dislodged crystal retains the mountain's ambient virtue for some time, a Medium is required to channel the mountain's power through the crystals."

Brechlin, who had watched the ceremony in silence, stepped forward to address Er Lomith. "We appreciate your help, but thirty warriors is a small number. And, I don't see the immediate application of these blue crystals. Would they be able to freeze an entire army?"

"Not hardly," said Er Lomith. "The power is not that extensive, but each one should be able to freeze some."

"But then the cadavers will thaw—so the crystals would only stop them temporarily," observed Chimber.

Er Lomith shrugged. "Yes. If you choose to use the power of the Blue Mountain in that fashion. That's for the leadership of Cegril's army to decide. All I can offer is the mountain's power. And remember, the life of these crystals is limited. They will lose their virtue more quickly if they are used to channel and direct the Blue Mountain's power."

"It is said that the power of two of the Gludemic Mountains can defeat the power of third," said Jern. "Isn't that the premise behind the Covenant?"

"So it is," replied Er Lomith. "But that is why Dran has taken Ferrin. And even with the White Medium back and Mount Krin active once again, how does that translate to an advantage? How can the power of healing and the power of freezing defeat an army of animated cadavers? The Covenant does not say."

"We thank you for your assistance, Er Lomith," said Chimber, conscious of Brechlin's disappointment.

"I wish I could do more," Er Lomith replied. "But hopefully it will be enough."

"Hopefully," said Chimber.

Chimber, Jern, Brechlin, and Flackard gathered their bags and were led to the waiting group of Lomitheri warriors, already gathered near the steps that led down from the valley. They were clad in leather bodices, boots, and elbow-length gloves.

"Thirty dwarfish women with pretty jewelry—our efforts to get here are questionably rewarded," whispered Brechlin to Chimber.

"That's thirty dwarfish *warriors*," called Schmie. As she was in front leading the Lomitheri band, her response surprised Brechlin. "Didn't you know? We have sensitive hearing."

Jern grinned at Schmie. "Really? You're truly a remarkable race."

"I'm sorry," said Brechlin. "I'm just concerned about our people. I didn't mean to disrespect you. And I do appreciate your help."

"We are under your charge and will do what we can," responded Schmie. "Your concerns may well be justified, but all we can do is all we can do."

Brechlin gravely nodded. "Of course."

"I don't want to sound negative, but there are wolves in yon forest," chimed in Flackard as they descended the valley steps. "Are you planning on freezing them?"

"Don't concern yourself, Flackard," said Delvisha, who had volunteered for the war party. "We have that problem ably solved."

And sure enough, as they approached the warm pool formed by the gushing spring at the head of River Muoki, the Lomitheri band pulled out several river canoes concealed under thick bushes crowding the bank.

Delvisha stepped into one and smiled at Flackard. "We ride to the Southern with the river current. We will reach Sleet Lake in two days' time."

"Thank Gludema," said Jern. "I much prefer riding. And, I must say, Schmie, that bodice looks quite fetching on you."

Schmie looked at him with puzzlement for a moment, shook her head, and pushed her canoe out into the small stream.

"Jern! Behave yourself," admonished Brechlin.

"What? I was just trying to make up for your insult," returned Jern. "Besides," he added in a whisper, "she's cute."

"Remember, she can hear you," snapped Chimber.

"Yeah? So what?" laughed Jern as he clambered into a canoe with Chimber.

Soon, the passengers in the canoes were able to relax as the growing current of the river whisked them south.

Brechlin's Return

"But, my Queen, if the siege lasts for more than several weeks, our food supplies will run low. I do not recommend it," insisted Tarmot, holding Queen Cirmar's hand.

"Tarmot, I will not leave my people out there to be subjected to the ravages of that swarm," said Queen Cirmar. "I insist that they all be allowed within the city walls—all of them." She spoke this last sentence with mounting authority.

"But think about the consequences..."

"My dear, have I not backed your decision to retreat behind these walls when my trusted advisers argued for assaulting the enemy at Gretly? Have we not agreed to leave our beloved homelands open to spoil from this macabre army? And haven't we, as you insisted, placed all our hopes on these walls in stopping the army? These are your decisions and yes, I stand behind them, but I will not abandon my people."

Tarmot opened his hand. "As you wish, my Queen. I'm only thinking of your safety."

As she kissed him on the forehead, there was a knock on the antechamber door. A young page entered the room, out of breath and excited.

"What is it, Magroy?"

"My Queen...Marshal Brechlin...she has returned."

"Great Gludema! Could it be?"

"Brechlin? Here?" asked Tarmot.

"Yes, My Lord. In the reception room," squeaked the excited page.

"Come, Tarmot, we must go to her at once," said Queen Cirmar, delighted with the news. But, as she walked toward the door, Tarmot grabbed her by the arm.

"My Queen, you see it would be folly to switch authority at this late stage."

"What do you mean?"

"I mean, I'm in charge of the city's defenses, and have created a coherent plan for its defense. If you give that authority to Brechlin now, at this late stage, she'll try to alter my plans and compromise us just as the enemy is upon us."

Queen Cirmar frowned. "Well, we will see." She hurried down the hall with Tarmot following her.

As Queen Cirmar entered the reception hall, she beheld a motley crew. Three men were standing with Brechlin, and all of them were filthy, ragged, and smelled of the forest.

"Marshal Brechlin!" exclaimed Tarmot as he walked up behind the queen. "How dare you come before the Queen and myself dressed in this manner! Have you no respect?"

"My Queen, I apologize for my appearance, but I deemed haste more important than decorum," responded Brechlin.

"Brechlin, don't concern yourself," replied the smiling queen. "I'm so happy you are alive and back with us. Tell me what happened, and who are your companions?"

"I will tell all, but first there is news. Our ship approached Capital Island from the south. As we made our way up Ger Strait to Cegril, we spotted Dran's cadavers embarking their transports. I believe they will cross the strait soon, perhaps even this day."

Queen Cirmar sat down. "So, it has begun," she said in a somber tone.

"Yes," continued Brechlin, "and when we landed and saw that the beaches and port were unguarded, we rushed here to give you the word. There is just enough time for our forces to get into position to strike at them as they disembark, for it will be then that they are most vulnerable."

"Our forces will go nowhere," intoned Tarmot. "You are welcome to take your friends and fend them off yourselves. Given your fragrant air, they may confuse you for one of their own."

In a flashing blur of motion, Brechlin unsheathed her sword and pinned it against Tarmot's neck. A droplet of blood was visible at the point as it pressed into his skin.

"Brechlin!" exclaimed Queen Cirmar.

Brechlin's tone was menacing and barely contained. "These men, and myself, have already fought battles in defense of this realm. I have met the army and survived. We have combated freezing cold and menacing wolves and have brought back allies from the Ice Shard Mountains. What, Tarmot, have you done for our city?"

Tarmot said nothing, and slowly Brechlin lowered her sword. He then backed off a couple of steps.

"Guards!" he shouted to the sentries guarding the entry to the reception hall. "Place this woman under arrest."

At once, Chimber, Jern, and Flackard drew their swords and crouched into their fighting stances. The two guards hesitated and looked at Tarmot. But, by this time, Queen Cirmar had gathered herself.

"Guards! Belay that order," she commanded. "Tarmot,

enough of your provoking comments!"

"But, my Queen, she threatened the marshal of your army with a sword," replied Tarmot.

"You? Marshal?" spat out Brechlin.

"My dear Brechlin, while you have been away, things have changed," said Tarmot with a haughty tone. "I've been given your office."

"Tarmot, please!" said Queen Cirmar.

"Is this true?" Brechlin asked Queen Cirmar.

She looked at Brechlin and then walked over to Tarmot and gently pushed him toward the door.

"Tarmot, my dear. Let me handle this alone. I assure you your authority is secure, but your presence is not helping things. Wait for me in my antechamber."

Tarmot cast a cold reptilian glance toward Brechlin and stomped out of the room without further words.

Queen Cirmar looked at Brechlin remorsefully. "Brechlin, we thought you were dead, killed in the defense of Keeman. We needed leadership and a strong voice, so I made Tarmot Marshal."

"I see," replied Brechlin, "and now that I have returned?"

"I don't think it wise to change leadership with the enemy at our door. You and he may not agree on many things, but he is no fool."

"But, my Queen, perhaps the reason he and I disagree so much is that I am an experienced commander and he is not. Are you willing to stake your kingdom on his good sense?"

"Are you saying his plan has no merit?" asked Queen Cirmar.

"That we not strike at them when they disembark, and just wait behind these walls?" queried Brechlin as she walked to a window overlooking the bay. She thought for a moment and continued. "If this were a conventional force, attacking them as they disembarked would be wise. At such a time, they would not be in defensive formation and would be vulnerable. But this...army...I don't know. Would capsizing their transports hinder them in any way? They would not drown."

She looked at Queen Cirmar and shook her head.

"The nature of this enemy forces us to rethink everything. The answer to your question is 'I don't know.' But it would have been an action we could have taken with small risk. Now, as Dran's army is approaching these shores even as we speak, we have little choice. Can an army of cadavers breach our walls? Maybe not. They are slow and uncoordinated. Yet, they built transport craft to carry them across the strait. I'm afraid we don't know of what they are capable."

"But if they are slow," pressed Queen Cirmar, "then as they approach the walls, we can pummel them with arrows and stones, and douse them with burning oil. Doesn't that make sense?"

"And as I mentioned to Tarmot, I have met this enemy. Arrows and fire are no matter to them, for they are animated *corpses*."

"We are committed, Brechlin. Let's hope you are wrong."

Brechlin let out a long sigh. "Well...on a different note, let me introduce you to my companions."

She turned around and gestured toward Chimber, Jern, and Flackard, who stood mutely through the conversation, somewhat awed by their noble surroundings.

"This is Chimber and Jern, citizens of Math. These two brave men rescued me from the field of battle as I lay unconscious. They nursed me back to health, and together we used Chimber's xebec to journey to Rolucca Peninsula in search of the

Medium of the Blue Mountain."

"But, she and the other Lomitheri dwell in the Ice Shard Mountains, way in the north of the peninsula," said the queen. "They avoid human contact."

"Yes, my Queen, we knew. And once we disembarked on the Roluccan shore, our chances of reaching them seemed remote. Until, that is, we encountered Captain Flackard, who was doing...service work...for citizens of Rolucca Bay. The followers of the pirate Desmondi had destroyed his brigade, and local authorities had detained him. I had him released, and he led us to the Ice Shard Mountains. And because he had nursed an injured member of that tribe, the Lomitheri gave us an audience with Er Lomith."

"I'm amazed," said Queen Cirmar. "What of Wolfglen Forest?"

Brechlin nodded. "It was a struggle, my Queen, but these are exceptional warriors. And now, we have allies."

"What does that mean?"

"Camped just outside of the town walls is a band of Lomitheri warriors. Their stature is small, and they number only thirty. But they wear pendants through which the power of the Blue Mountain can be channeled. I do not yet know how, but I would like to believe their aid could be a significant addition to our defense."

Queen Cirmar's eyes flashed with girlish curiosity. "A band of Lomitheri...here? Just outside the city?"

"Yes, my Queen," said Brechlin.

"I can't wait to meet them!" she said excitedly. "But for now..."

She walked over to Chimber and extended her hand.

"Honored to meet you, Your Majesty," said Chimber, bowing his head.

Queen Cirmar smiled. "And I you, my dear Chimber."

She proceeded to Jern and extended her hand to him. He bowed low with a flourish, kissed her ring, and said, "My most lovely Queen. I am your servant."

"Why thank you, Jern. Pleased to meet you."

Flackard, who had sworn an allegiance to the queen when he joined Cegril's armed forces, also bowed. "I am honored to return to your service, my Queen."

"And what a fortuitous time for you to do so. Cegril can use warriors of your character." She turned to Brechlin. "The city is crowded with citizens from the countryside, but please find a place for these three men within the palace walls. I'll go with you myself to welcome the Lomitheri warriors to our city. But first, I must console Marshal Tarmot. I'm afraid he may be upset by your return."

The Siege of Cegril

The next day, Jern and Flackard strolled across the open ground outside the city walls toward the Lomitheri's encampment—a cluster of tents under a copse of evergreens. A group of curious citizens was milling around the perimeter of the camp, staring in at the wondrous sight of a band of Lomitheri at their doorsteps. Several of Cegril's garrison, standing guard, kept the onlookers at a distance.

The sentry recognized them as they approached and let them through the perimeter. They found Schmie and Delvisha sitting down with several others under a towering tree, enjoying the relative cool of its shade. Feeling secure within their camp, they had discarded their leather bodices.

"Flackard," exclaimed Delvisha with delight. "You visit us!"

"Hello, Schmie," offered Jern with a big smile, admiring the unadorned bodies of the small but feminine Lomitheri.

"Jern," she said wearily as she stood up. "Flackard and Delvisha are friends, but why have you come? And do we need to dress, or can you contain yourself?"

"Just saying hello," he replied nonplussed. "And please, relax as you are. You are fine."

The other Lomitheri wandered off, quietly giggling among themselves, leaving just Schmie and Delvisha with Flackard and Jern.

"Did you see the queen?" asked Flackard.

"Yes, she visited our camp this morning," replied Delvisha. "Quite a fine, noble lady. Although, I can't say the same for that ill-disposed fellow who follows her around."

"That would be Tarmot," said Jern, "the newly appointed Marshal of Cegril's army."

"So we heard," said Schmie.

"How are you holding out in this heat?" asked Jern. To him, the outdoor temperature was not warm at all. He wore a jerkin over his shirt for added warmth.

"These amulets are doing their job," replied Schmie. "We are comfortable enough."

"Is there anything else that can be done for you? For we appreciate your coming to our aid and would want all of your needs attended to."

Schmie studied Jern's face after this comment. "You said 'we,' but is this an offer from Cegril? Or does it come from you personally?"

"Well, me personally," returned Jern.

"You, personally, would have all my needs attended to?"

"Well, yes," he said, a little self-conscious.

Schmie stood in front of Jern and looked straight into his eyes.

"Should I take it you have interest in me? That you wish to lie with me?"

"Well," said Jern, somewhat put off by Schmie's directness. "I do find you attractive."

"Hmm," she replied, looking Jern up and down. "You are rather large for our kind, but your face does not displease me. Yet you must realize that even should I find you attractive, and even though it has been nine years since I have last mated, you could never act on your interest."

"Um, yeah, I have heard something like that. That the heat of passion is not something you desire."

"On the contrary. The problem is we desire passion too much. The heat of an erotic encounter literally overwhelms us. So only when its heat is tempered can our bodies withstand the strain. Only when the Blue Mountain's power chills the mating chambers sufficiently can a Lomitheri let her emotions go without heed of the danger to herself. You see, for Lomitheri, our fires of passion are all-consuming."

"That sounds interesting, but it must be a miserable existence to have so few encounters," suggested Jern.

"We are used to it. And it makes the few erotic experiences we have especially fulfilling."

Jern bit his lip. "If you say so."

Schmie looked briefly at Delvisha and then back at Jern. She then took one of her ample and exposed breasts in her hand and massaged it seductively as Jern watched with interest. Her full nipple became erect.

"Would you like to touch my breast?" she asked Jern. "Please, touch my breast."

"What?" asked Jern, still puzzled by Schmie's actions. "Just...put my hand on your breast? Right now?"

"Um, better just a finger. Don't you want to touch my breast?" she asked with a demure smirk.

"Okay." He reached his hand toward her breast, drawing his finger across her aureola.

"Ouch!" he exclaimed as he looked at the tip of his finger. It was burned and blistery. "What happened?"

Schmie pointed to her breast. The track his finger had

followed was now reddish and swollen.

"Your finger has burned me from the heat, and I have burned you from the cold. Now, are you sure you want to lie with me?"

Delvisha snickered, and Flackard let out a low rumble of mirth.

"I...maybe not," said Jern, "but I still think you're cute."

As he spoke, two Lomitheri came running up to the small group. They said nothing but pointed to the southeast. The land that stretched to Cegril's south was generally flat, dotted with stone fences, a few trees, and an occasional farmhouse. As all eyes turned toward where the Lomitheri were pointing, they could see a long dark line along the horizon.

"The enemy has disembarked to the south of the city and is advancing," said one of the Lomitheri.

"A black line," mused Jern. "The color of death."

"You two should get back inside the walls and alert the city," said Schmie. "We must break camp and get into position."

Flackard gave Delvisha one quick look. "We'll see you inside." They waved to the others and hurried back toward the city gate.

* * *

The first light of the next morning found Brechlin, Chimber, and Captain Labrok in position above the city's main gate. All along the wall facing the southeast, a thousand uniformed soldiers stood, swords and bows in hand. They stared out at the thickening line of black as the slow-moving army made its way over the flat expanse between Cegril and the coastal area south of the harbor. It was a large force—it was, after all, the entire population of Bewel Island—and strange. Every animated

243

corpse, whether a man, woman, or child, was a deadly threat.

As they stood guard and watched, the hours passed. By afternoon, the cadaver host had come close enough for observers to make out individual bodies and faces. At this point in their campaign, the forces of Keeman and Gretly had horribly disfigured many of the cadavers. Some were missing limbs. Others had eyes or partially severed fingers dangling free. But, what most horrified the observers lining Cegril's outer wall was the realization that pieces of the cadavers, hewn from the bodies of the macabre horde, were part of the advancing mass. A leg here and an arm there, inch-worming along with the other bodies as if they were keen not to miss the show.

"I see no siege equipment," said Captain Labrok, peering into the dark mob. "How do they plan on overcoming our walls?"

"I suspect Dran has a plan in mind," replied Chimber.

Brechlin stroked her chin. "I'm sure of it."

As Dran's army moved closer to the walls, she felt a cold dread. Mangled and severed bodies, animated child corpses, and the large size of the force affected her spirit. This was an enemy unlike any she had encountered before. Ugly, evil, and apparently invincible—how, she wondered, were they to survive? At least the city walls separated the living from the dead. It appeared there was no way these awkward, slow-moving cadavers could get past them.

Her confidence was short-lived.

Without pause, the army advanced. Once in range, the archers along the wall launched wave upon wave of arrows. The cadavers carried no shields. They made no effort to avoid the rain of shafts, many finding their mark. But, as was feared, they had no effect on the progress of these animated corpses.

Onward they came, unperturbed and steady.

Those tending the heavy cauldrons of boiling pig oil watched attentively as the large mass of the enemy lumbered next to the base of Cegril's wall. Poised near the edge of the upper battlement, the cauldron-tenders had no difficulty drenching the cadavers with boiling oil. All along the wall, they emptied the contents of their boiling pots upon the amassed corpses, but although there was physical damage to the bodies of the corpses, such as poached, flayed skin, it had no effect on their actions. The smell of fried flesh wafted along the wall.

The cadavers, once in position, used whatever weapons they carried to hammer against the base of the stone wall.

"They have got to be kidding!" exclaimed Captain Labrok as he looked down on the cadavers, their skin and clothes smoking from the burning oil. "Do they plan on hacking their way through solid stone?"

Brechlin was watching intently but said nothing.

"Is it possible that will work?" asked Jern, who had wandered up to the parapet to join Chimber.

"I would wager it has never been tried," suggested Chimber. "No living army will stand there and hammer away while arrows, rocks, and burning oil rain down upon them."

"These walls are two feet thick!" exclaimed Captain Labrok. "How can mere swords and pitchforks ever hope to bring them down?"

"I wonder," said Brechlin. She looked up and down the front wall of the city. Thousands of cadavers were crowding the base of the wall, and the wild cacophony of the sound of their metal implements—mostly swords—striking the stone echoed throughout the city.

"These corpses never get tired, they don't need food or

water, they don't heed our missiles," she mused. "And they have time on their side. I don't know if a sword can bring down a stone wall, but while they are preoccupied with their chore, it might be time for us to do what we can to hamper them."

"What do you have in mind?" Labrok asked.

"Let's discuss an idea I have," she replied. "Captain, assemble all available officers. Let's meet in the palace assembly hall."

"But, General Brechlin," responded Captain Labrok in an awkward, embarrassed tone. "I would be happy to do as you bid. But what you command is outside the purview of a field general. Only the Marshal can order a gathering of all officers."

"Ah, yes...damn. I forgot. Sorry, Captain Labrok. In that case, I suppose I had better find Marshal Tarmot and share my ideas with him. Hopefully, he will then order an assembly of officers. Perhaps I shall shortly see all of you in the assembly hall."

Brechlin made her way through the dense throng of uniformed men positioned along the city wall, voicing comments as she went. She was no longer their Marshal, but she knew most of them respected her and would appreciate her words of encouragement.

She took the ramp down from the parapet wall and entered the city proper. She observed that, for now anyway, the city seemed to carry on as usual. Most merchant stalls were open, and carts still rumbled along the cobblestone streets. She made her way up the double-wide pathway that led to the palace and to Tarmot's command center.

Had she remained Marshal, she would have set up her command center in the common room of the officers' barracks.

But, Tarmot preferred the palace environment. She wondered whether he had yet made the trip down to the city walls to view the enemy army.

She entered the command room to find Tarmot surrounded by several men he had promoted to aides-de-camp. The nature of their conversation puzzled her. It was light and laughter-laced.

"Ah, General Brechlin," called Tarmot, smiling at her over the shoulders of his comrades. "Come in, come in."

"It sounds like I've missed joyous news," she said.

"Haven't you been at the walls to see our pitiful enemy?"

"I have."

"Then you realize all that fretting was for nothing. Next time, you and Alipharem will be more receptive to my ideas, eh?"

"Tarmot..."

"Marshal Tarmot, if you please."

"Marshal Tarmot, I'm afraid I do not follow."

"Haven't you seen the ineptitude of Dran's army? My aides tell me they have brought no siege equipment. They carry swords and farm implements, so they have no way of breaching the wall! Soon enough, they must disband," finished Tarmot with more than a hint of triumph in his voice.

"Have you seen what they are doing?" asked Brechlin.

"Doing? They are pitifully hammering swords against solid stone. Ha! What a laugh! And you and that wizened piece of leather the Queen uses as an adviser wanted us to recklessly waste the lives of our men assaulting them in the open." Tarmot got up and motioned for his aides to leave as he walked around the large table and rested his backside against its edge. "But don't let your petty grudge against me lead you to not enjoy our good fortune," he said with great complacency.

"Don't you think your celebration a little premature?" asked Brechlin.

Tarmot shrugged. "The enemy can't get in. I don't know how long they can stay out there, but the gray powder will eventually weaken. In the meantime, we are adequately provisioned and can wait them out."

"Marshal Tarmot," began Brechlin, "even as we speak, several thousand animated cadavers are relentlessly hammering away at the base of our defensive wall. True, with swords and scythes, but that doesn't matter, for they are impervious to anything we can do to them. We shoot arrows at them, and they continue to hack. We pour hot oil over them, and they continue to hack. No living army could use this tactic for breaching our wall, but a dead army can. If we do nothing, then eventually—say, in a week's time—they will have pulverized the base of the wall, and our defenses will crumble."

At hearing this line of thought, a dark cloud passed over Tarmot's face, but only briefly. "That's ridiculous," he managed. "Swords cannot take down stone walls."

Brechlin shrugged. "A chip here, a chip there, and the wall comes down. But, I have an idea."

"Of course you do," replied Tarmot with a smirk.

"While they are preoccupied with their efforts on the wall, the time is right for us to strike. They are slow in their movements, so we can sally forth from the front gate and attack before they react, especially since they are stretched out along the base of the wall. And, if they mass for a counterattack, then we can use the Lomitheri's powers to temporarily freeze them. This will allow our forces to retreat to safety inside the gate, and it may even allow us to slice up the affected cadavers. After all, they cannot defend themselves if they are frozen."

"Why do you insist on exposing our troops to harm?" returned Tarmot. "Why risk losing lives on the basis of such wild conjectures?"

Brechlin blew out her cheeks. "Tarmot, listen, if we sit here all safe and cozy and hope the enemy eventually leaves us alone, we are doomed. We may be doomed anyway, but as defenders of this realm, it is our duty to do what we can to stop them. Every single warrior under our banner would agree. So let's assemble the officers and plan our first assault."

Tarmot waved his hand in a dismissive gesture. "Okay. I have no time for those tedious strategy sessions, but if you and your men want to get yourselves killed, go right ahead."

"So, we have your permission to plan and implement my suggestion?"

Tarmot heaved a long, showy sigh, crossed his arms, and peered out the window for a long moment. Then, with great gravity, he turned toward Brechlin.

"I give you permission," he said, obviously enjoying his display of power over Brechlin. "And feel free to take your little fairies with you."

Brechlin made no response but bolted out the door and headed toward the garrison headquarters.

Tarmot's True Character

Over the next two weeks, General Brechlin and her forces re-peatedly sallied forth outside the city walls, bravely attacking the busy cadavers as they worked hammering away at the stone fortifications. The results were always the same. The group of cadavers near the attacking force would leave their positions along the stone wall and fall upon the horses and men, hacking randomly but relentlessly. Cegril's troops would stab and slice but to little effect. It took less time than Brechlin had expected for the enemy to mass their numbers, especially around the gate, evidently attempting to prevent the troops from retreating inside the walls.

Every time, it was the efforts of the Lomitheri that enabled them to escape back inside the city gate. Positioned along the upper wall, they would launch into the air and, using their flying abilities, hover just above the flailing swords of the enemy. By directing the power of the Blue Mountain through their pendants, they would freeze as many of the cadavers as possible. Although this caused little direct harm to the cadavers, it froze their animated flesh, causing their motions to cease. This would allow the retreating troops the time to avoid their malice and re-enter the gates.

Because of the help of the Lomitheri, there were few casualties. And, on some occasions, Brechlin's men would converge on the frozen cadavers and hack a few of them into smaller pieces. But, their icy flesh was difficult to cleave. The various component pieces, when defrosted, returned to their animated state, sometimes resuming undermining the walls if there were any way for the dismembered limbs to grip a sword or implement.

It became clear to Brechlin that their efforts at distracting the enemy from its task were having minimal impact. As the days passed, the effect of thousands of cadaver swords on the base of the stone wall became ever more manifest. A deep recess along its length had formed in front of the cadaver host, and Cegril's engineers were concerned that the weight of the walls could cause them to collapse even before the swords had hacked their way entirely through them. It was on day eleven that the first section of stone fell forward near a corner tower. It was a small section, and while the Lomitheri froze the advancing cadavers in place, workers quickly filled in the gap with loose materials on hand. The breach had been temporarily repaired, but it had become clear that the fall of the city's walls was imminent. Moreover, the pendants of the Lomitheri, due to their heavy use in assisting Brechlin's sorties, were losing their power.

A few hours after the fallen section of wall had been repaired, Brechlin secured an audience with Queen Cirmar. She found the queen in her inner chamber sitting on her bed, teary-eyed and emotional.

"My Liege," said Brechlin, "I apologize for insisting on this meeting, but Tarmot has made himself unavailable, and time is getting short. We must plan the evacuation of the city."

"Leave? The city? Our new home?" she asked, speaking as

if she were a child.

"Yes. The enemy moves slowly, and I believe we have a reasonable chance of moving the citizens to Drumel. Maybe there—"

"Tarmot won't come out of his chamber!" blurted Queen Cirmar in a cascade of tears. "He won't talk to me!"

Brechlin sat next to her and took her hand. She had compassion for her, despite the pressing events at hand.

Queen Cirmar looked thankfully at Brechlin. "You have always been a faithful friend, haven't you, Brechlin?"

"Yes, my Liege. Till my last dying breath."

Queen Cirmar clasped Brechlin's hand with both of hers and looked earnestly into her face. "You will talk to him, won't you? He must come to me. We must face this adversity together. Talk to him."

"My Queen, I...I don't think my involvement would help."

"Please try, Brechlin. For my sake. I can't stand this treatment—his ignoring me."

Brechlin looked away. She could not hide her feelings well and didn't want the queen to see the disgust in her face. It had been obvious to her the first time she met Tarmot that he was a manipulating, cowardly weasel. It wouldn't help to say this to the queen, especially now. But she wouldn't be surprised if this didn't turn out well for her.

"I will go to Tarmot's chamber," she said firmly. "I will try to reason with him. For your sake and for the sake of the city. For he is marshal of our army, and we cannot begin our evacuation without the cooperation of the army. But I tell you this: don't expect much. I suspect he fears the enemy's sword and has revealed his true character."

She left Queen Cirmar in a swell of sobs and walked down

the hall to Tarmot's personal chamber. There, she found two guards barring the way.

"We have orders from the marshal," said the larger one. "He is not to be disturbed."

Brechlin didn't blink. "It is of the utmost importance I speak with him. I take full responsibility."

"I am sorry, General Brechlin," continued the large guard, "but if you make any move toward this door, you shall be..."

Brechlin's frustrated rage erupted. Before the heavyset guards could react, she drew her sword from its sheath and rammed the hilt deep into the solar plexus of the larger guard. As he bent over in agony, she whipped the tip of her sword next to the other guard's neck. The guard froze, his sword still not fully removed from its sheath.

"Like I said," began Brechlin, her angry face indicating to the guard that this was a dangerous situation, "it is of the utmost importance I see Tarmot. The safety of the city is at stake. Must I take your life to gain access?"

The guard raised his hands above his head. "No, my General," he managed and backed away.

Brechlin placed her boot on the backside of the larger guard, still doubled over, and roughly pushed him aside. She banged on Tarmot's door with the hilt of her sword as loudly as she could, but there was no response. She turned to the guard still standing.

"Open it," she said.

"But I have no key," he responded.

"I don't give a damn!" she exclaimed, once again brandishing her sword. "Get that door open, now!"

The guard slammed his shoulder into the door, but it was heavy oak, and it took minutes to break through. Brechlin rushed through the antechamber and into Tarmot's office.

Normally filled with expensive knickknacks and tapestries, it had been stripped bare. And, as she had already suspected, Tarmot was nowhere to be found. She went back to the guards at the doorway. The larger one was groaning on the floor. She turned to the one still on his feet.

"Where is he?" she demanded.

"He left," he replied with uncertainty.

"I can see that!" exclaimed Brechlin. "Where did he go?"

"He left yesterday. He said he had a meeting outside the walls and that it was important for the morale of the city that it seem like he were still here."

"Did it make sense to you that it would be good for the morale of our city for the marshal to lock himself inside his office during a siege?" asked Brechlin incredulously.

"It is not mine to question," said the guard.

"Fool!" exclaimed Brechlin, shaking her head in dismay. She shoved the man aside and proceeded back down the hall.

Jern's Solace

"Perhaps he did leave the city for a meeting," said Queen Cirmar in a pathetic whine. "Maybe he caught wind of an alliance."

"No, my Queen," replied Brechlin in a solemn tone. "He would have mentioned it to someone. And besides, who else is there?"

"The pirate tribes of the Southern Cays! Yes! He had a meeting with Desmondi!"

"No, my Queen!" said Brechlin, more firmly than Queen Cirmar had ever heard her speak. "He is gone. He feared the doom of the city and has abandoned us...and you. I dislike speaking to you so, but our time is short. We must save our people."

Queen Cirmar stared at Brechlin with an uncomprehending gaze. Brechlin watched her lip quiver, and then the queen burst out in a spasm of sobs, pressing her face into her hands. Brechlin gave her a few minutes before continuing.

"My Queen," she said in a soft but firm voice, "I suggest you appoint someone as marshal of the army so we can begin our exodus to Drumel. These walls may fall at any moment."

Queen Cirmar uncovered her teary face and look beseechingly up at Brechlin. "I'm sorry for my treatment of you, my dear Brechlin. But the city needs you. Will you please re-assume the duties of marshal?"

"I will tend to everything," replied Brechlin. "I will come to you when it's time to leave."

Brechlin bid the queen farewell and softly closed the door behind her. She hustled toward garrison headquarters.

* * *

Later that afternoon, Flackard entered Chimber's and Jern's chamber just outside the garrison barracks. He looked around appreciatively. They had a small cottage to themselves, complete with a spacious fireplace and two berths filled with hay for sleeping.

"Pretty decent accommodations," he observed. "Especially compared to what most of us grunts in the garrison get—a cot in a large room with thirty other farting grunts."

Chimber snorted. "It's comfortable. Better than Wolfglen Forest, anyway. But I still have a farting grunt in the room," he added, pointing at Jern.

"Well, time to get uncomfortable," said Flackard. "We're leaving the city. Evacuation begins first thing tomorrow morning."

"Tomorrow morning!" cried Jern. "We're leaving Cegril to those...things?"

Flackard nodded solemnly. "The walls are compromised and will collapse any minute, so we can't stay. We'll make a stand at Drumel. And we'll need your help to move as many of our citizens there as possible."

"We'll be ready," said Chimber. "It's not like we have a lot to pack."

"Happy to serve the queen," added Jern, "and to tell you the truth, I would value the opportunity to put some distance between ourselves and that constant clanging."

"There is more," said Flackard. "Tarmot has fled the city. Brechlin is now Marshal Brechlin once again. She is meeting with city leaders and officers at the palace assembly hall at seven today. She invited the two of you to join her."

"So, we're now considered leaders of Cegril," observed Chimber with a bright smile. "Hey, Jern, we're moving up in the world."

"They say that the cream rises to the top, no matter how big the urn," replied Jern with a smirk.

Captain Flackard shook his head. "Don't let it go to your heads," he said as he made for the door. "See you when the temple bell tolls seven times."

* * *

The meeting went on for hours.

Wooden benches with no backs filled the room. They were occupied by the anxious leaders of Cegril's citizenry. The logistics of moving the entire body of Cegril's population was of no interest to Jern. At first, he escaped the tedium by trying to catch the eye of Schmie, who was sitting several benches behind him, but other than a brief wave and smile when they first settled into their places, she steadfastly ignored him. Frustrated and bored, he urged Chimber, who was sitting next to him, to leave the meeting.

"This is important, Jern," he replied in a whisper. "Pay attention!"

Jern tried to listen for a few more minutes but finally could stand it no longer. He left his seat and meandered out into the palace corridor before slipping through a side exit and into a beautiful courtyard. The sun was low, so he sat on a marble bench and took in the delightful fireflies and the refreshing breeze. It was a welcome retreat from the ponderous tedium of the meeting.

Above where he sat was a balcony, its balustrade intertwined with vines and abloom with purple flowers. The chirp of crickets filled his ears. The din of the dead army hacking away at the city's walls was white noise in the background.

Moving an entire city requires lots of planning, thought Jern. *I'm glad it's not my responsibility. But why, I wonder, is Chimber making it his?*

As he sat there, he found his thoughts wandering back to Saffral's quiet smile. He wondered how she was faring. *I'll find a way. I must get her off that island.*

As he pondered what his life with Saffral would be like, he heard a soft sobbing coming from the balcony over his head. He looked up but saw nothing through the balcony's balustrade, as it was thickly covered with vines and the light was fading. He could tell it was a woman's voice, and the deep anguish expressed in those sobs moved him to pity. Perhaps someone lost a loved one in the battle. Or maybe there were simply distraught over the thought of leaving their home unprotected to those walking sacks of meat.

Unable to restrain himself, Jern deftly scampered up a vine-wrapped column to the balcony. He peeked over the balustrade and there he saw Queen Cirmar herself, lost in her sorrow and sobbing into her hands.

Jern, whose notions of proper decorum and court etiquette were vague, followed his soft heart and plopped over the rail.

"My Queen, you are distressed. Can I be of any service?"

Startled out of her sorrow, Queen Cirmar gave a frightened jump backward as she looked up to see Jern suddenly standing beside her.

"I am Jern, my Liege. I was with General Brechlin when she returned with the Lomitheri."

The queen wiped her eyes with her handkerchief.

"Jern, of course," she managed. "I remember you. What are you doing here?"

"I heard sobbing and wanted to see if I could help. I'm sorry if I'm not being proper."

"No, no. It is I who am sorry. I shouldn't have been sobbing so loudly. Not very dignified of me, is it? But thank you for your concern."

Jern plopped down next to her on her short bench. "Tell me what's troubling you."

Queen Cirmar's eyes opened wide at this brazen act, but she relaxed as she looked into Jern's sincere and open face. "I'm so weak. Tarmot has left me. He has abandoned the city to its fate. I was such a fool." Once again, she succumbed to a wave of sobbing spasms. "I thought...he really...loved me," she managed between breaths.

As with many people, Jern had guessed Tarmot's true mettle soon after meeting him, but he appreciated how powerful a force love could be.

"Pine for your loss, my Queen, for that is pure. But do not despise yourself, for we all know that love is blind."

"And blind I was! And now the city is in peril. Had I not listened to him—"

"Tarmot did not summon this macabre army, and we see now that there is little we could have done to stop them. You bear no burden or responsibility for our predicament."

"Thank you," said Queen Cirmar. "I know you're right. But still...if only he had stayed, we could have faced them together."

Once again, the tears washed over the queen. Jern sat quietly beside her, venturing to hold her hand and let the waves of emotion surge through her body. After a few minutes, she settled down enough to speak. "I have to get control of myself. My people need me."

"You needn't worry yourself, my Queen," replied Jern. "General Brechlin and the other leaders have things well in hand."

Queen Cirmar folded her hands in her lap and looked down at them. "Of that, I'm sure. But despite the deep pain in my breast, I must be strong. As queen, I can do much for the morale of the people."

She stood up at these words, her fists clenched in determination, but a second later, she collapsed again in sobs. "Oh, God, I hurt so badly."

Her honest sorrow moved Jern. He fumbled into his shirt for his pendant. "My Queen, there is something I want to give to you, something that has eased my pain. Though your pain is not from a physical wound, perhaps it will ease yours too." He placed the necklace around her neck. "It is called the Tear of Life."

Queen Cirmar held the pendant in her hand as she looked it over.

"It has magical powers," added Jern. "It stopped my pain."

Queen Cirmar continued to examine it closely, all signs of her distress having left her face.

"Where did you get this?" she asked, looking deeply into

Jern's face.

"From Pith Isle, my Queen. From a lady there. I was injured and she..."

"But where did *she* get it?"

"Oh, well, if I must tell all, she's the wife of the prison warden. She got it from some special prisoner they had—"

"Ferrin!" interjected the queen.

* * *

For the third time in his life, Jern was on the deck of a ship as the morning sun appeared above the horizon. The sudden chain of events had excited him, but he was also exhausted and even overwhelmed. In a flash of insight, Queen Cirmar had realized that the special prisoner held at Pith Isle Prison was Ferrin, the Medium of the White Mountain. Dran was keeping him alive, for if he had not, the Gray Mountain would lose its power. So instead, Dran had him imprisoned in the bowels of Pith Isle, far away from Drumel and the White Mountain.

When Jern first spoke to her, Queen Cirmar had been a pathetic figure. But her realization that Ferrin was found had transformed her and given her new purpose. She led Jern to the barracks of her elite Royal Guard, and they had immediately launched the city's war sloop in the cover of darkness. Her plan was to confront Kruuger and free Ferrin, and then return to Capital Island as soon as possible.

"With the White Medium restored to power, it just might tip the balance in our favor," Queen Cirmar had said as the sloop had set sail.

"But why the secrecy?" asked Jern.

"I don't want the citizens to think their queen is abandoning them. I left a letter for Marshal Brechlin. With a little luck, we'll be there at Drumel when they arrive, and with Ferrin at his post. That could change everything."

"Pardon my lack of insight, but I don't really understand. With Ferrin at his post, our wounded troops will heal much faster and return to battle more quickly, but how does that help us destroy that which is already dead?"

"Truly, I cannot say," replied the queen somberly, "but it is written into the Covenant that the power of two of the Gludemic Mountains will overcome the power of the one. We have the Blue Mountain already working for us. We need to figure out how both the Blue and the White can overcome Dran."

Now, with a new day blooming, Jern leaned back against the rail and took in the morning sun. Around him, several large, armed men were asleep on the deck and steadily snoring. Queen Cirmar, who was down below in the cabin, would lead their group to free Ferrin. And, Jern hoped, Saffral. So, he relaxed as the rising sun brought its brilliance to the day and let his hopes for Saffral's liberation grow.

Exodus

The sharp rap at her door in the early morning annoyed Brechlin. Exhausted from the long and tedious hours of yesterday's planning, she and Chimber had collapsed together on her bed with barely a caress between them. For decorum's sake, she had always urged Chimber out of her chambers before her officers came calling in the morning hours, but now it was too late.

Oh, well. Chimber in my bed will surprise no one. Besides, there's much to be done today. I'd better get started.

She opened the door and was surprised to see a palace messenger rather than an officer. Apologetically, he handed her a sealed envelope, bowed, and departed. Brechlin read through the brief message and sat down on the bed next to Chimber's sleeping form. She ran her fingers through his dark hair as he awoke and looked up at her with his bright smile.

"Good morning," he said. "I see I'm still in your bed."

She looked at him fondly. "It is fitting, for it may be our last opportunity. It's a pity, however, that all we did was sleep."

"We were exhausted. But today is a new day," said Chimber with a mischievous grin, and his hand reached out to caress her bare thigh.

Brechlin smiled but sighed. "We must seize the day. We

have an entire city to evacuate. And there is news."

Chimber sat up in the bed. "News?"

"It concerns Queen Cirmar and your friend, Jern. Apparently, the two of them, along with members of the Royal Guard, have left the palace under the cover of darkness."

"Jern!" exclaimed Chimber. "Abandoned the city?"

"No, not abandoned. They are going to Pith Isle. Queen Cirmar believes Ferrin is imprisoned there, and they intend on freeing him and bringing him back to us."

"The White Medium on Pith Isle? We were just there."

"We must keep their departure secret. The city's morale is bad enough as it is without our citizens thinking their queen has abandoned them."

Chimber squeezed Brechlin's hand and kissed her on the cheek. "Looks like you're in charge, my dear Marshal. Let's get it done."

* * *

Many of Cegril's frightened citizens had gathered in the town plaza. At this early hour, it would normally have been filled with market stalls, but on this morning, it was filled with panic and fear. Groups of people, some angry, others distressed, were clustered together in tight groups, speaking energetically. Over their excited din could be heard the sound of the cadaver swords chipping away at the city's walls.

Brechlin and Chimber climbed up on an elevated podium with their backs to the wall. Chimber banged together two swords to get everyone's attention.

"Citizens of Cegril," bellowed Brechlin in a loud voice, projecting over the now muted crowd. "As you all know, the walls of our fair city are in danger of being breached at any moment. The macabre host outside bears a deep malice toward us, and we believe they will kill every man, woman, and child once they enter our gates. There are no terms of surrender offered. Nor will they offer any. They are a mindless, killing mass, and the time has come for us to abandon our city and make for the safety of Drumel."

"But our homes!" rang out a voice in the crowd. "Are we to just leave them in the hands of the enemy?" A cacophony of other voices echoed similar concerns.

"Yes. We abandon Cegril to save our lives," said Brechlin, "and we are not here today to debate the issue. This was done for hours on end yesterday by the city's leaders."

"If you choose to stay, you do so at your own peril," added Chimber, still standing at Brechlin's side.

Brechlin glanced at the wall behind her. "Now listen, all. We must leave without alerting our enemy, and this is possible since they seem to be intent on only one thing—taking down the city walls. We must leave through the west gate and take the Lackal road before veering south along the old Drumel Pike. If we are careful, I believe we can escape detection. They will hopefully be preoccupied with their task long enough to allow us to reach Drumel. But, should they pursue us, they move slowly, so we should be able to stay ahead of them, assuming we march without rest."

"That's over thirty miles!" cried a merchant. "Surely you don't expect us to march that far without stopping?"

"It will be difficult, but we have no choice," replied Brechlin. "We will carry the feeble and sick in wagons. All others must walk or, if you have them, ride horses. Bring no other livestock. Take with you only what you can carry on your backs or the backs of your pack animals. There will be food at Drumel."

"But they will raze the city," cried out another voice.

"They may," returned Brechlin. "That's what they did to Keeman, and they dismantled many buildings at Gretly to build their transports. But there's nothing that can be done about that. We flee for our lives and hope that Drumel will offer us a chance to overcome this unholy menace. The evacuation begins in one hour. We will turn back anyone attempting to carry more than a few essentials. It is for your own good."

Brechlin left the podium as the frightened crowd erupted with objections. Chimber banged his two swords again with a loud crack and announced, "You have one hour. Do not mill around here, or we will leave you behind. And there will be no army here to protect you."

Chimber felt for the despairing people before him. He had seen what the enemy did to Keeman after overcoming its walls, but there was nothing he could do other than evacuate the citizens as smoothly as possible. He, too, left the podium and made his way through the crowd to his chambers to pack up what few belongings he possessed.

* * *

The port city of Cegril was located at the northeastern corner of Capital Island, which had a narrow coastal plain that widened as one traveled farther south. Behind the city, to the west, rolling hills dominated the landscape. Through these hills, a lightly used road meandered from the city to the town of Lackal, on the western shore of Capital Island.

Brechlin and the troops of Cegril's army watched as a long snake of humanity poured forth from Cegril's west gate and made their way along the narrow road. Led by a small band of officers at the vanguard, including Captain Flackard, the plan of the exodus was to veer south at the tiny village of Bluer, which was little more than a cluster of shacks and sheep corrals, and follow a trail south across open country all the way to Drumel.

Brechlin had positioned mounted scouts so they could watch the cadaver army, but the city walls shielded the evacuation from their view. If a section of the wall were to give way, there would be no army available to clog their advance. If the enemy left their positions along the east wall and advanced to the other side of the city, the people of Cegril would be vulnerable. The result would be a massacre. She knew that she, and those under her, would likely have to give their lives to protect the fleeing citizens, but the gamble had to be taken, for the alternative was the certain doom of all.

Brechlin hoped that the last of the populace would pass through the west gate by day's end. *There will likely be people left behind,* she thought. *But what can we do?*

She sat on her mount, watching the people stream out of the gate and occasionally glancing toward the corner of the city walls from whence the enemy would approach, making sure all was clear. While she watched, her thoughts turned to what they would find at Drumel when the population of Cegril arrived. Two years ago, Drumel had been a bustling, crowded town. The oldest city in all the Dalmeer Islands, it contained great convalescence halls packed close to the base of Mount Krin. Back when the White Medium was at his post, injured citizens filled the roads to Drumel—broken limbs, bleeding wounds, painful burns—doing their best to make their way to the healing powers of the White Mountain.

The convalescence halls were close enough to the mountain for its ambient healing powers to affect them. The White Medium, however, could focus the powers of Mount Krin and heal most wounds in short order, typically within hours. But now, since the White Medium had been missing for two years, the convalescence halls lay mostly empty. Many of those citizens of Cegril most in need could be housed there. The less fortunate would sleep in the streets or, if lucky, a spare bed in the home of one of Drumel's residents.

The most important consideration, however, was that Drumel had city walls. Undamaged, solid stone walls, made in the old style. They were not as large or sturdy as Cegril's great walls, but they would delay the enemy for a while longer. Maybe by then, they would have figured out a way to defeat an army of malignant corpses.

Dran's Drumel Stratagem

Ilsher had just descended the many steps leading down from Dran's lofty perch on the shoulder of the Gray Mountain and entered the Ascension Chamber. There, Ginthar intercepted her. He was excited and out of breath, his face lined with worry.

"Why so distressed, Ginthar?" she asked, looking him over with some concern.

"I have to get to Dran," he replied in a loud, breathy whisper. "After I catch my breath...I've been down at the wharf...word has reached us that the people of Cegril...are leaving through the west gate. If Dran acts quickly, he can turn the host upon them. They would be vulnerable."

"You will do no such thing," said Ilsher. "I have attended to his needs and given him direction. All is in good hands."

"But... Are you forbidding me to go to him?"

"That is correct. Sorry if I wasn't clear."

"But the city? Our window of opportunity is narrow. We should strike!"

"No," replied Ilsher. "We will not. I, too, received word that the citizens were leaving. I instructed Dran to let them leave and to focus on taking the city."

"Why? Now is our chance," insisted Ginthar, his gravelly whisper more of a growl. He paced back and forth with uncertainty, glancing up at Dran's high perch through the windows of the chamber.

"Ginthar, if you disobey my direct order and disturb Dran after I said not to, I will have you severely punished. Do you understand?"

Ginthar did not answer but continued pacing. And then he threw his arms into the air in a gesture of exasperation. "But why must you meddle?" he mumbled. "All of our efforts and hopes come down to this moment. The city itself counts for nothing. It is the people we must defeat."

"Ginthar, I think you have little confidence in my judgment. And your tone of voice troubles me."

"Blast you!" cried Ginthar, shaking his head vigorously and speaking with an articulation unusual for him. "You are ruining everything. Why does Dran allow his meddling child to interfere with our carefully laid plans? Unbelievable!"

Ilsher looked down at the floor, while slowly rubbing her temples. "Ginthar, my dear, you have crossed a line." She quietly walked to the doorway leading down into the compound's living area and beckoned the guard stationed on the other side.

"My good sir," Ilsher said to the guard after he entered the room. "Please hold the blade of your sword to the throat of this man."

The guard looked at Ilsher with puzzlement for only the briefest of moments. He pushed Ginthar back against a column and held the sword point at his throat while holding him by the breast of his stained tunic.

"Ilsher," gasped Ginthar, "I am only thinking of Dran's best interest."

Ilsher smiled. "I know you think so, Ginthar, but you must never question my judgment. You want to attack the citizenry of Cegril now, as they leave the city. Our slow-moving cadaver army would destroy many, but many others would disperse. Perhaps even most, especially if Cegril's army sacrifices itself in their defense. It would take weeks to find them all, and by then, the gray powder will have lost its virtue and Dran would have lost control of the cadavers."

"But if we killed enough..."

"Silence!" snapped Ilsher. "I encouraged Dran to let the people leave, for they will try to make one last stand at Drumel. But Drumel's walls, just as Cegril's, will fall. And then, my dear Ginthar, what will the citizens do?"

"They...well, Drumel is built into a walled valley. Yes, I see now."

"Yes, Ginthar. Now you see. Once the walls of Drumel are breached, the people of Cegril will be trapped. We can destroy them all if we wish or threaten them with total annihilation in exchange for whatever concessions we ask."

Ginthar lowered his eyes. "Yes, it is a good plan. I was wrong to question your judgment."

"Yes, you were, Ginthar," replied Ilsher in a sweet, almost cheerful tone. "And you must be punished. I will take a finger."

"What?" said Ginthar, his eyes wide, his expression uncomprehending.

"I will take a finger, as a sincere token of your remorse. But I will allow you to choose which finger. We owe you as much."

"But," said Ginthar. He attempted to move away from the guard's grasp. The guard pressed the point of his sword deeper into the folds of Ginthar's neck.

"Do not attempt to move, Ginthar," Ilsher said, shaking her head. "You may irreparably damage yourself."

"Dran will hear of this! This outrage will not—"

"Ginthar, choose a finger, or the guard will choose it for you."

"No. Please no." Ginthar began shaking. He looked up at the guard and at Ilsher. "Please, no. I will never dispute your judgment. Never."

"I know you won't," sang out Ilsher. She nodded at the guard and walked to the rail, where the waves of the sea surged a hundred feet below her, hurling themselves against the rocky cliffs along the shore. The crashing sound of the turbulent waters filled the room, and Ilsher listened with fascination as Ginthar's high-pitched scream pierced the low-pitched rumble.

Pith Isle Incursion

With the sloop anchored just out of view from Pith Isle's small village, Queen Cirmar, Jern, and the five guards rowed to shore behind a jutting headland. They climbed the low ridge that separated their landing from the village and looked down on the small cluster of buildings below them. It was peaceful and quiet. Just beyond the village, they saw the low-lying gray prison walls, and next to it, along the riverbank, Kruuger's ornate three-story home.

"The guards number twelve, maybe more," said Jern. "Do we have enough men to force the issue if they prove uncooperative?"

"Do not concern yourself over their number," replied Jarida, the Captain of the Royal Guard. "But we need to devise a means of entering their gates."

"Hmm," said Jern, gazing at Kruuger's home. "I have an idea. But we must pass through the town. It would be best for everyone to don their cloaks."

"Where are we going?" asked Queen Cirmar.

"To enlist the services of an angel, my Liege," answered Jern. "Are you joining us? They may resist. There may be a struggle."

"Yes, there probably will be a struggle, and perhaps there

is a chance I could be harmed. But, I am queen of these lands, so my presence may defuse the need for conflict. And, as you may have an opportunity to see, these men protect me well."

As the party mutely followed Jern through the town, he looked over the members of the Royal Guard. All five were large, well-built men. What impressed Jern most was their quiet self-assurance. They did not seem concerned about what might be an unbalanced fight. His own confidence rose, and he felt proud to be in their company, one of their team, and in the immediate service of the queen.

As they made their way through the little hamlet, the size of their party was large enough to attract the attention of the few villagers who were about. Since their cloaks hid their battle armor and identity, this attention remained mere curiosity rather than alarm.

"Has Kruuger hired new staff?" wondered one villager to his companion as they worked splitting wooden shingles for the village roofs.

"It looks like it," replied the other, wiping his brow.

The first gazed at the group and shook his head. "They are making them big these days," he observed before returning to the work at hand.

Jern led the group along the path that followed the riverbank and then to the rear entrance of Kruuger's home. "We had best break through quickly," he suggested. "If Kruuger is home, he'll sound an alarm if given the chance."

The men nodded, and two of them, whom Jern realized for the first time were identical twins, approached the door. With just a quick nod at one another, the twins slammed their muscled shoulders into the door with an exactly-timed movement. The door yielded to the force of impact, and the group entered the house, weapons bared.

Inside they found a lone woman. Their unexpected entrance startled her, and she backed away, but a bolted chain attached to her leg prevented her from going far. Her face was wet with tears and contained red whelps and bruises.

"Saffral, it's Jern!" cried Jern as he approached her, looking at the chain and her face with dismay. "What has he done to you?"

It took Saffral a minute to calm down from her fright. The members of the Royal Guard were still cloaked, but they were large and intimidating. Jern gently took her hand.

"It's me, the gravedigger. Remember, you gave me this?" he said as he showed her the Tear of Life. She studied his face.

"You—you're that naked little fellow," she said with a slight flash of a smile.

"That was me." Jern smiled, unembarrassed by the memory. "We're here to take you away from all this."

"But who are these people? And where is your gravedigger friend?"

Queen Cirmar approached Saffral and drew back the hood of her cloak.

"Do you recognize me?" she softly asked.

"Why, yes," she replied, looking at her in wonder. "You're Queen Cirmar."

She smiled at Saffral. "We have come not only to rescue you, as your valiant friend has said, but we believe that this prison holds the Medium of the White Mountain, and we hope you will help us gain entry within its walls."

Saffral looked over the group once again and back at Queen Cirmar. Those standing around her watched her look of fright and despair transform into something new. Her face became

275

angry and determined.

"Oh, I can get you in," she said eagerly, "and I know where they keep their special prisoner. But I doubt they will cooperate. Do you have more men?"

"It won't be necessary," said Queen Cirmar, confidently smiling at her. "Jarida, have this chain removed."

After the anklet had been removed from Saffral's petite ankle, Jern grasped her foot, bruised and swollen, and gently caressed it.

"Kruuger will pay for this," he said intently.

"Thank you, Jern, for thinking of me," said Saffral, now giving him her full smile. "I wish I had left with you when I had the chance."

"And now?" asked Jern.

"And now, I would follow you anywhere," she said as she got up on her feet. She looked at Queen Cirmar. "There is a side entrance, along the riverbank wall, that Kruuger and I use to access the prison. I will gain you entry."

The group followed Saffral along the river path, past where Jern and Chimber had taken a swim, and up to the rear wall of the prison. There, they found a small but solid metal door. There were no windows or other entrances along this side of the prison, so the group stationed themselves on either side of the door, out of view, while Saffral knocked. A guard pulled back a small panel in the center of the door, and espying Saffral, opened it to let her in.

"Thank you, Turb," she said as she stepped past him while he held the door open, but as he released it, a large booted foot blocked the door, preventing it from closing. Turb looked up in astonishment to see the hooded Jarida with sword drawn and several hooded figures behind him. He released the door, and with catlike speed dashed off down the short hall to the outer courtyard. Jarida pursued him for a step or two but then halted and turned back to the others.

"Quick little bugger," he said with annoyance. "He will sound the alarm, but we're inside now. We had better move but stay prepared. Your Highness, you and Saffral please follow behind us. Jern, you guard the rear."

Jern was not inclined to complain about this unglamorous assignment and fell in with the rest of the group as they passed from the hall into the bright courtyard. It was empty until they were about halfway across, when the prison guards started filing out of the L-shaped building on the far side. There were twelve of them, including Turb, and they formed a line with Captain Charkol standing in front. He wore a smug, confident face. After all, the prison guards outnumbered this unknown band by more than two to one.

"Is that you, Saffral?" asked Charkol. "I don't know who your friends are, but they have trespassed upon these prison grounds, and I'm afraid we must arrest them. Please lay down your arms, and no one will get hurt...much."

Queen Cirmar pushed Jarida aside and moved to the front of their group. She removed her hood and cloak, revealing her ornate clothing, and stood before them exuding authority.

"It's the queen!" gasped one guard.

"I am Queen Cirmar, your rightful sovereign," she announced. "We believe you are holding Ferrin, the Medium of the White Mountain, and I command you bring him to us at once."

Captain Charkol chuckled. "Well, if you command us and all...but the problem is that we serve a new ruler now. And what have you done for us, anyway? Dran pays us gold, and plenty. And he has promised us land on Capital Island."

"We'll be lords," blurted out Turb.

"Yeah, we're gonna be lords," repeated Charkol. "A new regime is coming, and your time has come and gone, Queen Cirmar. So, I say this to you respectfully—surrender or die!"

Queen Cirmar looked over the group of prison guards and shook her head. They were strong men but oafish, yet they were confident and defiant, even before their queen. No doubt they were used to bullying those around them when in a tavern or down in the cells.

In a different tone that could only be described as haughty, Queen Cirmar continued. "I wanted to avoid bloodshed, but since we're all doomed to die at your hand, I think it proper I introduce you to my escorts." She turned and waved her hand at the men standing behind her. "These men are my Royal Guard. Selected from among the champions of our land. They dedicate their swords and their lives solely to the protection of the royal family. The man on my immediate right is Jarida. He has been witnessed to kill four men with one swing of his sword."

At the mention of his name, Jarida deftly threw off his cloak, revealing his ornate suit of leather and armor. He whipped his heavy sword through the air with amazing speed and then came to attention with a distinctive smile of glee on his face, sword extending in front of him at a menacing angle.

"The man on my left is Murmlo."

She gestured to a tall man who also discarded his cloak, revealing a bare, muscle-laden torso with a painted sarong wrapped around his waist. In his large hands, he held a long, stout spear.

"He can throw his spear through a solid oak door. And

behind him are the twin brothers Lavil and Brem."

The twins shed their coats with their swords coming to the ready. Their bulging and defined muscles shone with sweat. Both men growled.

"They are both the strongest men in the land," continued the queen. "Each can rip off a man's head with one arm. And to the right of them is Que Barth, who has been Capital Island's champion swordsman for sixteen years straight."

Que Barth discarded his cloak to reveal his elegant garb of braided leather and silver plate, and with a precise and controlled flourish of his sword, assumed his fighting stance.

"And last, but not least," began Queen Cirmar, looking back at Jern, "is Jern the Valiant. Small in stature, but powerful in character."

Jern smiled and waved but opted not to remove his cloak.

"Now," said Queen Cirmar, turning back to the prison guards, "all we want is Kruuger and Ferrin. And even though we are outnumbered, if you stand in our way, every single one of you will die, and these men will barely lose breath."

As if on cue, the five champions uttered a deep visceral grunt and, in unison, whirled their weapons in the air, abruptly coming to a ready stance. They walked to the front of the queen, forming a single line of imposing warriors. Queen Cirmar stood next to Jern and Saffral in the rear. Jern noticed that both women now brandished swords and thought it best to draw his own.

The guards looked somewhat unsure. Although they all had military training, they had never faced the likes of those who stood before them. Jern guessed that some of these elite warriors may have been sufficiently well-known that their deeds were discussed in local taverns.

But Captain Charkol was made of sterner stuff. He shouted to his men.

"Have no concern. They men may have reputations, but we outnumber them and can take them down. You will be the talk of the land. Sergeant Jikes, your ear."

Charkol exchanged a few words in a whisper with Sergeant Jikes. The sergeant went back to his station and spoke in muted tones to several of his men. The men spread out in a wider front, with Charkol and Turb on either flank.

"Now!" cried Charkol. Abruptly, ten of the guards ran straight toward the five champions while Charkol and Turb held back. There was a clang of metal and the weapons of both sides whirled through the air. While the Royal Guard was engaged, Charkol and Turb dashed around the flanks of the warriors to reach Jern, Saffral, and Queen Cirmar at their rear. The idea was sound. If they managed to hold Queen Cirmar under their sword point, they could compel her Royal Guard to do as they wished.

But almost immediately, there were loud cries of pain from the prison guards. And as Charkol and Turb fell upon Jern, Saffral, and Queen Cirmar, they were surprised to find that all three stood their ground and brandished their swords with conviction. Charkol and Turb swung their swords aggressively, but the three defenders parried their initial blows, though they began to back away. A second more, and the strength and training of Charkol and Turb would have overwhelmed Jern and the women, but their surprising stand had given the Royal Guard all the time they needed.

Jarida and Que Barth, having dispatched two men each, quick as light fell upon Captain Charkol and Turb, who immediately had to divert their attention away from the queen. The other three champions, whose immediate opponents had either fallen or run, stood before the remaining guards, protecting the back of Jarida and Que Barth.

Jern saw Que Barth's sword blur through the air and heard the clang of metal as it struck Charkol's hilt. Before the prison Captain could reposition his sword, Jern saw another blur, and Charkol's severed head tumbled through the air. His headless body, spurting blood everywhere, ambled a few steps before collapsing. Turb had turned to face Jarida, and from his position behind Turb, Jern saw the tip of Jarida's sword emerge from Turb's back. Jarida withdrew the sword, and Turb slumped to the ground, his gurgling scream fading.

Jarida and Que Barth joined the other three guards, but there was little to do. Most of the prison guards lay lifeless on the ground, but across the courtyard, two guards who had escaped the fray were desperately trying to open the main gate. Murmlo pulled his massive spear out of the body of one of the fallen guards and threw the missile with incredible force, catching one man in the back, piercing his plated torso and pinning him to the wooden gate. The last guard scurried over the top of the gate to dash away and tell the story to any who cared to listen.

It had all happened so fast that Jern's head was reeling. But, his first concern was Saffral.

"Are you okay?" he asked her, looking over her from head to toe.

"My little warrior, looking after me once again," she replied, smiling at him. "I'm unharmed. The blood on my leg belongs, I think, to him," she continued, pointing to one of the slain guards.

"We must find Kruuger," announced Queen Cirmar.

"His office is this way," said Jern, and he led them to the main door of the administration building.

Kruuger's Hell

As Jern, Queen Cirmar, and the rest of their party burst into Kruuger's office, all they found was a frightened clerk sitting at a small side desk.

"Where is Kruuger?" demanded Jarida, a demand he accented by pointing his sword at the man's face.

"He's...he's gone!" said the assistant. "He went to town to...get a drink at the Saber Slash. Find him there." The man's eyes nervously darted from Jarida to the other warriors in the group.

"I know where he is!" cried Saffral. She pointed to the wall. "He goes in here to count his money." She pushed her shoulder into what appeared to be a nondescript section of paneling, and the wall rotated to reveal a small interior chamber with a desk and chair, and at the desk was the tall, thin frame of Kruuger. He jumped up, obviously afraid, but trying to sound outraged.

"What is the meaning of this!" he cried, sounding passably authoritative. "You are trespassing on prison property!"

"Which is owned by the crown," retorted Queen Cirmar. Kruuger recognized her with a shock. "Your game here is over," she added.

Kruuger noticed Saffral standing next to the queen. "You

vile bitch!" he yelled. "You will pay for your treachery."

At this, Jern walked up to Kruuger and slapped him so hard on the face that he crumpled to the floor. "I've waited a long time to do that," Jern said with evident pleasure. As Kruuger got up on all fours, Saffral ran up and kicked him solidly in his side. Once again, he crumpled to the floor.

"You are the one who'll pay!" she said with great intensity.

"That's enough!" said Queen Cirmar. "At least for now. Kruuger, we know you have Ferrin here. So take us to him now, or your agony is just beginning."

"I don't go into the cells," whined Kruuger, now utterly defeated. "My poor vision doesn't allow me—"

"The queen said *now*!" growled Jarida, advancing his sword point to Kruuger's neck. Kruuger nodded and got to his feet. "Lead!" the captain commanded.

Hunched over and now timid, Kruuger led them to a lonely building in the middle of the prison courtyard. It was similar to the one in which Jern and Chimber had spent the night during their earlier visit to the prison, but Jern knew it housed the opening to the lower cells. Kruuger opened the door, and a blast of warm, fetid air rushed over the party. The odor was so foul that Queen Cirmar retched.

"Good Gludema, that's awful!" cried Jern, also on the verge of losing his meal as well.

"Are you okay, my Liege?" asked Jarida. Queen Cirmar nodded.

"Do you see what I mean?" asked Kruuger. "I would recommend sending—"

"Move it!" sternly interjected Jarida, pushing him in the back.

They waited for Queen Cirmar to wipe the traces of vomit

from her mouth, and all entered the small building, which contained nothing but a few chairs and a table. On the table were playing cards and dice, obviously where the prison guards spent their time. In the center of the floor was a large, weighted stone slab attached to a system of ropes and pulleys.

"He's down there," said Kruuger, pointing to the slab, "with the other prisoners."

"Under that slab?" Queen Cirmar asked. "How do they get air?"

"They're prisoners, my Liege," said Jern, "and prison ain't for fun. So I was told by the captain of the guards. You know, the one now missing his head."

Kruuger pulled on a cord, and the slab cantilevered back to reveal a dark opening and a renewed blast of foul air.

Jarida lit a torch and held it over the opening as he looked down. "The entrance is steep. There are no steps. Just a ladder. I'll go down with Kruuger. It's safer if the rest of you stay here." He turned to Kruuger. "I see side openings leading off the main shaft. I assume these are tunnels to the cells."

Kruuger nodded.

"Are there no lights?"

"Light would encourage prisoners to escape."

Jarida scowled. "A stinking, black hell. How far down is Ferrin?"

"The last one," replied Kruuger. "You can't miss it. Just go down to the bottom of the ladder, and you will find the opening."

"Don't worry, you will be leading the way," returned Jarida.

"But..." managed Kruuger. He looked over his captors with resignation and nodded. "If I must, but we must be careful. The prisoners' waste is dumped down the main shaft and has been piling up for some time. I have been told that it has accumulated to a high level."

"This shaft is where you dump their filth!" exclaimed Queen Cirmar. "No wonder it smells so foul. And they have to breathe it, with no circulation..." Her voice trailed off.

"They are prisoners, Your Majesty, enemies of the crown," whined Kruuger.

"Poor Ferrin," said Queen Cirmar, her face reflecting her thoughts about the horror of the Medium's situation.

"It was Dran, Your Majesty," stressed Kruuger. "He paid us gold, and lots of it, to keep Ferrin and keep him alive. We had to make sure he lived. So it stinks down there, sure, but we fed him regularly and gave him water. And it was just last week we let him come out of his cell and bathe in the guardhouse."

Queen Cirmar looked at him coldly. "Your generous nature tells us a lot about your character."

"Just a servant of the crown, Your Majesty," replied Kruuger, missing Queen Cirmar's sarcasm.

"A servant of Dran! Now, proceed down into that fetid hole and retrieve Ferrin. If he has perished, you will soon follow."

"Yes, Your Majesty."

Kruuger, then Jarida stepped down the ladder with torches in their hands. Jern peered down the shaft from above, watching the torch lights become dimmer and dimmer as the echoes of their steps on the ladder rungs became more distant. After many steps, the torches, now just dim points of light, shifted to the right and disappeared.

"I think they've entered a side shaft," Jern informed the group.

Queen Cirmar nodded. "How could someone like that man have achieved such a position of responsibility under my regime?"

"Don't blame yourself, my Queen," said Jern. "Blame Dran. Gold can bring out evil in many men who are otherwise a decent sort."

"Kruuger was never a decent sort," burst out Saffral. "Although, he is skilled in hiding his true nature."

"They're coming back up," said Jern, peering down the shaft.

After a few minutes, Jarida and Kruuger emerged from the opening with a pathetic, rail-thin person, nearly unrecognizable as a human. Naked, shaggy-haired, and covered with filth, he was breathing heavily from the exertion. Jarida, who had carried his emaciated frame up the ladder, gently released the old man as he collapsed on the floor, gasping convulsively. He squinted in the dim light of the guard shed.

Kruuger gestured toward the figure. "See. He lives."

Queen Cirmar's face became distorted with anger and pity.

"Your Majesty, the living conditions in the cells are indescribable," relayed Jarida. "It is a miracle he survives. The excrement dumped into the main shaft had risen above Ferrin's cell tunnel. The foul filth had contaminated it and was spilling into his cell."

"But no one informed me of that!" cried Kruuger.

"Silence!" exclaimed Queen Cirmar, her voice cold and menacing. "If I hear another word from your foul mouth, I will have you killed instantly!"

Kruuger nodded his head in assent. Queen Cirmar kneeled to Ferrin and placed a hand on his shoulder. "Ferrin, it's Queen Cirmar. Do you recognize me?"

Ferrin's breathing leveled off somewhat, and his eyes adjusted to the light. He looked at the queen.

"Your Majesty...why, yes," managed Ferrin as he looked from Queen Cirmar to the others standing there, and then down at his filthy, naked body. "I'm not...presentable...please, forgive..."

Ferrin sobbed. Jern draped his cloak over Ferrin's shoulders.

Queen Cirmar stood up and gazed furiously at Kruuger.

"When this is all over," she began, "I will investigate who hired you to administer this prison."

"Why, as to that, it was the General Counselor himself," replied Kruuger with a note of pride. "We were business associates in the past. We go way back."

"My God," said Queen Cirmar. "Tarmot!"

"Yes," said Kruuger, confused by Queen Cirmar's tone. "General Counselor Tarmot."

Tears welled up in the queen's eyes. "I was such an idiot!" She knelt once again beside Ferrin, shook off her tears, and took his hand. "It's all okay now, Ferrin. We've come to free you."

"Free me? Yes. It's been so long," said Ferrin, looking around once more.

"We'll take you back to Mount Krin," continued the queen. "To once again fulfill your office as Medium of the White Mountain."

"What did I do, Your Majesty? Why was I imprisoned?"

"No, Ferrin, you are not here for anything you did. It was Dran. He had you sent here while he attempts to take over our lands. Even now, he attacks Capital Island."

"Dran? We made him Krakul Gat. I suspected...we should have waited."

"Ferrin, now we need your help," said Queen Cirmar. She stood up and looked at Jarida. "Get Ferrin cleaned up, properly fed, and into a bed. We will let him rest in comfort this evening, but no more. We must return. In the meantime, remove every other prisoner from this hole and find a suitable place to keep them."

"Yes, Your Majesty, but what about the remaining prison staff?" asked Jarida.

"Take everyone associated with this facility and put them into those rank cells until we decide what to do with them, including that man!" exclaimed Queen Cirmar, pointing to Kruuger.

"But, Your Majesty," said Kruuger, "please be merciful. I'm not just a lowly administrator. Tarmot himself assigned me."

"Well then," said Queen Cirmar, her cold look unwavering, "a special person such as yourself deserves special accommodations. I think we have just the place."

Kruuger's eyes widened in horror. "You can't—"

"Oh, yes we can," said Jarida, smiling at Kruuger.

Jern and Saffral each took one of Ferrin's shoulders and gently led him out of the dim shack and into the bright light of the exterior.

Rearguard

Chimber caressed the mane of his mount as he braced himself against the steady wind. Perched atop a small knoll, he studied the long narrow valley that connected the city of Drumel with the the broad plains dominating the central region of Capital Island. He surveyed the progress of the long string of civilians who wearily plodded the last few miles through the valley floor. To Chimber's eyes, they seemed to move as if they were walking through a mud bog, though their path was dry and firm.

The string of civilians was several miles long, stretching from Drumel's gate to the mouth of the valley and then out into the open plain itself. As slowly as those in the valley seemed to move, the citizens who formed the rear ranks were slower still. Some were on foot, while others were pulled along in heavy, crude carts by mangy, ill-looking beasts. Most of Cegril's army lined the shoulders of the road, urging them onward and helping where they could, but there was little he or the others could do about the fact that the citizens were exhausted. They needed more time.

Chimber shifted his gaze north toward the dark line growing on the horizon. Still at least ten miles away, the slow-moving cadaver host was advancing steadily. In a few hours, they would reach those civilians in the rear, including the aged, ill, and those burdened with small children. The most vulnerable of Cegril's citizenry.

They couldn't adequately defend themselves, and he wouldn't stand by while they got massacred. But what could be done? Slight panic started to rise in him as he observed the crawling pace of the final laggards making up the rear.

He looked down to see Marshal Brechlin urging her steed up the side of the knoll to join him at its apex.

"It's no good," said Chimber as Brechlin reined in her mount next to him. "I fear we'll have to buy the last of the citizens some time."

Brechlin watched the civilians entering the valley and the dark mass of cadavers across the plain.

"I don't know, Chimber," she said. "They might make it. Perhaps if we aggressively prod those in the rear, and carry what we can of their burdens, their pace will quicken."

"But see how weary they are?" asked Chimber. "If the fear of a horde of walking dead at their heels won't speed up their pace, I doubt your troops will do much better. Perhaps we should think about how we should deploy the troops."

"Sweet Chimber," said Brechlin with a smile. "Always attentive to precaution. I assure you there will be sufficient time to form up the ranks if need be. But let's hope there will be no need. We can only slow the pace of the enemy at the cost of many lives. And, even then, they'll barely hesitate. This evil horde is unstoppable."

As they gazed down at the slow-moving stream of humanity passing below them, they noticed a chubby older man leave the procession and approach several of the officers positioned along the shoulder of the road. One officer turned and pointed up at them. "It's Alipharem," Brechlin said to Chimber. "Let's see what he wants." She led her mount down the knob and dismounted next to where the old man was standing. Chimber did likewise.

"My dear Brechlin," said the old man, beaming an affectionate smile at her.

"My dear Alipharem," replied Brechlin. "Good to see you are still as spry as ever."

"Just an extended morning stroll," quipped Alipharem, whose flushed face showed that his overweight frame was not used to such a walk.

Brechlin nodded at Chimber. "Let me introduce you to Chimber, my right-hand man."

"Yes, every time I see you these days, riding along the city walls or positioned along the ramparts, I see this young man at your side." He extended his arm. "I'm glad to make your acquaintance."

Chimber grasped Alipharem's hand warmly, for the man had a kind and wise demeanor.

"Alipharem is the leader of the Council of Sages," said Brechlin. "And Queen Cirmar's most trusted adviser. At least, he was while Queen Cirmar was with us."

"Ah, my dear Brechlin, she will be with us again soon, for my old feeble eyes spot a small band of riders coming from the east."

Brechlin and Chimber followed the old man's gaze. There, indeed, was a small group of riders heading toward them from Capital Island's eastern coast, four miles distant from Drumel.

"It seems your feeble eyes best those of my lookouts," exclaimed Brechlin, who at that moment heard the lookout's cry of approaching riders.

"It must be Jern and Queen Cirmar!" burst out Chimber.

"My Gludema, I hope so," said Brechlin. "Her presence would boost the morale of the people."

Chimber, Brechlin, and Alipharem stood and waited for the riders to approach. They could discern details of individual faces. Chimber made out Jern's thin form and Queen Cirmar's, but was uncertain of the others. One other rider looked vaguely familiar.

"Why, that's Saffral!" Chimber exclaimed.

"And Ferrin is with them!" cried Brechlin. "They've found Ferrin!"

And Ferrin it was. He was clean, newly dressed, and free. He, along with Queen Cirmar, Jern, Saffral, and the Queen's Royal Guard pulled up on the reins of their mounts as they approached Brechlin, Chimber, and Alipharem.

"And so, the White Medium returns," announced Alipharem.

"My Liege," said Brechlin. "You are safe. Your note was so cryptic, we were all worried."

"My apologies, Marshal Brechlin," said Queen Cirmar. "But time was short. And if that ominous black band I see on the horizon is Dran's host, it would appear that I was right to be in a hurry."

"Yes, Your Majesty," replied Brechlin. "It is Dran. As you can see, we are gathering in Drumel for a last stand. And with Ferrin now in our ranks, perhaps the stand will hold. But, we may need to engage this evil horde before all of Cegril's citizens are inside Drumel's walls."

Queen Cirmar peered at a wobbling cart making its way in front of them. "Yes. They are moving slowly."

"They are weary from the march," said Brechlin, "and those in the back cannot move any more quickly than those in front of them. But please, My Queen, follow me up this knoll. I have an idea."

As Brechlin remounted and led the queen up to the top of the knoll, Chimber walked over to Jern, who, along with Saffral, had dismounted. "So, now you are Queen Cirmar's sidekick, I see."

"Well, since you became so tight with the Marshal of Cegril, I needed to do a little social climbing myself," replied Jern.

"Not too bad for a couple of gravediggers," observed Saffral in her sweet voice.

"But what I would like to know—" began Chimber, but Brechlin's war horn cut him off mid-sentence. She sat on her mount at the top of the knoll. As the echoes of the sound faded away, the long line of civilians halted and looked up at her.

"Queen Cirmar has returned!" bellowed Brechlin at the top of her lungs. "The White Medium has returned! Drumel awaits us! We now have both Mount Krin and Mount Lomith at our side, and so we shall defeat the Krakul Gat! Let us join Queen Cirmar and Ferrin in Drumel!"

There was a scattered cheer, and slowly, the halted line of civilians regained their momentum toward Drumel. Brechlin and Queen Cirmar rejoined the group at the foot of the knoll.

"I hope it helps," said Queen Cirmar.

"Oh, yeah. I already see them picking up the pace a little," replied Jern, trying to sound positive.

Brechlin looked over at Ferrin, who had been in close conversation with Alipharem, and then back at Queen Cirmar.

"My Liege," she said. "I think our best strategy is for you and Ferrin to ride on ahead to Drumel. Ferrin, you need to prepare to once again to enter into the heart of the White

Mountain and get ready to focus its healing power on our ailing forces. And Queen Cirmar, we need your presence and leadership in the town. Space will be at a premium, and everyone will be irritable and afraid. Your being there can help calm them."

"I will do as you ask," replied Queen Cirmar.

"As will I," added Ferrin, "but first, you should listen to what Alipharem has to say."

Hope

Chimber, Jern, Brechlin, and Queen Cirmar all turned toward Alipharem, who was gazing at the White Mountain, its milky crystal tip visible above the natural wall of the narrow valley leading to the gates of Drumel. He looked weary, but there was a light in his eyes.

"Soon," he began, "we will have ensconced ourselves behind the thin walls of Drumel, once again waiting for the inevitable. The presence of Ferrin and the Lomitheri may delay it, but Dran's army will destroy us all—it's just a matter of time. We all know that."

"But we can't just lay down our swords and die," replied Brechlin. "As long as we survive, there may be a way."

Alipharem stroked his chin. "Yes. There may be a way. It is uncertain, and exposes your army to great risk and loss of life. But I believe it is a better option than awaiting our inevitable doom."

"It sounds like hope," said Queen Cirmar. "Please continue."

Alipharem gazed back up at the White Mountain. "Well, with Ferrin once again at the helm of Mount Krin, he could focus its healing powers on the cadaver army."

"Heal our enemy!" cried Brechlin. "For what purpose?"

"Don't these cadavers have enough advantages already?" asked Jern.

"Recall that the Krakul Gat's power to animate only affects cadavers," said Alipharem. "Which is why he and Ginthar laced the black cloud with poison. He not only extended the reach of the Gray Mountain's power with the gray dust of the mountain, but he had to also kill his victims to have something to apply his power to. I believe that if these cadavers come within reach of the power of the White Mountain, with Ferrin focusing all of its virtue upon them, then yes, he can heal them. And once they have returned to life, once they are no longer cadavers, Dran's power becomes inert."

"But the White Mountain can't bring the dead back to life!" exclaimed Chimber. "At least, I've never heard of it done, and as a gravedigger, you might say death is my profession."

"What the power of the White Mountain cannot do is reverse natural processes like disease or decay," said Ferrin. "It can only affect those aspects of a being counter to the natural course of things. That is, injuries, burns, and the like."

"Or poisoning," added Alipharem.

"Or poisoning," repeated Ferrin. "Normally, a deceased body would have experienced decay before being exposed to the White Mountain's healing forces. It doesn't take long—a matter of hours. Therefore, Mount Krin cannot revive the dead under normal circumstances. But the Gray Mountain not only animates inert flesh, it also prevents decay. Otherwise, the cadavers working in the mines of Kromul Island would disintegrate from rot in a matter of days."

"My apologies for saying so, my dear Alipharem," said Brechlin, "but this sounds wildly implausible, if not downright impossible."

"No, not impossible," said Ferrin. "There was a ward attendee working the convalescence halls in Drumel who fell while holding a freshly sharpened cleaver. The blade of the cleaver severed the arteries in his neck, and by the time he was brought to my attention, the life force had left him. But since it was within minutes of his demise, there was no decay. I focused the mountain's power upon his body. The wound healed, and his life force returned."

"You were certain he was dead?" asked Brechlin.

"Yes. His corpse was utterly lifeless, drained of blood."

Brechlin nodded, biting her lower lip. "Okay, so these walking dead are poisoned and somewhat sliced and burned, but the powder that allows Dran to animate them has also prevented their decay."

"Yes!" said Alipharem. "These cadavers, dead and hacked though they are, are wholesome."

"What an odd thought," quipped Jern.

"This is an intriguing idea," said Brechlin, her voice tinged with excitement. "I know they have to be stationary, but once they reach the walls, they will stand in place for days while they hack away. It might work!"

Ferrin and Alipharem looked down and were silent for a moment. "I'm afraid it's not that easy," said Ferrin finally. "I cannot focus the power of Mount Krin as far as the city walls."

"But once they breach the walls, the enemy will destroy us," said Chimber.

"Yes," said Ferrin. "Once the walls are breached, we are doomed. We cannot allow the enemy to reach the walls."

Brechlin brow crinkled. "But how?"

"There is only one way," returned Alipharem. "This valley, as it winds its way up to the front gate of Drumel, passes within the shadow of the White Mountain about a half mile before the walls. Since the cadaver host will have to pass through the valley to assault Drumel, it will briefly enter the shadow of the mountain."

"Right, but the subjects have to be stationary," said Chimber, "and I presume it would take time for them to heal."

Ferrin nodded gravely. "Yes."

"How much time?" asked Queen Cirmar.

"Well, to heal them completely, to repair their battle damage and cure the poisoning, for several thousand people, many hours," answered Ferrin.

"But, there is no way..." began Chimber.

"However, we need not heal them completely," said Alipharem. "It is enough to bring them back to life for Dran to lose control."

"How long will *that* take?" asked Jern.

Alipharem looked at Ferrin, who shrugged.

"I don't know for certain," he said. "It would depend on how well I focus the power of Mount Krin, and how stationary you kept them."

Alipharem turned to Queen Cirmar. "There you have it. The longer your army can hold the cadaver host in place under the shadow of the White Mountain, the more of them will be healed. If we heal enough, then the tide could be turned, for healed cadavers would be lost to Dran's control."

Queen Cirmar turned to Brechlin. "Can it be done?"

Brechlin looked at the approaching enemy, still several miles distant, and then down the long line of civilians passing into the valley opening. It was a mile to Drumel from the valley mouth, and the valley itself was only fifty yards wide at places. Her troops could block the passage of the host, in theory. "If only we had more time. We could construct some kind of barrier."

"What about the reservoir's dam?" asked Chimber. "If we released its waters, would they delay the enemy?"

"Not likely," said Brechlin. "The volume of water in the reservoir is not great, and the valley is wide. If we destroyed the dam as they approached, I doubt the water would rise more than a few inches, and it would quickly drain away."

"And I might mention that if it failed to work, Drumel would be without its water supply," observed Alipharem. "The defense of the city would be compromised."

"Can't you construct some kind of barrier?" asked Queen Cirmar. "We have a couple of hours before they reach the mountain's shadow. Wouldn't that be enough time?"

Brechlin looked over the valley. "It would be difficult. We would have to wait for these citizens to pass before we completely seal the barrier, and I fear the enemy would be upon us. Besides, the valley is so open and flat. What would we fill it with?"

Queen Cirmar opened her hands. "Wooden furniture? Dismantled gates? Wagons? Isn't it worth a try?"

"Yes, My Liege," said Brechlin, nodding thoughtfully. "It's worth a try. I'll have my troops gather up anything they can find and pile it in the valley."

It pleased Brechlin that her queen was thinking more like a resourceful leader now instead of a desperate and abandoned lover. It was a side of her she had seen before, but not so much recently, and she had been concerned that Tarmot's departure made things worse. If they all managed to survive, this would be a good experience for the queen. It would help her build the confidence that a competent ruler required.

But that's if we manage to survive.

"I think it's our only hope," added Chimber somberly. "We must wait for the last citizen to pass, pile up anything we can find, and close up our ranks behind the barrier. We must hold the enemy as long as possible under the shadow of the mountain."

"Many will die," said Queen Cirmar.

"It doesn't matter." Brechlin glanced at the queen. "If we fail to delay them, we all die anyway."

"My Gludema," said Ferrin. "I hope my strength holds. My years in prison have not been healthy ones. Even now, I feel exhausted."

Queen Cirmar took Ferrin's hand. "I believe in you. Your first order of business is to focus the power of Mount Krin on yourself. You don't have long, but we will need you as strong as possible." Then she turned to the others. "We shall try Alipharem's plan," she announced. "Chimber is right. It is our only hope."

Desperate Measures

After their impromptu meeting by the knoll, Queen Cirmar, Ferrin, and Alipharem mounted their horses and raced off to Drumel, with Queen Cirmar's Royal Guard following.

"Damn, I wish we had an army of those guys," said Jern, watching the queen's champions ride down the valley road.

Brechlin assembled her officers and told them of the plan. Two brigades would stay back and assist the citizens in any way possible reaching the gates of Drumel. The rest of the troops would scour the town for anything suitable that could be carried and added to the barricade.

With a specific plan of action in mind, the leaders of Cegril's army moved with a purpose. They were no longer delaying their inevitable demise but were working toward possible salvation. And, it didn't take long for word of the plan to reach the citizenry. It was whispered with a new hope—the Medium of the White Mountain would save the day. The weary, slow-moving line of citizens picked up their pace. Morale revived.

Jern joined Chimber and Brechlin as they mounted up and rode down the valley to survey the terrain. Along the way, Chimber looked at Jern and smiled.

"I don't know how you pulled it off, Jern," he said. "But nice work."

"What do you mean?" Jern asked.

"Getting Ferrin off Pith Isle and saving Saffral. How did you figure out Ferrin was there?"

"Well," said Jern, beaming from the praise. "In all fairness, it was Queen Cirmar who figured it out. When she saw the Tear of Life, she knew it had to have come from Ferrin and, basically, put two and two together. So off we went. And boy, what a ride it was!"

"What happened to Kruuger?"

"I'll tell you more details later, but he got what was coming to him. At the moment, he is personally enjoying the comforts of a Pith Isle prison cell."

Chimber looked at his small-framed companion with a good deal more respect. "So how did you take the prison? I am sure the prison guards put up—" he began, but Brechlin interrupted his question.

"Gentlemen, we approach that part of the valley that Alipharem referred to."

The three riders, moving alongside the stream of civilians, had entered a region of the valley that was slightly narrower than what had preceded it, but still over fifty yards wide. They peered around them, looking for any advantage in terms of terrain along the valley floor, but there was nothing. A small stream created a shallow gorge along one side, and in the middle ran the road to Drumel's gate.

"As I suspected," said Brechlin. "Nothing we can use to our advantage."

"There's the tip of Mount Krin," said Jern, pointing above the valley wall.

Chimber looked up at the spire of white crystal with awe. "I've never seen the White Mountain."

Jern snorted. "You're a gravedigger. They don't like your kind in these parts."

Brechlin crossed her arms over her chest. "Once the cadavers move beyond this area, they will no longer be in the healing shadow of Mount Krin. Its power will no longer affect them. Here is where we have to hold them."

"How do you delay an unstoppable army?" pondered Jern.

Brechlin eyed several of her soldiers as they passed through Drumel's main entrance and approached them carrying items—a wooden settle and a gate. "I don't know. Perhaps the barricade will help. At least we have a fighting chance. If Dran's cadavers subdued Cegril's stout walls, then Drumel's demise, too, would be a matter of time. And then, where would we go? With the city backed up into the head of the valley, there would be no escape, so we must make our stand here, in the shadow of the White Mountain. And we can't be concerned about losses, even if we lose every man. If we don't stop them, we lose everything."

Brechlin instructed the soldiers where to place the settle and the gate. "You two," she said, speaking to two of the soldiers. "Station yourselves here and make sure everyone stacks their items over to the side. We can't erect the barricade over the road until these people have all passed by. And hopefully, there will be a lot more items coming."

Brechlin, Chimber, and Jern then rode back up toward the mouth of the valley, offering words of encouragement to the exhausted populace still plodding toward Drumel's main gate. Once back at the valley's entrance, they rode up to the top of the knoll and looked to the north. The enemy was surprisingly close—only an hour away. Brechlin instructed nearby officers to command their troops to be more aggressive in prodding any stragglers near the end of the civilian train. Increased morale and fear were already doing wonders in urging the trailing travelers onward, but the army would need time to close the barricade once the last citizen had passed.

Brechlin left Chimber and Jern on the knoll to keep an eye on things and rode her mount up to the band of Lomitheri gathered on the far side of the road leading into the valley. As she looked over them, it was easy to see they were nearly spent. Their pendants still worked for now, but they were fast losing their virtue, and the exertion of their journey to Drumel in the heat of Capital Island had taken its toll.

She hailed Schmie and dismounted next to her. Schmie looked up with a haggard smile.

"How are the Lomitheri holding out?' asked Brechlin.

"Our crystal pendants weaken," replied Schmie. "But not our spirit. We are ready and willing to sacrifice all that is necessary."

"Have you heard of our plan?"

Schmie nodded her head soberly in assent.

"We need to hold the enemy's approach to Drumel for at least two hours under the shadow of the White Mountain. If we fail, it's just a matter of time until the city falls. But if we succeed, we can turn this tide."

"I understand," replied Schmie.

"What I need to know from you is if we go for broke and the Lomitheri use all of their remaining power, can you freeze enough of the cadavers to matter?"

"I don't think so. Although a frozen cadaver needs an hour or two for their limbs to thaw, it takes a good deal of focus to fully freeze a single cadaver. It is such a shame we cannot touch them directly without great risk. Mount Lomith's power is much reduced when projected through the air."

"I need a number. What's reasonable to expect?"

"If we use our wings to hover above the approaching enemy and exhaust the power of our war kernels to freeze as many as we can, we may delay several hundred of the enemy. Leaving, I fear, thousands more unimpeded."

Brechlin nodded slowly. "You're right, that isn't many, but it is our only real hope. Be prepared to slow down all you can. Once the crystals are drained, I want your people to retreat behind the city gates. You will be vulnerable and would not stand long, I fear, in armed conflict with the enemy."

Schmie looked over her comrades and all nodded their assent.

"We will do as you ask," said Schmie, "but you should know that once the pendants are drained of their power, we will all perish soon thereafter. Our bodies will not be able to withstand the heat of this southern climate."

Brechlin thought about saying something appropriate in response, but what could she say? She had known it before she had asked—the Lomitheri party would all die. They would sacrifice their lives for the sake of these civilians, a race of beings to which they did not belong.

She felt great admiration for these courageous beings fiercely battling alongside her to the very end. It touched her soldier's soul to be losing her new sisters. She looked into mighty little Schmie's eyes, hoping to convey her true respect. Then, uncharacteristically, she felt the desire to embrace Schmie and reached for her shoulders before realizing that bringing Schmie's freezing body into contact with hers would be painful for both of them. So she contented herself with a rigid salute.

"We are honored to have you as sisters-in-arms," looking over Schmie and her colleagues.

As she climbed back upon her steed, she noticed that a small piece of ice had formed on the edge of Schmie's eye. She wondered if it were uncomfortable for a Lomitheri to cry.

* * *

Chimber and Jern, still stationed on top of the knoll, saw a rider approach from the direction of Drumel and recognized the plump form of Alipharem. He directed his mount up to the top of the knoll.

"I wanted to see for myself how near the enemy host has come," he said.

Jern balled his fist and shook it in the direction of the black line of cadavers. "They do not tire, nor do they stop for food or drink. They are vile, unholy things."

"Aye, that they are."

Chimber looked pensively at the approaching enemy. He turned to Alipharem. "There's something I wonder about. The Covenant that binds the three mediums seems to assume that the power of two will deter the power of any single one. Yet here we stand with both the Blue and the White Mountains among our allies, and our plight is a desperate one."

"True," Alipharem said, "so maybe our plan will succeed. And, if it does, we shall say the designers of the Covenant were correct."

"Do you think it will succeed?" asked Chimber, again gazing at the approaching swarm of cadavers.

Alipharem didn't hesitate. "I have faith in the wisdom of the Covenant. And so should you."

307

Dagger

Ilsher studied her father's face as she handed him pieces of fruit. Dran stared out into space, barely noticing the morsels of food he was placing into his mouth. He sat on the bench near the entrance to the tunnel into the Gray Mountain. He hadn't left the cleft for weeks and had slept little. His hair was unwashed and unruly, and the black circles under his eyes were pronounced.

"Poor Father. This is taking such a toll on you."

Dran shifted his gaze to look at his young daughter as if seeing her for the first time. The slightest crinkle of a smile touched the rim of his eyes. "It has, my dear. But I'll survive it. And it will all be worthwhile."

"Of that, I'm sure," she replied. "As long as my father, my hero, is not lost to me. For we will wish to speak of your glory as we gather around feasting tables."

Dran's weather-dried lips formed a shallow crescent.

"But," continued Ilsher, "are we truly near the end? Does our awful ordeal near its close?"

"We are truly near the end," replied Dran as he stretched his legs out in front of him. "Once the people of Cegril join the citizens of Drumel, we have won. Their walls won't hold back our army for long, and once we breach them, they'll have no place to retreat. They'll be bottled up like a pilfer fish in a net, and I'll be able to assert my will."

Ilsher looked into the basket she carried and slowly pulled out a dagger. "That is so splendid to hear!" she said with much enthusiasm. "Then I guess there is little need for this." She handed Dran the dagger.

Dran looked at it and then at his daughter with a puzzled expression. "What's this for?"

"You know me, your dutiful daughter," sang out Ilsher, and she bounced up off the bench and brushed crumbs off Dran's clothes. "I knew you would want it, in case you failed."

"In case I...what do you mean?"

"Well, if you fail, all is lost. You would be captured and no doubt tried and executed. How humiliating to us all. I knew you wouldn't want to put your loved ones through all that."

"And commit suicide!" burst out Dran. "You think I would want to kill myself if this fails?" He threw the dagger to the ground.

"Wouldn't you?" said Ilsher, her words dripping with sincerity.

Dran stood and walked over to the edge of the cleft, looking out to the sea, his hands on his waist. After a second, he looked back at her.

"I haven't contemplated failure," he said quietly. "It's too unbearable to even conceive." Then, after hesitating, he continued. "But I don't know about suicide. Besides, all of that is irrelevant. Barring some unexpected calamity, you shall soon be the princess of the Dalmeer Islands and live in Queen Cirmar's new castle."

"Yes!" exclaimed Ilsher. "And get off this godforsaken dot on the ocean." She walked over, picked up the dagger off the ground, and placed it carefully on the bench. Then she turned back to her father. "I have the greatest faith in you. And so would Mother, if she still lived. We know you won't let us down."

She smiled at her father, lightly caressed his cheek, and left the cleft, descending the stairway. Dran felt a strange sense of relief at her departure. *Why do I let her trouble me so?* he wondered. Then, with a sigh, he ambled back to the tunnel entrance and entered the bowels of the mountain.

All In

Chimber and Jern rested on their mounts next to the barricade and watched the last wooden cart pass through the barricade's opening, its rigged rear wheel wobbling and threatening to fail once again. It seemed like everyone stationed at the rear of the human convoy had spent all the last hour quickly repairing wagon wheels and shifting loads and invalids from unstable vehicles to stable ones. And now, as the citizens were behind him and no longer his concern, he looked up to see the dark, lurching mass of walking dead—crowded from one side of the steep-walled valley to the other—approach their position. Chimber regretted not having time to mentally prepare himself for what was to come.

He and the rest of the rearguard slipped through the opening, and Cegril's army rapidly moved the remaining wooden wagons and odd pieces of furniture into the gap, wedging the smaller pieces into place. Chimber and Jern rode up to Brechlin and looked over the line. At nearly a thousand strong, they stretched from one end of the valley to the other in a double line, positioned directly behind the wagons and piled furniture. Behind them stood a ragged assemblage of volunteers from among the citizenry, most holding farm implements. There were not enough to stretch from one end to the other, so they clustered near the center road. The Lomitheri spread out at the back of this human defensive barrier.

The plan was that once the cadavers breached any section of the barricade and pressed forward, the Lomitheri would use their flight to hover above the cadavers and freeze them into place. The hope was that if enough were strategically frozen, their unmoving mass would fill the freshly opened gap, clogging up the advance of those behind them.

Chimber once again looked over the terrain. He wanted to make sure that the ground behind the barricade had been cleared of all debris that might trip up retreating troops. A painted pole with a banner had been planted at the edge of the valley perhaps fifty yards behind them. It marked the point at which Mount Krin's power would no longer remain effective. If the enemy got beyond that point, the game was lost. The survivors might retreat to Drumel, outrunning the slow-moving cadavers, but it would only be a matter of time before the enemy host would destroy Drumel's thin defensive fortifications and fall upon the people inside.

High on the wall that separated the valley from the white crystal of Mount Krin, Chimber saw a lone figure holding a large signal horn. His job was to let Ferrin, stationed on the shoulder of the White Mountain, know that the enemy had entered the effective range of Mount Krin. He would then assume his position within the depths of the mountain and direct its healing force into the valley and, all hoped, heal enough of the cadavers to turn the tide. For a healed cadaver was no longer a cadaver, and no longer under Dran's control.

Chimber studied Brechlin's face and found that he admired her more than ever. He could see she was afraid. Only a fool wouldn't be. But, she was also determined, with a fierce light burning in her eyes. As he looked up and down the line of troops and citizens, he got a similar impression from most of the others. They were afraid but determined. Every one among them knew the consequences of failure. He looked back at the Lomitheri, now mere shadows of their previous selves—they were haggard and pitiful. But again, they were committed to what was to come.

If this was the end, he was going out in good company. Good company, indeed.

He thought about how different his life would have been had he not taken Brechlin's unconscious body from the battlefield. Likely, they would never have met. But now, he knew she was the one for him. Strong, courageous, and confident, he admired her and loved her. His love for her filled his chest and radiated out to his limbs. He wanted to hold and protect her, yet follow her at the same time. A contradiction she was, and the most unique human being he'd ever known.

If only this wasn't the beginning of the end.

"It should take the enemy at least an hour to break through our barricade," mulled Brechlin, considering the structure. "If we manage to hold them in place for two, it might do the trick."

"How many would we need to eliminate from their ranks, do you think?" asked Jern. "I mean, what would be enough to make a difference?"

Brechlin silently considered the question. "As many as possible. I don't know a number." She studied the approaching swarm. "There are several thousand cadavers in that swarm. Can we stop merely a thousand? I don't know."

Chimber glanced over at the nearby dam holding back the city's drinking supply and once again wished there was enough water behind it to create some kind of advantage. It held back a small pond, no more. Yet, something tickled in the far reaches of his brain.

He cast these unformed thoughts aside. They had a plan in place, and they had done all they reasonably could to prepare for its implementation. Therein lay their best chance for success. As he rode his horse behind the ranks, looking things over, Jern joined him.

"Is everything to your liking?" he asked.

Chimber shrugged. "Everything looks in order."

"Good ol' Chimber. Fastidious and ordered to the very last."

Chimber allowed a smile to crease his grave face. "It's when things count the most that one must be most prepared. And nothing counts more than this."

"But don't you see, this is battle! Once our blades clash with the enemy's, nothing is preordained. Anything can happen. And by being flexible and spontaneous, one can react. Your rigid plans go out the window."

"Maybe," said Chimber, looking once again all around the terrain and down the line of soldiers. "But you do what you can."

"You know, the timing is terrible," said Jern after a few minutes of watching the enemy approach down the narrow valley, now only a hundred yards away.

"Is there a good time to be obliterated by a cadaver army?" asked Chimber.

"I meet the girl of my dreams, save her from her horrible predicament, and then I go and volunteer to be a dead hero."

"Yeah, I can relate," replied Chimber, "but if we don't stop them, then Saffral will die, along with everyone else in Drumel."

"I know. But still...the whole thing reeks a vile stench."

"You know, maybe we'll live. Have you considered that option?"

"Yes, of course," said Jern, his voice full of sarcasm. "Every time I peer at yon black mass of undead indestructible warriors bearing down upon us, I think that very thing."

"You must have faith in the wisdom of the Covenant," said Chimber.

"Bah, the Covenant!" Jern pointed back toward the stretched-out line of Lomitheri. "Look at those pitiful creatures. They're near their end. Schmie told me her pendant will lose its virtue at any time now, and the same is true of her comrades. And without the power of Mount Lomith to cool their bodies, they will perish within the hour—win or lose. And regarding Mount Krin, just look how close that pole marker is. Ferrin, who is a mere shadow of his former self, has that long to save our hides."

"It looks grim," agreed Chimber.

"And what idiot built Drumel's walls beyond the reach of Mount Krin's power?" continued Jern, now on a roll. "Couldn't they have anticipated an assault by an army of undead upon their city?"

Chimber grunted. "Yeah, shortsighted architects."

"I know I'm rambling," said Jern, grinning at Chimber. "But damn, I had a lot to do yet in my life. I guess I'm just not ready."

"Well, you'd better get ready," replied Chimber, nodding toward the approaching enemy. "The festivities are about to begin."

"I didn't mean ready in that sense. I'm ready to fight. I'm not ready to, you know, end it all."

"Jern! For Gludema's sake, will you shut up and get your game face on!"

"Some game," quipped Jern, but then he unsheathed his sword. "If this doesn't end well, good buddy, I'll see you in the land between."

The men of Cegril's army watched the approaching horde through gaps in the barricade and braced themselves. The wind quieted, and a distant thunder could be heard rolling across the southern sea.

There may be rain later, thought Chimber.

And the black mass of undead warriors was upon them.

On the Brink

Chimber watched the ranks of walking corpses bunch up next to the barricade, extending from one side of the valley to the other. They didn't hack at their wooden obstructions but instead filled in their ranks until they were nine or so cadavers deep along the entire front of the barricade.

The longer they wait to hack at the barricade, the better, he thought.

The frantic blowing of the signal horn overhead caught his attention. Then he felt it. A slight surge of energy through his body. It was subtle but discernible. Ferrin was at work, directing Mount Krin's power into the valley. Chimber's hopes rose.

"Can you feel Mount Krin's power?" asked Jern, sitting on his mount next to Chimber. "This scrape on my arm is starting to tingle."

"I can feel it. Let's hope the cadavers do, too."

"But why aren't they hacking?" asked Jern. From his seat on the saddle, he could see over the jumble of wooden furniture and wagons.

"Whatever the reason, it's a good thing," said Chimber.

"Oh, my Gludema!" Brechlin cried. She was a few yards away, watching the barricade.

"What is it?" asked Chimber.

"The barricade!" she said. "It's moving!"

She was right. Chimber understood now. They weren't hacking at the barricade because they had put their hands on it and were pushing. The whole barricade was moving backward.

"Everybody, push back!" bellowed Brechlin. "Jern, you ride to the left. Chimber to the right. Tell everyone to hold the barricade. We can't let them push us beyond the marker!"

Chimber and Jern bolted off, riding down the ranks of Cegril's army, yelling at them to push back on the barricade with all their strength. For a few minutes, the barricade held. But soon, the multiple ranks of animated cadavers, many times their number, overcame their strength. Once again, the barricade moved inexorably toward the marker. At several places, the stress of the pressure from both sides overcame the barrier's structural integrity, and it began to give and shatter.

As a few cadavers seeped in between the cracks, nearby soldiers gave up their grip on the barricade and wielded their swords in self-defense. As they did, the wall receded even faster.

Brechlin and the other officers dismounted and were pushing on the backs of the men in front of them in a futile attempt to hold ground.

"Chimber, Jern!" cried Brechlin. "Dismount and push!"

Jern was about to dismount when he noticed Chimber not moving.

"What is it, Chimber?" he asked. He wondered whether Chimber has lost his nerve. But his face was grim. There was no evidence of fear. "What are you doing? Dismount! Let's help!"

But Chimber sat there, stroking the stubble on his chin.

"Let's think this through. What will happen?"

"What? I don't have a clue." Jern let out a harsh breath. "We probably can't stop them from pushing back the barricade. There are too many. So I guess we take down as many as we can before we go."

"Not good enough." A thought had come to Chimber. A wild, reckless thought. He hesitated for a few seconds, looking once again at the dam, before he set his jaw and yelled to Brechlin.

"I have an idea," he cried. "I need Jern and a couple of others—quickly."

Brechlin looked at him, exasperated, pushing with all her strength.

"Chimber, we're losing ground fast! What are you talking about?"

"The dam! We must break the dam!"

A rickety old wagon crumbled with a loud crack twenty feet to their right. The men at behind the wagon began swinging their swords. They saw a flash of movement overhead as the Lomitheri flew over to plug up the gap.

"No, Chimber," cried Brechlin. "It'll do no good! And we will lose our water supply!"

"I have an idea! You must trust me!"

"Marshal," said Captain Labrok, positioned next to Brechlin and pushing mightily. "We have nothing to lose. We're doomed otherwise."

Brechlin looked at Chimber impatiently. "Dammit, Chimber! Go. Do what you gotta do. Take who you need. Just do it fast!"

"Jern! Flackard! You and you," he said, pointing out two nearby men. "Follow me!" Chimber looked at Brechlin. "Hold it as long as you can!" he called. "Do not retreat. Do not give up the barricade."

Brechlin did not say a word but grunted with exertion and nodded assent.

Chimber spurred his mount and led the small party to the far wall of the valley and toward the dam.

"Wow, Chimber," said Jern, galloping along with him. "When you decide to be spontaneous, you don't kid around, do you?"

"I learned from the best," Chimber called back.

As they approached the dam wall, a wooden structure seven feet high and thirty feet long, Chimber yelled out to the others to use their swords to hack through the supporting beams. Heavily muscled arms wailed away, but the weathered, waterlogged boards only slowly responded to the blows.

"Quickly!" urged Chimber. "We must release the water!"

At that instant, Flackard's mighty sword severed the beam he had been working on, and a thin stream of water gushed through. The men moved aside as the wooden structure collapsed, overwhelmed by the weight of the flowing water. For a couple of seconds, Chimber watched the rush of water begin to fill the valley. Then he and the other members of his party galloped back to Brechlin at the center of the barricade. The water splashed as they came up, just barely above the feet of the soldiers. The wall kept moving backward.

"It's having no effect," cried a grunting Brechlin, "except now my footing is unsteady."

"A few inches more," said Chimber.

"Our water is lost, and we are nearly out of range of the White Medium. What is your damn plan?"

Chimber said nothing but watched Jern, whom he had sent to fetch the small band of Lomitheri.

"Do you remember when we first met the Lomitheri, back in Wolfglen Forest?" Chimber said.

Instantly, Chimber's idea was crystal clear. "You mean to use the Lomitheri to freeze the water! To trap the cadavers in place!"

"Precisely," replied Chimber with a beaming smile. "Do they have enough power left?"

"I don't know," said Brechlin. "But they would be able to put their crystals directly into the water instead of projecting its power through air. So maybe."

Schmie and the remaining band of Lomitheri came running up to Chimber, Brechlin, and the receding line of Cegril's army.

"Schmie!" she called out to them. "You must freeze the water. Trap the enemy in place. Use everything you've got."

Schmie was breathing heavily and clearly overheated, but she nodded somberly.

"But before you do..." said Brechlin. She pulled out a horn she wore on a chain around her neck and blew heartily. It was the signal to retreat. The men all left their stations at the back of the barricade and ran toward Drumel's gate.

Brechlin, who knew what was coming, jumped up on Chimber's steed.

"Now!" she cried.

Before action could be taken by the Lomitheri, a swarm of cadavers came surging through the now-untended barricade. Chimber, Brechlin, and Flackard quickly dismounted and wielded their swords. They dismembered several of the cadavers, but the enemy surrounded them, and all three took several vicious wounds to their body. Chimber crumbled to his knees, blood gushing from his wounds.

He then heard a strange cracking sound, and all was black.

The Wisdom of the Covenant

Chimber opened his eyes and slowly resolved his surroundings. He no longer lay on the battlefield but upon a bed in one of the convalescence wards of Drumel. To either side of him lay other beds. As he looked closely, he recognized Brechlin's form in one of them. She turned to look at him, herself awakening, and smiled.

"It appears we live," she said.

"What happened?" he asked. At that moment, Jern walked up to their beds.

"Jern!" said Chimber. "You're alive, too! What happened?"

"Why, Chimber, you old clod, you saved the day," said Jern, sitting on Brechlin's bed. "And let me tell you guys, you missed it!"

Brechlin sat up and peered around her. The convalescence hall contained two hundred beds, and every bed was occupied. Scores of pathetic moans echoed from all directions. "Dran's army—was it destroyed?" she asked.

"Hardly," replied Jern. He gestured casually to the beds arrayed around them. "They are once again citizens of Bewel. Ailing and confused, for sure, but no longer under Dran's control."

It was too impossible to grasp. "Are you saying that Ferrin

succeeded?" asked Chimber. He looked up to see Alipharem approaching them.

"My dearest Brechlin. And brave Chimber. You seem to do well," he said, beaming.

"Is it true?" asked Chimber, still incredulous.

"What? That our faith in the Covenant was justified? Yes, it is true. The White Mountain converted the inert but preserved flesh of Dran's army back into living, breathing people. So you see, my boy, not only did your last-minute spontaneity save the citizens of Cegril from ultimate destruction, but it also brought back to us many whom we thought we had lost."

"You should have seen it," said Jern. "It was a sight to behold! Those hacked up cadavers, stuck in ice, first lost their pale pallor and then returned to life. Although it was no fun for them. Along with the return of the spark of life, they all felt the extreme agony of pain."

Alipharem nodded gravely. "It is a good thing they have no memories of their actions. For then there would be more than their bodies to heal."

"And there were more than a few cases of frostbitten feet," added Jern.

"I fell...in the middle of a swarm of cadavers," recalled Chimber.

Jern sat on the bed next to Chimber. "Yes, and you were stuck in the ice. But fortunately for many of us, Dran's cadavers hacked at the ice, trying to free themselves instead of continuing to administer punishment to those still within reach."

"The ice was solid," added Alipharem, "and no doubt Cegril's stone walls had blunted their blades. Ferrin had enough time to work his magic."

Chimber lay back on his cot and smiled. "It is amazing how things can change," he pondered. "And thank Gludema for Ferrin and his return. He saved our skins."

"Indeed. He had to focus the mountain's power on so many for so long," added Brechlin. "I'm sure it was no easy task."

Alipharem lowered his head. "No. It was not. In fact, he has collapsed from the exertion and is, I fear, dying. The two years at Pith Prison sapped his strength. Frankly, I was amazed that he kept at it as long as he did."

"He's dying? Here? Under the shadow of Mount Krin?" asked Chimber.

"Ironic as it may sound," replied Alipharem, "since he lies unconscious, he cannot project its healing powers upon himself."

"That's why we've been worried," added Jern. "You were both cut up pretty well. All the folks in here will have to get well without the White Medium's help."

"But this hall and the others lie in the shadow of the mountain, and its ambient power will help some, even without Ferrin," said Alipharem. "But if he passes, its power will wane over several weeks and will eventually become dormant."

Jern looked at Chimber. "And you, ol' buddy, had extra help."

Chimber reached toward his chest and found what he had expected—the Tear of Life, dangling from a chain around his neck.

"The Tear of Life! But no, let Brechlin wear it. I'm just fine. Let me..." Chimber was sitting up and reaching for the chain around his neck when a shot of pain flashed through his left side. He fell back to the bed.

"Best stay down, Chimber," admonished Jern. "Brechlin

is much better, but you had a particularly nasty gash in your side. You need more time with the pendant."

Brechlin managed to sit up in bed. "He's right, my dear. I'm weak, but nothing hurts particularly. I believe I could get up. If I had to."

"Isn't that precious?" quipped Jern. "The Marshal of Cegril's army called you 'dear'."

Chimber carefully sat up, supporting his back on his pillow. "It is a shame these beds aren't big enough for two," he said, looking over at Brechlin.

"Well, it's not exactly private," replied Brechlin, smiling. "But I will look after you for a change. Of course, I'll have to send for a jar of Frakar's ointment."

Chimber took a long look around the infirmary ward. "How badly off are these people?" He recalled how sliced and burnt many of the cadavers were. And, if he was still this sore with the help of the Tear of Life, he knew that many of them would be much worse.

"Many will die," answered Alipharem, "and although this place is well equipped to deal with convalescents, the sheer numbers have overwhelmed this community. The streets are lined with makeshift pallets, occupied by the ailing citizens of Bewel Island. Their road to recovery will be long, but if we can get a new White Medium in place soon, that would help."

"My God, is there no hope for Ferrin?" asked Brechlin.

"My pendant," cried Chimber. "Let him wear my pendant!"

"No, Chimber," said Alipharem. "It is generous of you to offer, but the Tear of Life is simply a kernel of Mount Krin. Ferrin's bed lies on his work platform, already as close to the White Mountain as possible. But, alas, Mount Krin's ambient virtue may not be sufficient."

"The Lomitheri!" exclaimed Chimber, suddenly recalling their plight. "What about Schmie and the others?"

Alipharem and Jern stared at the floor for a moment. "Ferrin kept them alive as long as his strength held out," said Alipharem. "But when he collapsed, well..."

"Schmie lives," added Jern, "and four others. Their pendants retained some of Mount Lomith's cooling power. But the others have perished, including Delvisha, Flackard's friend."

"What's being done to help those who live?" asked Brechlin. "We must save them. Without their help, Chimber's plan would not have been possible."

"They're being taken care of," assured Alipharem. "Even as we speak, they are in transit to Rolucca Peninsula. With a little luck, they'll make it to cooler climes in time. And they will notify Er Lomith of the likely need to reconvene on the Plain of Nubinor to install Ferrin's replacement. We should have a new White Medium as soon as possible."

"He's not the only Medium we'll have to replace," added Brechlin with a stern edge to her voice. "A trip to Kromul Island is in order. Dran will pay for what he has done."

She threw her legs over the edge of the bed and sat up, grimacing but looking determined.

"Alipharem, please let my remaining officers know that I am better and that I would like to confer with them all this afternoon."

"Now, don't overdo it, my dear," said Chimber. "I can see the scabs covering your legs."

"I won't," replied Brechlin, "but it's time for justice to be served."

At that moment, a nurse walked up to Alipharem and whispered into his ear. Alipharem nodded and turned somberly to the others.

"It is as I feared," he said. "Ferrin has passed."

After a few minutes of solemn silence, Brechlin slowly stood up.

"He must be honored," she said. "Before we depart Drumel, we must honor the man who gave his life to spare us all."

Alipharem nodded. "I agree. Queen Cirmar has yet to leave the city, so I will speak to her. Let us honor Ferrin's memory in the Sanctivius Colonnade."

Ferrin's Final Journey

The next morning, in a high meadow just beyond Drumel's city walls, many of the important citizens of the Dalmeer Islands gathered around two rows of forty white marble columns—the Sanctivius Colonnade. Erected in ancient times, these rows of columns framed a cobblestone pathway that ended at a great cleft in the gray wall of a towering mountain. Inside the cleft, niches had been carved in times past to hold the remains of revered citizens of Drumel and, since the time of Narr, the bodies of the past Mediums of the White Mountain.

All along the edges of the cobblestone pathway, the onlookers stood just outside the columns. Jern and Saffral were there standing side by side. Nearby sat Chimber in a chair that Jern himself had hauled up the steep trail to the meadow. Every spectator wore a loose white robe.

At the far end of the Sanctivius Colonnade, the Royal Guard lifted Ferrin's coffin upon their shoulders, and they carried it down the pathway, their steps in slow, smooth unison. Alipharem led the procession, slowly speaking an ancient prayer for all to hear. Behind the coffin walked Queen Cirmar, with Brechlin at her side, along with other important personages of Queen Cirmar's court. As they approached the great cleft, the coffin bearers shifted their load from their shoulders to their waists and entered the cavern, dimly lit by candlelight. The trailing entourage followed into the relative darkness.

As Ferrin's body entered the darkness from the light, symbolizing Ferrin's passage to Gludema's Realm, the somber spectators began singing an old hymn of passing.

And now we give to thee
  Oh Queen of all the Queens
  The treasured memory
  Of a soul now serene

To you he is released
  Oh Queen of all the Queens
  Escort him in peace
  To the land of in between

As was customary in the land of the Dalmeer Isles, the hooded onlookers all grasped hands as the hymn came to a close and knelt upon the ground, looking deeply into the soil. It was said that the land in between lay deep within the fragrant earth, where dwelled the all-powerful Gludema, pouring forth her life-giving force into the plants and animals of the world as well as the powerful Gludemic Mountains. And now, as a proper tribute, the people of the Dalmeer Islands gave back to Gludema the body of one they loved and honored.

As the members of the procession came back into the light of the meadow, the crowd dispersed. Chimber, waiting for Brechlin, looked up at Jern.

"What do you know of Ferrin's designated successor? He has big shoes to fill."

Jern didn't respond at first and, in fact, looked somewhat

uncomfortable. "Tingle was killed. Dran's thugs took his life when they captured Ferrin."

"I didn't know," returned Chimber. "But what will they do? Who will be the new White Medium?"

"Um, well..." managed Jern. He looked at Saffral, who gave him a big smile.

"The queen has asked Jern if he would take the job," she said. "And he has accepted."

"What?" exclaimed Chimber, nearly falling from his chair. "Jern? The White Medium? You can't speak the truth!"

"It's not final," replied Jern, unfazed by Chimber's incredulity. "It'll have to be approved by the Council of Sages."

Chimber could think of nothing more to say. He stared at Jern, dumbfounded.

Jern withstood his stare for a few minutes before responding. "I know what you're thinking. Irresponsible Jern. But things are different now. I've matured. I've matured a lot in these last weeks. And the queen recognizes my talents. If it wasn't for me, we wouldn't have had Ferrin on our side. Plus, I now have Saffral to keep me in line," he added, squeezing Saffral's hand tightly and looking fondly into her face.

Chimber shook his head. "Of all the audacity in the world, for you to believe you can be..."

In that moment, Brechlin walked up and stooped down to Chimber's chair to give him a hug.

"Now he's on his journey to Gludema's Realm," she said, referring to Ferrin's passage to the land in between. She looked up at Jern and Saffral. "On a happier note, have you heard the news?"

Jern frowned. "Um, I'm not sure..."

Brechlin smiled at Chimber. "It is official. Chimber has

been designated as Vice Marshal of Cegril. He'll give up his membership in the Gravedigger's Guild and lead the troops of Capital Island by my side."

"Chimber! Second in command of Cegril's army?" asked Jern. "Are you being serious?"

"Yes, I am," replied Brechlin. "He has shown quite an aptitude for leading our forces. And he is a hero for his bold action with the dam."

"Congratulations," said Saffral.

"Why, thank you, Saffral," said Chimber. "At least someone around here has manners."

"And what about the Gravedigger's Guild?" asked Jern. "No more digging holes?"

"Guess I gotta give that up. Turn a page. Start a new life."

"Chimber, a vice marshal," pondered Jern to no one in particular.

"Jern, the Medium of the White Mountain," countered Chimber.

"Yeah, I heard about that," said Brechlin. "It has to be cleared first, but it's probably a go."

"My, my, how things change," said Jern, placing his arm around Saffral's waist.

"You two make a nice couple," said Brechlin, looking them over. She then turned her attention to Chimber. "My dear, there is unfinished business on Kromul Island, and I must depart and return to Cegril. I don't know what to expect when we arrive at Kromul, so we must be prepared with a sizable force."

"But Dran has no army," said Chimber. "Must you go personally?"

"Access to the island is notoriously difficult. There is no

place to land the boats and disembark except within the narrow confines of the tiny harbor. Dran still has cadavers working the mines, so he may use them to attack us as we disembark. Given the situation, we'll need a large enough force to counter such a move."

She hugged Chimber again and looked at Jern. "Take care of him while I'm gone. I'll see you all back at Cegril in a week."

Brechlin discarded her white robe and handed it to a nearby assistant, then hurried down the steep path to Drumel.

Journey to Kromul Island

Sitting on a crosstree of the sloop's mast, Brechlin carefully scanned the horizon. Above her, perched above the sails, another pair of sharp eyes was scanning the heavens. Everyone was watching for unusual weather phenomena, such as black clouds. But though they remained alert, the sky ahead remained clear.

Brechlin had arrived two days earlier with three war sloops and several transport craft, carrying a total of four hundred of Cegril's now battle-hardened troops. They had kept just out of sight of Kromul Island during that time, waiting for the wind to shift. Brechlin had no wish to beat upwind into another one of Dran's poisonous clouds.

But now, the wind was blowing to the northwest, carrying away any potential threat, and they had approached near enough to see many of Kromul's towering peaks. No poisonous cloud was forthcoming.

Brechlin assumed Dran would try to contest their disembarkation with the mining cadavers still employed within Kromul's mines. She knew how difficult it would be to overcome even a handful of dead soldiers, and they had to be prepared, especially considering how narrowly confined the disembarkation area was.

She looked over the huddled troops who now lined the deck of the sloop and glanced back at the other war sloops and the troop transports. The greatest challenge would be to get her men on shore, which would be difficult if Dran's murderous cadavers were waiting on the quay. Once beyond the harbor area, where a wide valley followed the short road to Dran's compound, his men could get into formation and overwhelm the far smaller numbers of mining cadavers.

As the sloop rounded the bend and eased into the inner harbor, Brechlin espied no activity on the main pier. The area seemed deserted. They maneuvered the sloop alongside the pier and tied off, looking around intently for a surprise attack. But, all remained still.

Brechlin breathed a sigh of relief. Either Dran had given up or had some other form of resistance in store for them. Perhaps a trap or an ambush. Or perhaps they had constructed defenses around his home compound. Nevertheless, once her men were on land and in formation, she was confident of their success.

She sent a small reconnaissance party into the cluster of fishing huts and warehouses that made up Kromul Island's only community while the rest of the men got into position the best they could in the loading area just beyond the pier. If there were any traps to be sprung, the smaller party would spring it, allowing the main body of the force to respond appropriately.

But, as the reconnaissance party, led by the ever-capable Captain Labrok, entered the village, no attacks were made. A few citizens were milling about the alleyways, attending to racks of drying fish or mending nets, but they retreated inside their huts, the sound of the shutters banging shut echoing through the quiet town. Once Labrok and his men reached the far side of the little community, he signaled Brechlin to bring the main force forward.

Once in the wide valley beyond the village, Brechlin felt more comfortable. Dran's compound was less than a half mile away on the opposite side of the island, and there weren't many places he could hide. Things would come to a head soon.

She looked up at the giant smoky mountain of crystal rising up among several impressive peaks. Brechlin saw the cleft where Dran's perch was located but spotted no figures or movement. With her men on high alert, she ordered her four hundred soldiers to move toward Dran's living quarters.

In minutes and without incident, they reached the outer limit of Dran's compound, abutting the base of the Gray Mountain. Still there was no sign of resistance. They tested the heavy iron gate that lead to the interior courtyard, and Brechlin astounded that it opened. It had not been barricaded.

The courtyard was clear, so her men filed inside. Before them stood the main entrance to the living area of the compound.

Captain Labrok and a handful of nearby soldiers walked up to the wooden doors.

"The door is ajar," called back Captain Labrok.

Brechlin frowned. *What was Dran up to?*

She walked up to Captain Labrok and gestured for one of her men to open the door. It was eased open and they looked inside. Brechlin saw that the atrium, lit by skylights, was nearly empty. In the center of the atrium, a body lay upon a table, and standing beside the table she saw the figure of a slim young girl. The girl was smiling and obviously expecting them.

"Please come in," she called. "There is no danger."

Brechlin did not sense danger but would play it safe. Two doorways stood several feet behind the table, and it was possible that a wild rush of attacking cadavers would come pouring through at any moment, so she had her men circle around the table, facing the doors in ready stances. Brechlin then approached the young girl.

"Your precautions are unnecessary," assured the girl. "The situation has been defused."

"Who are you?" asked Brechlin, sword in hand and on ready alert.

"My name is Ilsher," she said. "I'm Dran's daughter and designated successor to the office of Krakul Gat. And this," she said, gesturing toward the body on the table, "is Dran. The perpetrator of great crimes against the people of our land."

Brechlin looked at the sallow face of the cadaver, still wearing a faint trace of surprise. It was Dran's body. A pool of blood had formed under the body and was visible on the table. Brechlin lifted the body up and saw a wound on his back.

"What happened?" asked Brechlin, still cautious.

"I killed him," Ilsher said simply. "He would not do it himself, so he came down from the mountain and I stabbed him with a dagger." She looked into Brechlin's face gravely. "He was a bad man," she said. "I knew what he had done, and I wouldn't let him do any more harm."

"I see," said Brechlin. She looked from Ilsher then to Dran and then back to Ilsher. Then she sat down, studying Ilsher's face.

"You killed Dran? Your own father?"

"I did," Ilsher replied. "And I had Ginthar imprisoned, awaiting the judgment of the Council of Sages."

Brechlin looked upon the contained, confident young girl

with some amazement. What Dran had done was as horrible as anything in the history of the Dalmeer Islands, and he deserved to die. In fact, after the judgment of the Council of Sages, he surely would have been put to death anyway. But that this young girl had taken his life with her own hands was astonishing. Her actions had, without doubt, saved them much loss of life compared to what would have happened if Dran had defended the island.

She ordered the men to search the rest of the rooms in the compound while she continued to sit beside Ilsher. "My dear, you are a brave girl, and I am sorry to say that you are right about your father's character. We all appreciate your sacrifice. It saved many lives. But how are you feeling? It must be hard to lose your father."

"Thank you for your concern," she replied with a solemn expression, somewhat out of place on her young face. "But as the days went by, it became clear that somewhere along the way I had lost my true father, and this...this criminal, this person who I no longer recognized, had replaced him. So, although I feel very sad that my father was lost to me, I feel no remorse taking this man's life."

Brechlin stared at the little girl for several seconds, amazed. Then she took her hand—only thirteen years old, she guessed—and placed her free hand upon her shoulder.

"My dear Ilsher," she began. "I'm sorry for your loss."

"You're Brechlin, aren't you? The Marshal of Cegril's army?"

"I am she," Brechlin replied, "and now we must temporarily assume control of Kromul Island. You will, I'm afraid, be asked to account for your actions before the Council of Sages, as will Ginthar and any others involved in all this."

"I understand," said Ilsher, humbly bowing her head.

"But fear not, my dear," added Brechlin and caressing Ilsher's hair. "Your actions will be deemed just and correct, I'm sure."

Ilsher looked sweetly up to Brechlin's face and smiled.

"So," said Brechlin, smiling back, "our first step is to gather up all the citizens of Kromul Island so we can determine exactly what happened. With Dran deceased and Ginthar in prison, who would you say is now in charge of this community? A town elder or mining supervisor, perhaps?"

"That would be me," replied Ilsher in a matter-of-fact tone.

"But dear..."

"I am the Krakul Gat designee. Everyone in this town knows that. They listen to me. Tell me what it is you wish, and I will have it done."

Once again, Brechlin looked at Ilsher with astonishment. "Can you have all the citizens summoned to that clearing down by the wharf?" she asked.

"Yes, just tell me when."

"Well, right away. In one hour, say."

At that moment, one of Cegril's officers came through one of the two doors at the back of the room and walked up to Brechlin.

"Aside from a couple of older servants, the compound is empty," he reported.

"So you see, there is nothing to be afraid of," said Ilsher. "So please, Marshal Brechlin, have your troops stand down. We want no unfortunate accidents."

"Okay, my dear. Once my men secure the island, I will, as you say, have my men stand down. In the meantime, I will count on you to gather up the citizens of this island. They will be safe."

Ilsher bowed to Brechlin and gracefully exited the room. Brechlin watched her with interest. *That little girl will be somebody one day,* she thought.

* * *

Two days later, Brechlin sat wearily down as the sloop glided away from Kromul Island. For hours upon hours, she and her officers had listened to the testimonies of the island's citizens. They were full of fear and concern, but it had become clear that those culpable for the crimes of the cadaver army were Dran and Ginthar. Any other persons who performed services for these two did so because they were ordered, not for any gain of their own. And now Dran was dead, and they had imprisoned Ginthar in the hold, awaiting trial back in Cegril.

For good measure, she also had detained Dran's mining supervisor and two town elders—old fishermen no longer able to handle a fishing craft—so that they could provide their statements directly to Queen Cirmar and the Council of Sages.

However, she had opted to leave Ilsher on the island. Brechlin recognized that, despite her age, she truly commanded the respect of the island's citizens. They obeyed her commands without hesitation. Brechlin had decided that Ilsher's authority would be needed to oversee the cooperation of the locals with the officers of the garrison force now stationed on Kromul Island.

As Brechlin looked out at the receding shore, Captain Labrok strolled up and stood next to her.

"Things went as smoothly as we could have wished," said Labrok. "Queen Cirmar will be pleased."

"I am certain she will be pleased," replied Brechlin, "but this is ugly business. I hope Ginthar's trial is over quickly. Our nation needs time to heal."

"I suspect that the Council of Sages will mete out its justice promptly."

Brechlin nodded in reply but was lost in thought. "I hope we did the right thing by leaving Ilsher on the island," she said, staring out at the small town whose buildings were still discernible.

"You don't suspect that young child of being responsible for any of this?" asked Labrok.

"Not that, exactly, but her statement could have been helpful to the Council."

"Well, if she's needed, she won't be going anywhere except to the Covenant Stone to take over as the Medium of the Gray Mountain," said Labrok. "If the Council allows it."

Brechlin shook her head pensively. "It's not under their jurisdiction. She is the legally designated replacement for Dran. And as long as she has committed no crime herself, she will succeed her father, despite her father's actions. Don't forget, her grandfather made a fine Krakul Gat." After a moment of further thought, Brechlin added, "And she is only twelve years old. What harm can a twelve-year-old do?"

Labrok shrugged and looked up into the awnings. A fresh breeze cooled their faces and billowed the taut sails. He looked at Brechlin.

"A nice breeze. If it stays out of the north like this, home will only be a few hours away."

"Even the winds are eager for us to return," Brechlin added. "The time has come for us to put this heinous chapter of history to rest."

Brechlin listened to the sound of the rigging as the increasing wind played musical notes. The bracing coolness of the northern wind felt good. But, as she relaxed to let the satisfaction of a job well done sink in, she heard the maniacal laughter of Ginthar from his cell in the hold. For a moment, she felt strangely tense, but soon the sound of the wind whistling through the rigging and the bustle of the ship's crew drowned out the laughter, and she calmed herself.

After all, she was homeward bound, and there awaited her beloved Chimber.

* * *

Thank you so much for reading **Cadaver Swords**. I hope you enjoyed visiting the Dalmeer Islands and confronting the cadaver hordes.

Would you like to be the first to hear the latest author news? Please go to my website (**emmettswan.com**) to sign up for the mailing list. I'll send you word whenever I have some new announcement or write a new blog post.

My next release is a science fiction novel entitled **Eden's Shadow**. In this story, Charles awakes in a primitive village with fifteen strangers. The village is in the middle of a vast wilderness with no sign of civilization anywhere to be found. No trash in the river. No planes in the sky. Nothing.

Survival is possible. But only if they commit to relearning the technology of the past and work from sunrise to sunset. Yet they remain in the dark as to why they were placed in their false Eden to begin with.

They gradually discover that their world contains strange,

unnatural phenomena, and begin to question whether they are truly alone in the wilderness. Are they being watched? Studied? What they ultimately discover leads Charles and his comrades to re-evaluate the future of humanity.

Available in November, 2020, go to emmettswan.com purchase your copy of **Eden's Shadow**.

Authors love reviews. If you enjoyed reading **Cadaver Swords**, please consider leaving a review on Goodreads, Amazon, or your website of choice.